Goalie Tandem

TIERNEY ROSE

For Luke Prokop, who lives his truth with unflinching conviction and gives great hugs, and Aidan Sutter, who welcomed me into his world and made a place for me there. You both inspire me daily.

One

THE FIRST THING Theo thought when he met Niklas was, *holy shit he's tall.*

The second thing he thought was, *so this is who's taking my job.* He'd opened the door to find his agent, Hannah, on the other side with Niklas shifting his weight beside her, clearly brimming with nervous energy. He towered easily eight inches above Theo, lanky where Theo was compact, all elbows and knees like a gangly colt not quite sure what to do with himself.

Hannah smiled at Theo. "Theo Wallin, meet Niklas Stromberg, your new backup. Niklas just landed, so he's pretty jetlagged, but he wanted to meet you before I took him to the hotel."

Niklas beamed at him, brown hair flopping into bright blue eyes, and thrust one huge hand out. Theo silently accepted it.

"It's such an honor," Niklas blurted in Swedish. His eyes were huge and earnest. "I became a goalie because of you. I wrote—"

Hannah cleared her throat. "English," she said gently, and Niklas's face fell.

"Sorry," he said in heavily accented English. "Ah... nice... meeting?"

Theo kept his face blank. "It's nice to meet you too. Will you come in?" He stepped aside and Niklas ducked his head and sidled past, followed by Hannah. Theo led them into his kitchen and Niklas turned in a circle, eyes wide at the vaulted ceiling, the gleaming utensils on the magnetized racks above the counters, and the spotless marble counters. "Are you thirsty?" Theo asked.

Niklas shot an uncertain glance at Hannah, who was tapping something on her phone. Theo could sympathize—Hannah was intimidating even to people who knew her. Niklas chewed his lip, darting a look at Theo and shifting his weight.

"Water is okay?" he finally said.

"Sure," Theo said. He busied himself filling two glasses and put them on the counter as Hannah scowled at her phone and then swore.

"Theo, I'm so sorry, I've got a fire to put out right now. Can you take Niklas to his hotel and get him settled in?"

Theo wavered as he set down the second glass before swallowing a sigh and nodding. He followed her out the door to get Niklas's gear and she was peeling out of his driveway before he had the strap over his shoulder. Niklas, right behind him, grabbed the bag as he babbled apologies.

"You not—is okay, I'm get—"

"She's gone, you can speak Swedish," Theo said shortly, and Niklas heaved a huge sigh of exaggerated relief.

"I *do* know English," he said, looking embarrassed. "But she scares me, and it just... *poof*, you know?"

Theo jerked his head for Niklas to follow him back inside. "She scares everyone. It's why she's so good at her job. Are you hungry?"

"*Yes,*" Niklas said fervently, right on his heels.

Theo showed him where to put his bag and then offered him a stool at the kitchen counter. Niklas hooked his feet around the rungs and watched as Theo pulled a lasagna from the refrigerator.

"It's a little early for dinner, but something tells me you need the calories," he said, mostly to fill the silence.

Niklas made a small affirming noise and Theo glanced up. Niklas immediately looked away, his cheeks going pink.

Theo went back to cutting a slab of lasagna and plopping it on a plate. "So, uh, how was your flight?" he asked to fill the silence as he put it in the microwave. When he looked up, Niklas jerked his eyes away again, cheeks turning even pinker.

"It, uh, was fine," he told the ceiling.

"What did you write?" Theo asked.

"Huh?"

"Earlier. You said 'I wrote—'," Theo said helpfully. "Wrote what? A school report about me?"

"More than one," Niklas admitted, ducking his head.

Theo sighed and grabbed two beers from the refrigerator. He set one in front of Niklas, then popped his and drained half the can without stopping for air. When he put it down, Niklas was staring at him again, his eyes huge.

"Get it over with," Theo said. "You'll feel better once it's out."

"You're the reason I'm here," Niklas said immediately, clutching the edge of the counter. "I saw you play in the Olympics when I was eight—" Theo managed to hide the wince, but just barely. "—And ever since then I just *knew*. I knew I was going to be a goalie. I knew I was going to play in the NHL. Play with *you*."

"Technically, you can't play *with* me, not if we're both goalies," Theo pointed out dryly, but Niklas didn't seem to register the sarcasm.

"I have posters of you on my walls," he said, eyes earnest.

"I've watched every single one of your games. At least all the ones I could find, and most of them more than once. You're my favorite player in the whole *world*."

They stared at each other for a minute. Niklas didn't seem inclined to say anything else, and Theo didn't know *what* to say. The ding of the microwave startled them both, and Theo coughed as he turned to retrieve the food.

Putting the plate in front of Niklas, he handed him a fork and then leaned back against the counter, arms folded.

If you think I'm so great, why are you here to take my job? He didn't say it, kept the words locked behind his teeth with an almighty effort. It wasn't the fault of the young man currently digging into his pasta like he hadn't eaten in a week. But Theo couldn't help the jolt of resentment in his chest, like the kick of a mule when he looked at Niklas's big hand folded carefully around the fork that looked so small in his grip.

In a way, Theo understood. The team needed to get bigger. Faster. Stronger. They needed a brick wall in net to make up for their inconsistent defense, and that brick wall was eating Theo's food, utterly oblivious to the conflict in Theo's head.

"You're not eating?" Niklas asked, looking up.

Theo shook his head. "I'm not a growing boy."

Niklas visibly bristled. "I'm nearly twenty-three."

"And I'm thirty-four," Theo said, grimacing. "You're fully grown, sure, but you're also still filling out. At least I *hope* you're fully grown, how tall are you, anyway?"

Niklas ducked his head, looking abashed. "Six five," he mumbled. "Sorry."

"For what, being tall?"

Niklas glanced up. His blue eyes were unhappy. "You're not."

Theo flinched. "Thank you?"

"Sorry," Niklas blurted. "Sorry, I didn't mean it that—"

He shoved a hand through his hair. "I wanted... to be like you. And I'm...." He gestured vaguely at himself.

The light dawned. "You can't help your height," Theo said. He scowled as he searched for the words. "And your height helps *you*. It means you can make the big saves with less effort, cover the net more efficiently. I have to work twice as hard to cover as much ground."

"You make it look easy," Niklas said, glancing up again.

"Well, I've been doing it for a while. Besides, you can't play like me. You have to play like you."

Niklas sighed and nodded.

After a moment of awkward silence, Theo spoke again. "So tell me about yourself."

Niklas's eyes went wide. "Oh," he managed, "I'm not really interesting."

Theo raised a brow. "Really? What do you like to do in your off-time? Surely you've got some hobbies?"

"Not much," Niklas mumbled. "I play Call of Duty some, I guess."

Doesn't everyone these days? "Anything else?"

Niklas ducked his head, a blush dusting his cheekbones. "No," he told the counter.

Theo watched him narrowly for a minute but didn't press. Whatever Niklas wasn't telling him, it wasn't his business.

"As long as it's not illegal, I don't really give a shit," Theo said, glancing at the clock above the stove. "We should probably get you to your hotel, you must be exhausted."

"I'm okay," Niklas insisted, then immediately yawned.

Theo bit down on a small smile. "Okay, whatever you say."

Niklas slid off the stool and took his dishes to the sink, where he proceeded to wash them over Theo's protests.

"A good guest cleans up after himself," he said, chin

jutting out as he scrubbed, and Theo gave up, reluctantly impressed. At least the boy had manners.

He watched him for a minute as Niklas frowned at the dish in his hand. He didn't *want* to like this young man, his replacement and physical reminder that Theo was getting closer to retirement every day, but he couldn't really help being intrigued. Niklas seemed earnest, sincere, and it didn't hurt that he was easy on the eyes.

Soft brown hair fell over his forehead, looking both silky straight and cornsilk fine. His bright blue eyes were narrowed in concentration, tongue peeking from his mouth, and Theo had seen dimples when he smiled.

Theo wondered idly about his sexuality, picking absent-mindedly at a patch of loose paint. Did he like men or women? Both? Niklas didn't read as gay, but he played hockey. He'd have learned to conceal it from an early age, act like the others, even flirt with women to keep his secret.

Or maybe that was just Theo. Niklas had finished the dishes and was drying his hands, looking at him expectantly.

"Do you have a place to live yet?" Theo asked.

Niklas shook his head. "Hannah said she would show me some places for rent. Maybe tomorrow. I don't want to buy anything yet, I'll probably be sent down soon, you know? And what if I don't fit? If I get traded, I don't want to go through all that."

Theo regarded him. "You've got a good head on your shoulders," he said, the words pulled reluctantly from him.

Niklas blushed. "My mama taught me a lot."

"Not your father?"

"Eh, he's okay," Niklas said, flapping a hand dismissively. "Not really involved, you know? He was always busy with work."

"Do you want to stay here?" Theo asked, and then snapped his mouth shut, horrified with himself.

Niklas's eyes went huge. "You—really? Do you mean it? *Really*?"

What was he going to say? *Haha just kidding, let's get you to the hotel?* Theo was an introvert, not a monster.

"Of course I mean it," he said out loud with conviction he didn't feel, and the smile that spread over Niklas's face was almost worth the regret in his gut. "Just for a while, yeah? Until you find a place of your own."

Niklas nodded fervently. "I'll be so quiet," he promised. "I'll clean—every day. And do laundry. Dishes. Whatever you want."

"You're a guest, not my maid," Theo said, startled. "I mean it, don't you dare try to clean my house because you feel grateful or something."

"I won't," Niklas said. "But if I see something that needs cleaning?"

"Then I guess you can clean it," Theo said, amused in spite of himself. "Come on, you can pick a room."

* * *

He had three guest bedrooms to choose from, each one decorated by an interior designer who'd worked closely with Theo to figure out his likes and dislikes.

"The house is too big for me, really," Theo admitted, opening the door to the yellow room. "But I like having room to move around, and it's good when family comes to town."

Niklas peered inside, making an interested noise. "It's very pretty." There were fresh daffodils on the dresser and an antique quilt in shades of gold and green on the four-poster bed.

"You should see the others first," Theo said, so Niklas followed him to the next room.

He made an involuntary face of distaste at the art deco

style, the gleaming silver accents and bright primary colors, and Theo laughed out loud.

"It's my least favorite too," he admitted. "But my mother loves the style, so it's where she stays when she and my father visit."

He opened the door to the third room, and Niklas's lips parted in wonder.

"Oh," he said, and stepped inside as if not realizing he was moving.

The room was paneled in hardwood—floors and walls both—with an antique dresser painted white against the wall. A metal pitcher with white lilies in it stood on top of the dresser, and an off-white hand-knitted blanket was folded on top of the wooden chest at the end of the bed.

Niklas turned in a circle, eyes wide. He stopped to stare at the lacy wrought-iron canopy over the bed with fairy lights woven through it, and Theo couldn't resist bending to flip the switch. They sprang to twinkling life, sparking against the metal and bathing the bed in a warm glow.

"*Oh*," Niklas repeated. "I—oh, is it okay if—"

"Of course," Theo said. It was impossible to dislike the boy, dammit. He was so polite, so respectful, so *grateful*, and a little more resentment slipped away at the smile on Niklas's face.

Niklas eased himself onto the edge of the bed and smoothed a reverent hand over the blanket at the end.

"My mother made that," Theo offered.

"It's beautiful. The whole room—it's so beautiful. Why isn't it yours? It's so…." Niklas gestured vaguely. "It feels like… home."

"My room's actually pretty similar, just a little bigger," Theo said. "The artist who did that canopy did one for my bed as well. There's a bathroom there—" He pointed. "Let's get your bags."

* * *

Hannah laughed at him when he called to tell her. Put the phone down and laughed and laughed, the tinny sound of her mirth echoing from the speakers until Theo hung up in disgust.

She called him right back, still hiccuping. "I'm sorry," she said, a faint wheeze in her voice, and Theo glared at the wall. "It's just—God, lovey, you're just so predictable!"

Theo hung up on her again and let it ring through to voicemail twice before he answered the third time.

"I'm done, I'm done," she said. "Swear."

"Uh huh."

"No, really! I think it's wonderful you're taking him under your wing. You know he worships you. Like to an alarming degree. I think he might need therapy."

"I'm not above hanging up on you again," Theo warned, and Hannah giggled.

"Seriously, though. It *is* good of you. Help him ease into rural Canadian life—it's going to be some real culture shock for the kid."

"Saskatoon isn't *that* rural," Theo protested, mostly for show. He could hear Niklas moving around in the living room. It sounded like he was exploring, looking at Theo's trophies and pictures. "I'll call you back, Hannah," he said. "And I'll bring him to practice with me tomorrow."

In the living room, Niklas was looking at a photograph on the wall, awe in his eyes. "Is this really an autographed picture of Jacques Plante? Did you get Jacques Plante's autograph?"

Theo stared at him. "Just how old do you think I am?"

Niklas looked away, guilty. "I didn't mean—"

"Relax," Theo said. "I didn't meet Plante in person, no. But I did meet his son, and that picture is one of my dearest possessions."

"Can I get *your* autograph?" Niklas blurted, and blushed a deep red, all the way to his ears.

Theo felt a smile tug at the corner of his lips and barely suppressed it in time. "You're *living* with me. Give it twenty-four hours. If you're not regretting all your life choices by then, sure. I'll give you my autograph."

Niklas's smile was brilliant. "I could never regret being here."

"Give it time," Theo said, and he couldn't stop the note of bitterness that crept into his voice. He shook his head and forced a smile as Niklas shifted his weight, looking worried. "Sorry. It's just—Saskatoon isn't exactly New York City or Portland. No one *wants* to come to this team. It's a pothole in the road to success. We suck, to put it mildly."

"But you're here," Niklas said softly. He looked bewildered. "You've been here for ten years. Why do you stay if it's that bad?"

Theo shrugged. "I didn't say *I* didn't like it here. I get along well with the coaches and staff. I'm not bothered when I go out, not that I do very often. I love my house, I love the game. Players come and go, but I'm comfortable here. I'll retire with this team, if they'll let me, even though we'll never win a Stanley Cup."

Niklas's eyes were sad. "You deserve a Cup, Theo."

Something turned over in Theo's stomach. "Don't pity me," he snapped.

"I'm not!" Niklas protested. "It's just—you've done so much. Worked so hard. Represented Sweden at the World Cup and Olympics. You should have the Stanley Cup, too. It's —it's not *right* that you haven't won it yet."

"'Right' doesn't enter into it," Theo said, unable to keep the harshness from his voice. "It hasn't happened. It won't. I've made my peace with it." He turned away, breathing deep and centering himself. "Sorry," he said over his shoulder and bent to straighten a pillow on the couch before turning back. "So I should tell you about the team."

"I've been reading about them," Niklas said immediately, voice cautious. "But anything you can tell me will help. I want them to like me."

"They'll like you," Theo said. He sat down and gestured for Niklas to join him. Niklas folded himself onto the couch, knees together and hands in his lap. "Trust me, you're way too sweet for them *not* to like you. Although they'll definitely prank you."

To his surprise, Niklas blushed bright red again. "You think I'm sweet?"

"Kid, you're going to give me diabetes if you keep it up," Theo said wryly, and somehow Niklas went even redder. Theo watched, reluctantly delighted, as Niklas squirmed and clearly couldn't think of anything to say, but finally took pity on him.

"So we don't have a captain right now. Haven't for a couple of years, since Mike retired. There are a couple of A's in the room though. Rudd Orsher—Orshie—is second line center. He's had an A for about two years—definitely deserves it. He's got two little ones at home so he doesn't go out with the team much, but he's a good guy, solid and dependable."

Niklas nodded. "I recognize the name. He's pretty good—needs more confidence with the puck though, I think."

"Yeah?" Theo asked, surprised. "I've thought the same thing for a while, actually. He tends to play it safe instead of taking risks."

"Who else?"

"Rainer Sündstrom is Swedish—we call him Sunny. The North Americans think it's clever, playing on his name. He's got twins, a boy and a girl, and Inga will feed you real Swedish food anytime you ask. I think he's the best fit, personally, but he says he doesn't want the responsibility."

Niklas perked up at that. "Swedish food is always good. Not so many Swedish restaurants around here, I guess?"

"Not so many," Theo agreed, lifting a shoulder with a faint smile. "Then there's Foz or Fozzy Bear. D-man, first pairing, the third A. Not very fast *or* graceful but he's one of the most well-liked guys there is. Always has a kind word for fans, loves to talk to kids especially."

"He protects you well," Niklas said. "I see a lot of him. Always screening shots and taking hits to keep you safe."

Theo nodded. "The others could learn a thing or two from him, honestly. So those are our A's. I don't know if or when they'll choose a captain, but those three are all good candidates."

"What else should I know? Anyone I should watch out for? Anyone not fitting in or not good teammates?"

"Eh...." Theo considered, rubbing his forearm. "Xander—Ivy—will probably be a douche to you, at least at first. He comes from money and thinks he deserves a better team than the Sentinels."

"Ivy?"

"He came from Harvard. Americans call it the Ivy League.Thinks he's hot shit. He's fourth line though, third if he's very lucky. You'll get to know the rest of them as you go. We'll have a lot of new faces in the lineup for training camp, and most of them won't stick around."

"What about the coaching staff?"

"Might as well be a revolving door." Theo grimaced. "Almost every year it's someone new. The last one lasted nearly two years, and his assistant took his place when he got fired after the season ended. He's a decent guy. Hard on us, but he's got a lot to prove. I think he's the youngest coach in the NHL right now. He knows his shit, and he'll listen if you have a problem."

"And the goalie coach?"

"We don't have one."

Niklas stared at him. "You're kidding."

Theo just shrugged. "Last one resigned at the end of the season. They haven't found anyone willing to replace him yet." He quirked a smile at the look on Niklas's face. "I've been doing this for a long time. They're looking for a replacement but in the meantime, I'll coach you or whoever else is my backup. Not officially, of course."

Niklas nodded. "Did you build this house yourself?" he blurted. "It's so beautiful."

Theo glanced around the room, with its floor-to-ceiling windows all along the east wall to catch the early morning sun. "Parts of it. I did a lot of remodeling when I bought it. You already saw the bedrooms and the kitchen—there's not much else except for the backyard."

"What's in the backyard?"

Which was how Theo found himself leading a wide-eyed young goalie through his sun-drenched back hall to the door that overlooked his pride and joy. He trotted down the back steps and along the cobblestone path, Niklas close on his heels, to his workshop, where he opened the door with something of a flourish.

Niklas stepped inside, glancing up at the twenty-foot ceiling and then around the room, registering everything in quick, flickering glances.

"This is... what you do?" He trailed a curious finger along the nearest workbench. Theo had built the bench first, when creating the room. It sloped just a little and one leg was a tiny bit too short, so he'd shoved a piece of folded up paper underneath to shore it up and stop the wobbling. He could have made a better one, but he kept it as a reminder of where he'd come from, how bad he'd been when he started and how far he'd come.

"It's just a hobby," Theo said. He touched the slat on the

bench beside him. He was building a rocking chair and it was slow going, every piece needing to be perfect before he added the next, but he thought it was turning out well.

"Furniture," Niklas said. It was hard to read his tone.

"Handcrafted, one-of-a-kind furniture," Theo clarified. "Each piece is different, matching the customers' broad specs but the details are my decision alone."

Niklas wandered deeper into the room. "Why haven't you told anyone?"

"My customers know," Theo objected mildly. "Even though there aren't many of them."

Niklas brushed this away with a quick movement of his shoulders. "I mean in the hockey world." He spun to face him. "You're an artist, Theo. You could sell so much more if you told your fans what you do. Can you imagine how many orders you'd have?"

"That sounds like a nightmare," Theo said flatly, and Niklas flinched. Theo gentled his tone. "I know you think you're trying to help, but look around. I don't do this for money. I have enough money. I could retire tomorrow and never lift a finger the rest of my life and I'd still be comfortable until the day I die. I do this for the love of it. I choose projects that appeal to me, that make me excited to work on them. If I had a backlog of customers and a waiting list of people wanting something, I'd be so stressed I'd never touch another piece of wood. It would take the joy from it."

Niklas shook his head, looking unconvinced. "But—"

"Would you want to play hockey if someone was looking over your shoulder at every second, telling you exactly how to move, when and where to play the puck, and all the little details of your game?"

Niklas grimaced.

"Exactly," Theo said gently. "I do this because it makes me

happy, just like hockey makes me happy. When it stops making me happy, I'll stop doing it."

Niklas examined his face. "And when hockey stops being fun?"

Theo hid the flinch and summoned something resembling a smile. "That will never happen, I think. Come on, get your coat. I'll show you some of the town before dinner."

* * *

They spent the afternoon driving around Theo's favorite spots. He took Niklas by the practice rink and then the gameday one, pointing out the players' entrance on the side.

"Can I walk with you tomorrow?" Niklas asked, fidgeting with his seatbelt. He never seemed to stop moving, but Theo didn't find it as irritating as he'd expected. He liked Niklas's energy, the way he absorbed everything Theo said and asked intelligent questions in response.

"Of course," Theo said. "They'll want to see us together anyway."

Niklas flashed him a brilliant smile. "I'm so happy I'm here," he said, looking out the window over the grassy plains.

Theo didn't say anything, just focused on the road.

Two

THEO MADE DINNER FOR THEM, meatballs and macaroni that he cooked from scratch. Niklas hovered, eyes anxious like if he didn't help enough, Theo would get tired of him and tell him to leave. Theo took pity and gave him a bag of carrots and a sharp knife. Niklas settled in at the counter and began to slice them, brow furrowed and shoulders hunched.

"Relax," Theo said dryly. "It's not rocket science, just cut them into chunks."

"Can I ask you something?" Niklas blurted.

Theo put the lid on the pot and rested his hips against the counter. "Go ahead."

"How come you never got married?"

Theo blinked. Of all the questions Niklas could have asked, that was one he hadn't expected.

Niklas ducked his head. "You don't have to answer," he said to the carrots. "I just... wondered."

"I guess I just... never found the one," Theo said after a minute. "This life—it's not easy for those not in it. I didn't want to make someone wait for me, or be dragged across the country when I got traded. It didn't seem fair."

"What about Anjali?"

Theo looked at him, but Niklas was still looking at the carrots.

"You really did do your research, didn't you?" Theo asked. *Sweet Anjali, small and dark and clever, her mischievous smile lighting the room. She'd never minded being his beard—she'd had her own reasons for wanting to be seen as a couple.*

"There were rumors that you were going to marry her," Niklas said.

"Don't listen to rumors," Theo said automatically. "We're still friends, you know. She's coming out to visit soon, in fact, once we can get our schedules lined up."

"So why—" Niklas broke off.

Theo sighed. "Our lives went different ways. That's really all there is to say." *Please drop it.*

Niklas hunched his shoulders. "Sorry. So no one important?"

"Not in the way you mean," Theo said. "What about you? Girlfriend back home?"

Niklas laughed. "She broke up with me when I told her I was moving to Saskatoon. I don't know if it was because of how far away it is, or because of you."

Theo dropped the meatball he was putting in the pan and it hit the floor with a dull splat. "Because of me?"

Niklas shrugged. "It's not like I ever stopped talking about you when I was with her." His grin flashed, brilliant and unrepentant. "She used to say she felt like the fifth wheel because I never shut up about whatever you'd done recently."

"Jesus Christ," Theo muttered, staring at the mess on his kitchen floor.

"Don't worry," Niklas hurried to add. "I only said your name in bed like once."

"*Jesus Christ*," Theo repeated faintly, and Niklas burst into peals of laughter, rocking back on the stool and clutching his stomach. His dimples flashed, and Theo felt like he'd been punched in the gut. He gathered himself and turned back to the meatballs, head spinning as he stooped to pick up the meatball on the floor and drop it in the trash.

Niklas composed himself, something almost like guilt slipping past the vestiges of laughter. "Did I make you uncomfortable?"

"No," Theo said immediately. He put another meatball in the pan and looked up. Niklas had put the knife down and was watching him, eyes worried. Theo mustered a smile. "Keep that sense of humor, kid. You'll need it to give the team as good as you get."

Niklas nodded, clearly relieved. "So, what kind of music do you like?" he asked. "And how do you feel about Swedish death metal?"

Theo let his head fall against the nearest cupboard with a soft moan and told himself the sound of Niklas's laughter affected him not at all.

Three

HE WAS HERE. Not just in Saskatoon, but in *Theo 'Brick Wall' Wallin's* house, sitting at his counter and watching him cook. His movements were as neat and contained in the kitchen as they were in net. He was shorter even than Niklas had anticipated, despite knowing his height to the centimeter, but his presence more than made up for his stature. *Poised*, Niklas thought as Theo stirred the meatballs and said something about music. As if Niklas didn't know all the bands Theo had ever mentioned listening to.

He wanted desperately to know what it felt like to be that comfortable in his own body, to move with such tidy assurance, no wasted movement or excess energy. Next to him, Niklas felt like a gangling scarecrow, gawky and unfinished. The nerves didn't help, of course.

No matter what Niklas thought of Theo, how it shorted out his brain just to be this close to him, perceived *by* him as if he was a real person with thoughts and actions and desires of his own and not just another faceless fan, he wasn't stupid. He knew he was there to eventually replace Theo, if things went well. He was a constant reminder to Theo that he was getting older and he didn't have much longer on his contract.

How Theo was even able to look him in the eyes, let alone smile at him, Niklas had no idea. But that was Theo's magic, wasn't it? Hiding his feelings, allowing only what he wanted others to see on his face. It was how he was so good on the ice, his gift of locking his emotions behind a wall, making himself nothing but driven purpose with only one objective in his head. Why couldn't Niklas be like that? Why did he have to let his emotions bleed out all over everything?

Theo said something and Niklas made an agreeable noise. Theo arched one brow faintly.

"Really?"

"Uh, really what?" Niklas asked. He thought desperately over the last several minutes but couldn't remember a word of the conversation.

"You really like marshmallows in your macaroni?"

Niklas made an involuntary face and Theo's lips twitched. "When did I lose you?"

"Sorry," Niklas said, hanging his head. "I didn't mean to be rude. I'm sorry."

"You weren't rude," Theo said, sounding surprised. He took a breath as if composing himself. "Kid, if you're going to stay with me, I think we need to set a few ground rules. Okay?"

Niklas nodded miserably and Theo slid onto the stool next to him.

"First of all, you're not my slave or my maid," he said, and waited until Niklas looked up before continuing. His gaze was compelling and Niklas felt trapped in it as he said, "I expect nothing from you except basic manners, okay? Clean up after yourself. Don't leave any room a sty. Preferably no loud music, at least not after ten p.m., and I'd like you to check with me if you want to blast it in any of the shared living areas. Similarly,

I'd prefer no guests after eleven, although I'm flexible on that as long as you check with me first."

Niklas swallowed and nodded again.

"*You're* a guest," Theo said, his voice gentling. "You're welcome to be here, to make yourself comfortable, and that includes daydreaming in the middle of boring monologues about my musical preferences."

Niklas could feel the blush crawling up his throat and Theo laughed quietly.

"I've seen you play, you know."

Niklas jerked upright so fast he nearly fell off the stool. "You what? *When*?"

"Sweden, last year," Theo said. "We didn't make the play-offs, no surprise, so I went over early. Thought I'd catch some Liiga action while I was there, see some of the new talent."

Niklas could barely breathe. "What day?" he asked urgently. "Do you remember the date?"

Theo looked distant for a minute, clearly thinking back. "Mid-April. Maybe the 13th or 14th? I'd have to check a calendar."

Niklas was already pulling out his phone to consult his. "The 13th was a Saturday. We didn't play Sunday. Home game, right?"

"Yes." Theo sounded amused.

"I was in net that day," Niklas said. "Oskar was backup. But I don't remember—"

"You won," Theo said.

"Oh," Niklas said. He chewed the inside of his cheek. What had Theo thought? Was he worth anything? Did he have promise, or was he all style and no substance? He had absolutely no idea how to ask.

Theo saved him. "You were amazing," he said quietly, but the admiration was clear in his voice. Niklas could feel the blush firing up again and he ducked his head. "Someone as tall as you shouldn't be that fast across the crease," Theo continued. "And your lateral angles are incredible. You need to work on your glove-hand and you favor your strong leg, you need to strengthen your weak one, but you don't get flustered even with a lot of traffic in front of you. You kept your composure no matter how bad it got and you never let the other team rattle you."

Niklas was going to shrivel up and die, right here in front of his childhood hero, just flake into mortified fragments and float off in the breeze. He had absolutely no idea what to say. Theo had been there. *Watching* him. Sitting in a seat like a regular fan, and Niklas hadn't had a clue. It was silly, but he should have, somehow. He should have known Theo was there, should have felt some inkling, when Theo was the whole reason Niklas was there to begin with. But it had just been another game.

"If you want, I can help you work on your glove-hand," Theo continued.

If he *wanted*? Niklas couldn't think of anything he'd ever wanted more, except maybe to kiss the man in front of him. He reeled that thought in abruptly, afraid Theo was able to read minds too—he wouldn't be surprised—and somehow managed to find his voice. "I wrote to you," he croaked.

Theo's eyebrows went up. "Oh, is that what you meant, earlier? When?"

"I was eight. You won a gold medal for Sweden in the Olympics. I wanted—" Niklas swallowed. "I wanted to be like you more than anyone else."

"What did I say?" Theo asked. "Did I respond?"

Niklas couldn't help the scoff at that. "Of course you did. It was handwritten. Three pages, front and back. You told me about your workout routine, what you ate, how you stayed focused, how you shook off bad games. You gave me advice if I wanted to be a goalie, and I've followed it ever since. I wanted… I guess I want to say thank you. That you took the time, it just meant… so much to me."

Theo's lips quirked and he tilted his head, looking at him. "You'll feel better once the hero worship fades," he said, and slid off the stool, graceful as ever.

Niklas was pretty sure it was never going to fade. How was he supposed to look and act and feel *normal* around this man? Theo was everything Niklas had ever wanted to be. There was no one he admired more, certainly not his father, not even his coach back in the Liiga. He'd had his sexual epiphany about Theo fucking Wallin, for fuck's sake—he was never, *ever* going to be able to be normal around him.

But he'd try, if it meant getting to stay. He could fake it, surely. He reached for the knife as Theo rounded the counter, but he misjudged how far away it was and knocked it off.

It fell with a clatter and Theo swung around, brows going up.

"Sorry," Niklas said helplessly, and nearly fell off the stool to retrieve it. He wanted to crawl in a hole and never come out, but instead he scooped up the knife and stood, taking a deep breath. "Just… have to wash it."

Theo gestured silently at the sink, but he didn't look irritated. More contemplative than anything, Niklas thought as he ran the knife under hot water.

Four

DINNER WAS QUIET, but it wasn't as awkward as Niklas had worried it would be. The jetlag was setting in, and he could feel the exhaustion finally overpowering the nerves and adrenaline, dragging at his limbs and making his motions slow, like he was underwater. His eyes felt gritty. He propped his cheek on one fist and ate mechanically, faintly guilty for not appreciating how delicious the food was, but far too tired to taste it.

He dozed off somewhere in there, and Theo cleared his throat. His eyes creased when Niklas jerked upright.

"Sorry," he said automatically, and Theo's smile slid into a frown.

"Stop apologizing."

"Sor—" Niklas snapped his mouth shut and stared at his plate. He couldn't think, his thoughts slow and sluggish. If he wasn't allowed to apologize, then he'd have to just not say anything at all.

Theo sighed. "Kid, look at me."

Despite the fatigue, Niklas had to stifle the jolt of resentment as he obeyed. He *wasn't* a kid. He'd led his league in save percentage, he'd been courted by leagues in four countries, he'd had a girlfriend and owned his own car and paid his own bills. He was a goddamn *adult*, the same as Theo.

Theo hadn't noticed his internal turmoil. "I really do think you'll be more comfortable once you've figured out I'm human," he said. "But in the meantime, I'm banning apologies for a while. Alright? No more cringing and expecting me to throw you out because you dropped something or think you said the wrong thing or acted the wrong way."

Niklas swallowed hard, blinking. "I j-just don't want—"

"You don't want me to regret having offered," Theo finished, and Niklas nodded.

"I know you don't like a lot of people around," he said. "And I'm—I'm *here*, in your house, eating your food, I'm imposing, and—"

"You're *not*," Theo said sharply. He pinched the bridge of his nose as if praying for patience, and exhaled through his nose. "I like you, okay? You're charming, you're funny when you let yourself be, you've got excellent manners. You're... delightful." He sounded anything but delighted, and Niklas peered at him, doubtful.

"I won't stay long," he said. "Maybe a week?" A huge yawn overtook him and he jammed a fist in his mouth, horrified.

Theo was smiling when he glanced back up. "Let's see how it goes. Now you need to go take a shower and go to bed."

"Oh no," Niklas protested as Theo stood to begin clearing dishes. "No, I'm going to wash up."

"You absolutely are *not*," Theo said, whisking Niklas's plate away even as he made a clumsy grab for it. "You're going to shower and go to bed and you're going to sleep like the dead for at least ten hours, so you're ready for practice in the morning. Camp starts tomorrow, you'll want to be on your game."

He chivvied Niklas onto his feet somehow without even touching him, and shooed him down the hall to his bedroom.

Niklas clung to the doorframe for a second, dragging thoughts together. "Theo—"

Theo looked at him, eyes patient. There was nothing but friendliness in them, kindness and sincere welcome. "Sleep well, Nik."

Five

CAMP WAS OVERWHELMING. There were at least forty players milling around when Theo and Niklas arrived, at least half of them looking as terrified and adrift as Niklas felt. Several gave Niklas sizing up looks, measuring him as Theo wove through the crowds, Niklas practically plastered to his back.

"The stall next to me is free if you want it," Theo said over his shoulder.

"Yes please," Niklas said instantly, and Theo shot him an amused look.

"Is that Theo Wallin?" someone demanded in what he probably thought was a whisper.

"Don't you mean the Asshole of Saskatchewan?" someone else said.

Theo stiffened, face going blank, as Niklas froze.

"You'll want to meet Coach," Theo said, tone clipped.

Niklas barely heard him, looking for the speaker. He was pretty sure it had been one of the group of gangly youths a few feet away, all of whom were currently staring anywhere but at Theo.

"Niklas," Theo said quietly, but there was something in his voice that begged him not to make a scene.

Niklas took another long, searching look at the group, all of them studying the ceiling with various degrees of interest, and turned to follow Theo without a word. He was too angry to speak, afraid if he opened his mouth everything he was feeling would come flooding out, drowning anything in its path.

Theo led him through the room to a door on the other side. It opened on a narrow corridor, and once through, Theo shut the door and took a deep breath.

"Why would they say that?" Niklas burst out.

Theo lifted a shoulder. "Because it's true?" His tone was wry but there was pain in the twist of his mouth, and Niklas clenched his fists.

"But it's *not*," he said. "*You're* not—"

"No, I am," Theo said quietly. "Sunny's the only one on the team who actually likes me. Everyone else either avoids me or hates me. Haven't you noticed that no one ever head-bumps me after a win? Not that we have very many of those to begin with."

Niklas wanted to hit something. "It's not right," he said, helpless and hating it. "Why can't they *see* you?"

"Or maybe they do see me," Theo said. He sounded resigned, more than anything. "Maybe you're the one who doesn't realize what I'm really like."

"No." Niklas shook his head. "No, that's not true. I know—Theo, I know I…." *Idolize you*, he didn't say. "A nice person wouldn't have invited me to stay with him. They're wrong."

Theo studied his face for a minute and finally the corner of his mouth quirked up. "You need to meet Coach."

Owen Benson wasn't a very imposing man, not even into his forties, slim-framed with just the beginnings of gray streaking the dark hair swept back from his temples. He studied Niklas with piercing gray eyes, seated behind his desk.

"Welcome to the Sentinels," he said after a minute. "We're glad to have you."

Niklas ducked his head and smiled at him. "Thank you. I'm glad to be here." He'd practiced that phrase in front of a mirror at least a thousand times.

"You probably know I'm new to the team too," Benson continued. "You'll learn how I want things run, but I've got no time for anyone who doesn't pull their weight."

Theo cleared his throat. "Have you heard about the—"

"Not yet," Benson said briskly.

Niklas glanced between them, confused, and Theo caught his eye.

"Remember no goalie coach right now?" he said, and then repeated himself in Swedish. "The last one got a better offer with the Ravens, middle of last season."

"Camp is for the goalies too," Benson said, making a note on the paper in front of him. Niklas wondered if it was about him, and straightened hastily when Benson glanced back up. "You're expected to work just as hard as the rest of the players. I have two other rookies looking to snag the seat behind Theo here. If you want it, you're gonna have to earn it. Is that clear?"

Niklas was listening as hard as he could to Benson's rapid speech, only catching about every other word. But the gist was clear. "Yes sir," he said. He'd earn that spot. He *would*. No one was backing up Theo but him.

"Theo," Benson continued, "can you help with the prospects?"

Theo grimaced. "There has to be someone more qualified."

"Not and wants to come here," Coach said, tone dry. "Just

work on drills with them, give them some guidance." His teeth flashed in a surprisingly charming smile. "Try not to scare them so bad they quit on their first day, yeah?"

"I can't promise anything," Theo said.

Benson snorted. "Go away, both of you. I'm busy."

Six

THEO TOOK Niklas to the locker rooms and showed him to the empty one beside his. Niklas stowed his gear bag and took a look around the room. It was a little dingy, the paint peeling in a few places, a cobweb clinging forlornly to one corner. The Sentinels' logo was on the rug in the middle of the room, faded and worn as if it had been walked on for years.

"Go ahead and get your gear on," Theo said.

Niklas obeyed as other players filtered in and out of the room. None of them spoke to Theo, although they cast curious glances at Niklas beside him as they suited up.

Finally, Theo deemed them ready and took him out to the ice. The practice rink wasn't very imposing, and there were already quite a few players on it, milling around, batting pucks back and forth to each other and talking loudly to disguise their nerves.

"Ready?" Theo asked.

Niklas squared his shoulders. He belonged here. He could do this. "Ready."

Seven

THEO KEPT an eye on Niklas as he warmed up in his crease. He was standing off to the side, talking to another goalie prospect Theo didn't recognize. There was awkwardness in the way Niklas shifted his weight and glanced around, his eyes more often than not landing on Theo briefly.

He'll be fine, Theo told himself, and started his drills. His body protested at first, unhappy with the exertion level even after his daily summer workouts, but soon enough his muscles warmed up and loosened. His right knee was a little *too* loose, a warning sign to keep a close schedule with the trainer and rekindle a relationship with ice packs, but he could bend it. He dropped to the ice. Pushed off and slid sideways, left and then right.

He was so focused on the comforting rote motions that he didn't notice the approaching player until he'd skidded to a stop and showered him with ice.

Theo popped back to his feet, his glare dissolving at the sight of Sunny beaming at him.

"Asshole," Theo said, no heat behind it as he shoved his helmet up on his head. "Why do you always do that?"

Sunny laughed and hugged him. "Because the rookies are terrified of you. And if they see me terrorizing *you*—"

"They might actually listen to you," Theo finished, slapping him on the back. "I hate that it makes sense. How are you? The family?"

"I'm good, they're good! Lilly and Oscar are in mite league. Inga keeps us all in line. She wants you over for dinner soon. How's tomorrow?"

Theo hesitated. "Ah... can Niklas come too?"

Sunny's eyebrows shot up. "Niklas... as in Niklas Stromberg? The goalie you're convinced is going to replace you?"

"He *is*," Theo snapped. "And yes. He's—" Sunny was never going to let him live this down, but it would get out soon enough. "He's staying with me for now."

Somehow, Sunny's eyebrows climbed higher. "He's *what*?" He looked over his shoulder at Niklas, running passing drills with the other prospect, and back at Theo. "I didn't hear that right. Surely you didn't invite your *rival*, the man you spent the last half of the season complaining about, the one you once referred to as your 'enemy', I believe, into your home? Tell me I just hallucinated that, Brick."

Theo punched him in the arm, hard enough to sting. "I might not have taken news of his signing well, but he's—" *Ugh*. "He's a good kid. It's not his fault."

"Do you want me to offer him Oscar's bedroom?" Sunny asked, sobering. "I know how you like your routines. Oscar and Lilly can share for a month, it won't hurt them."

Niklas laughed as he missed the puck, bright and clear over the sound of skates and sticks on ice.

"No," Theo said. He smiled when Sunny looked dubious. "Really. You'll see when you meet him. He's a good kid, a good houseguest. And it won't be for long. But thank you, really. Can we get back to hockey now?"

Sunny studied his face for a minute. "I suppose," he finally said. "But this isn't over."

"Is it ever with you?" Theo said dryly. "Dog with a bone, you are. Do some shooting drills, I need to warm up, and it always makes me feel better to watch you fail."

Sunny just laughed and skated away.

Theo spent the next thirty minutes stopping pucks. First from Sunny, then Orsher and Foster joined him. Theo didn't have time to acknowledge them, too busy reading their plays, but it wouldn't have mattered. Neither of them liked him anyway. Respected him, maybe, knew what he could do between the pipes, but there was no affection there.

Once Theo was fully warmed up, he beckoned Niklas and the others over.

"Theo, this is Finn Wilson and Alvar Koskinen," Niklas said as soon as he was within earshot, the two other prospects trailing behind him like nervous ducklings.

"English," Theo reminded him.

Niklas scowled but made his way through the introduction in halting but clear English.

Theo rewarded him with a nod before looking at the shorter boy. "Finn, I know you, don't I? Where are you from?"

"Calgary," Finn said. He was barely taller than Theo, slender even under his pads, with bright blue eyes and blond hair. "I've been playing for the Bandits, in North Battlefield. Even started for the last month or so of the season."

"And you?" Theo asked Alvar.

"Helsinki," Alvar said dryly. He had red hair, acne-pitted skin, and a mouth that smiled easily. "Finn and the Finn, yeah?"

Niklas laughed, the others joining him.

Theo allowed it for a minute but then cleared his throat. "You're here to learn, not make jokes." The minute it was out, he wanted to soften it somehow, make it less of a rebuke, but he couldn't find the words, so he just let them hang as Alvar and Finn sobered instantly, looking nervous.

A smile lingered on Niklas's face, though. He shrugged when Theo narrowed his eyes questioningly. "Nothing," he said.

"We'll start with positioning," Theo said, letting it go. "Foundation is the most important part of being a goalie. If your base is unsteady or lopsided, you won't be able to find your center quickly again after a big save. Every movement you make has to be deliberate and controlled. Alvar, show me your T-pushes."

Finn said something under his breath to Alvar, who stifled a snicker.

Theo fixed him with a look and Finn quailed, head going down and shoulders hunching.

"Sorry," he mumbled when Theo didn't speak. "It's just—we know this stuff."

"You may know it," Theo said, and Finn flinched at the granite in his voice, "but I don't know *you*. So you're going to prove to me that you deserve to be here. Alvar."

Alvar cleared his throat and got between the pipes. He pushed off with one skate and slid to the top of the crease, then rotated his body and slid back to the opposite post.

"What did he do wrong?" Theo asked Finn.

Finn looked baffled. "Uhh...."

"Dropped his glove-hand," Niklas said, *sotto voce* in Swedish.

Theo pointed at him without looking. "Again. In English."

"He let fall his glove," Niklas said more loudly. He

grimaced apologetically at Alvar, who shrugged as if he was used to it.

"Never let your guard down," Theo said to Alvar. "Again."

They spent the next hour working on shuffles and T-pushes, one at a time and then in a group as Theo watched, called out corrections, and made them start over every time someone made a mistake. Then it was bag skates to measure their endurance, one end of the arena to the other, timing them separately and together and yelling every time someone flagged.

Everyone was dripping sweat by the time he let them stop. Finn doubled over, hands on his knees, and Alvar opted for the simpler expedient of sprawling on the ice.

Theo arched a brow at Niklas, who shrugged.

"We go again?"

"Fuck off," Finn groaned.

"Not bag skates," Niklas said hurriedly. He frowned, clearly searching for the word in English. "Drills?" he finally said in Swedish.

"You're not human," Alvar said, rolling his head to glare up at him. "How come your English so shit, huh? Swedish schools that bad?"

Niklas flipped him off. "Busy playing hockey," he retorted. "Why your hockey so shit? Play so much video games?"

"Okay," Theo said mildly, before blood was shed. "They're getting ready for shooting drills. Nik, you can go first. You two, keep moving so you don't stiffen up; Alvar's next and then Finn."

. . .

He positioned himself off to the side, out of range of fired pucks, and watched as Niklas got in position. Like any good goalie, he had a ritual all his own to put himself in the zone. His seemed to consist of tapping the right post, then the left, then putting his elbows on the cross bar and lifting himself off the ice before dropping back to his skates and into a crouch, glove up and ready.

Theo nodded at Coach, who blew his whistle.

* * *

Niklas was good. Theo already knew that much from watching him play in Sweden the year before, but he'd improved since then even, his reactions faster and decisions unhesitating. Occasionally he made the wrong play and a puck slipped by him, but each time he shook it off and got back in position without wavering.

He needed seasoning, experience, and a lot more games under his belt, but he had what it took. The thought stung. It shouldn't, Theo knew that. He should want what was best for the team, someone the players genuinely liked and would try for. It was stupid and selfish to want that person to be him.

You had your chance, a tiny voice whispered. *If it hasn't happened yet, what makes you think it ever will?*

He watched as Alvar took up position in net, forcing himself to pay attention. He was struggling almost immediately, stopping one out of three shots and then only by scrambling desperately.

"You're wasting energy," Theo called. "Small movements, stop throwing yourself all over the place. *Focus*. You know where the puck's going to go if you just read the play."

Alvar, face flushed behind his mask, nodded and resettled himself. The next shot thumped solidly into his glove and he shot Theo a brilliant smile.

Theo gestured at the next player, advancing fast, and Alvar jerked around but it was too late. The puck sailed between his knees and into the net.

"What did I say at the start of practice?" Theo asked.

"Never let your guard down," Alvar muttered. He was as red as his hair, mouth tight with frustration.

"Finn, your turn."

"I want to go again," Alvar protested.

"You had your chance," Theo snapped. "Finn."

Alvar scowled but left the crease, muttering under his breath, as Finn took his place.

Theo nodded at Sunny, who was waiting off to the side with a puck. He scooped it up and started toward them.

It didn't take long to see that Finn was easily as good as Niklas, if not slightly better. He thought on his feet, read every play several moves ahead, and only let in two pucks.

That was good, Theo told himself. Having not one but two solid prospects in the pipeline meant they had options. He didn't want to look too closely at why he was disappointed by the idea of Finn backing him up instead of Niklas.

Coach blew his whistle, interrupting Theo's thoughts. "Bring it in!"

The players obediently gathered around him in a loose circle, Theo off to the side where he could watch their faces.

"I don't know what you've heard about me," Coach said. "Probably things like I'm too young, not enough experience, no proven track record of winning. Well, it's true that I'm young. Thirty-six years old and never coached an NHL team before. But that doesn't mean I'm going to go easy on you. I know what we need to do to get to the Final. And I know we have what it takes." He swept the group with sharp gray eyes. "Does anyone disagree?"

Theo scanned the players. A few looked dubious but no one was stupid enough to speak up.

Coach nodded. "Three-on-three scrimmage. Niklas in this net, Finn in the other."

So he'd noticed too. Of course he had.

"Sunny, Orshie," Coach continued, "you're the captains. Choose your teams and get started. Theo, with me." He turned away without looking to see if Theo followed and headed for the door off the ice.

Theo hurried after him as quickly as he could in his gear. Coach didn't take him down the tunnel, though. Instead he closed the rink door after them and turned around to face the players through the glass, milling on the ice as Sunny and Orsher made their picks.

"What do you think?" Coach said quietly, arms crossed over his chest.

"You've got a good core this year," Theo said. Niklas was on the end closest to them, going through his routine. "They need to learn to work together, though."

Coach grunted. "Goalies?"

"Finn's good," Theo said. Sunny was charging the net, bearing down fast on Niklas. Niklas stayed with him, mirroring his trajectory, and batted the puck away almost contemptuously.

"So's this one," Coach said. "Keep watching them. I want your opinion on who should be backing you by the end of the week."

He spun on his heel and walked away, leaving Theo watching the game without really seeing it.

* * *

"I'm dying," Niklas whimpered. His cheek was pressed to the short carpet, rough against his skin, but every single muscle in his body was on fire and he couldn't move. He was pretty certain he was going to die right there, passed out on the floor of the Sentinels' dressing room.

Someone nudged him with a toe. "Good showing, kid." It was in Swedish, so—

Niklas flopped his head sideways and peered up at Sunny, beaming down at him. He was a big, blond man with a huge smile, bright blue eyes, and perpetual cheeriness. It would be disconcerting except for how he so clearly meant it.

"I'm sure I'm impressing everyone right now," Niklas mumbled, and Sunny's smile widened.

"No one survives Coach's bag skates," he said. "Especially after Theo was so brutal to you." He held out a hand.

Niklas accepted it and Sunny hauled him to his feet without effort.

"So, I hear you're staying with Theo?"

Niklas nodded as he sank onto the nearest bench without looking at the nameplate. "He's been very welcoming."

One of Sunny's eyebrows notched up. "You think so?"

The room was filling around them, volume rising as guys filtered in, tossing insults back and forth with the ease of long familiarity. Theo was among them, arriving at his stall already half-out of his gear and keeping his back to the room. Niklas averted his eyes from the sight of Theo's back muscles and glanced back at Sunny, who was still waiting for an answer.

"He's nice," Niklas said.

"Nice, sure," Sunny agreed. He sat down beside him and nudged Niklas's thigh. "I love Theo," he began, and Niklas couldn't help looking across the room again. Theo had turned halfway to talk to a rookie, his fair hair slicked back and dark with sweat. At this angle, Niklas could see Theo's abs, far more defined than they had any right to be for a man his age, and he jerked his gaze away again.

Sunny was still talking. "—Swedes have to stick together," he said.

Niklas nodded.

"But Theo's more of a lone wolf. He doesn't really… *get* the team. They're mostly a little afraid of him, or at least in awe, especially the rookies. They look up to him. But he's not friends with anyone except me, not really. So when I heard he'd invited you to stay—well, I was skeptical."

"It won't be for long," Niklas said hurriedly. "Just until I know if I'm staying up or being sent down."

Sunny patted his knee. "Come to dinner. I think it's great. Maybe you can help pull him out of his shell a bit. Get him to come out with the team sometimes. You've noticed how they're scared of him?"

Niklas nodded. "It's not right. And it hurts him."

Sunny studied Theo, stepping into shower slides. "He's never seemed bothered by it before."

"I'm sure of it."

Sunny made a thoughtful noise as Benson stepped through the door and clapped his hands. "Good showing today, guys. Most of you impressed the hell out of me." His gaze swept the room as the rookies cringed, clearly afraid of his attention. "Shower, go home, be back in the morning ready to go. Tomorrow I want *everyone* to impress me. Think that's possible?"

"Yes Coach," they all chorused dutifully, and he nodded and left the room.

Theo caught Niklas's eye from across the room and raised a brow. Niklas smiled at him, not entirely sure what he was asking, just as a lanky young man in his early twenties stepped between them. Niklas looked up into a handsome face, sharply bladed cheekbones and piercing blue eyes. Niklas had seen him on the ice, but they hadn't spoken. He wasn't sure he'd ever seen someone quite so aware of how physically attractive he was. That and the mouth twisted in sour irritation ruined the overall look a bit.

Niklas blinked at him, and the stranger's glare intensified.

"Hi," Niklas said tentatively. He glanced at Sunny, who looked amused. No help there, apparently. "I'm Nik."

The man ignored the hand Niklas held out. "You're in my stall."

Niklas twisted to look at the nameplate. XANDER JAMES. *Oops*. He scrambled to his feet and took a step sideways.

"Sorry," he said, but Xander ignored him, stepping forward to strip out of his practice jersey. "Nice to meet you too," Niklas muttered in Swedish, and turned to his stall as Sunny snickered behind him.

Theo was completely naked now except for his shower slides, a towel slung over one lean shoulder. There was a space around him, like no one wanted to get too close. On Niklas's other side, another rookie was stripping, revealing pale skin dotted with freckles.

"Arkady, right?" Niklas asked.

The rookie turned and beamed at him. Brown hair fell over a high forehead and friendly green eyes. "You call me Kasha, yes?" He held out a hand and Niklas accepted it.

"You from Birds?" he asked as he pulled off his jersey.

Kasha's face fell briefly but he just nodded. "They're good team."

"Play with Saint, yes? What he's like?"

Kasha lit up. "Saint is *best*. So good player, so good person. Just so nice."

"So why you here?" Niklas asked.

Kasha lifted a shoulder, bending to pick up his towel. "Guess they have enough forwards. Need stronger defense now. Karma can't do all on his own, yes?"

Niklas slapped him on the shoulder, wishing he could

properly convey his sympathy for the trade. "Glad you're here."

Kasha smiled at him, honest and uncomplicated.

Niklas hurried to get undressed too and followed the rest of the players into the showers. It was raucous and cheerful, and even though he couldn't understand more than about half the conversation, he still found himself relaxing, tilting his face into the spray and letting the hot water drum the tension from his muscles. It felt like home, he thought as he lathered himself up.

* * *

"So how do you feel?" Theo asked as he drove them home.

"Sore," Niklas admitted.

"Did you connect with anyone? Make any friends?"

Niklas gave him a sideways glance, sparing half a thought to appreciate Theo's perfect profile. "It wasn't school," he pointed out.

Theo's mouth quirked. "Humor me. What did you think of everyone?"

Niklas slouched, getting comfortable. "Xander's delightful."

Theo laughed out loud at that. "He's fun, isn't he? If you pull the girls' attention from him when we go out, be ready for a tantrum. He prides himself on being the best looking one on the team, he won't be happy you're here."

Niklas blinked, staring at him. Theo thought he was good looking? *Theo thought he was good looking.*

"Who else?" Theo asked, and Niklas dragged his brain back into gear.

"Uh... Sunny's great, really. Invited me over for dinner soon."

"Sunny's probably my best friend on the team," Theo said,

nodding. "Couldn't ask for a better guy. We're going over tomorrow. Hope that's okay with you."

"I get the impression he's not easy to say no to." Niklas grinned as Theo made a rueful face of agreement. "He's good with the puck, too, especially for a d-man."

"He broke the franchise record for defenseman goals last year," Theo said. "Plus I always know I can count on him in a scrum."

"I remember that fight last year," Niklas said, grinning. "When you played the Racers and that one forward crashed into you? I thought Sunny was going to rip his head off with his bare hands."

"He gets a little overzealous," Theo agreed, returning the smile. "He'll do the same for you. Anyone else stand out for you?"

"Tanaka—Nathan?"

"Nate." Theo nodded.

"Good hands. A little... disorganized. Needs to focus."

"Agreed."

Niklas shifted in his seat, warming to the subject. "I think that new forward—Kasha? The one from the Seabirds?"

"Volkov," Theo said.

"Yes, him. He's good. Could be very good someday, but he needs experience. Sweet kid, though."

Theo laughed again. "I think he's a year older than you."

Niklas resisted the urge to stick his tongue out. "Gotta be hard for him, leaving the Birds—and Saint."

Theo nodded, sobering. "Want to invite him over?"

"Is that okay?" Niklas asked, startled.

"Sure. I'll make dinner. Anyone else?"

"For dinner, or that I noticed today?" Niklas teased, and Theo shot him a mock glower.

"Smartass. You know what I meant."

"They're not fast enough," Niklas said. "They need to be a

lot faster. And I know it's only the first day, but they don't... gel. There's no real cohesion. On the first and second lines it's better, but it's like everyone thinks they're the star instead of playing like a team. They don't pass enough, either."

Theo nodded again, looking thoughtful. "You're right, of course. How do you think we should fix those things?"

"Me?" Niklas asked. "I'm just a goalie. I can't fix them."

"You're not *just* a goalie. You're an impartial observer. You know hockey inside and out, and you've already proven you have a keen eye for players' strengths and weaknesses. Plus I'm interested in your thoughts."

"Kasha's fast," Niklas offered, doing his best not to dwell on the heady revelation that Theo Wallin was interested in his, *his*, thoughts. "He needs experience, like I said, but I think he could really help pull the others up with him. Maybe put him on Orshie's wing?"

"That's an idea. I want to see Orshie improve his speed *and* confidence. Maybe Kasha can help with that."

They discussed strategy and the team's flaws the rest of the way home. Theo made them lunch, and then after they cleaned up, disappeared to work on some of his waiting orders.

Left on his own, Niklas found a Jacques Plante autobiography on Theo's bookshelf and curled up on the couch with it.

He liked it here, he thought. The city was pretty and welcoming, the people friendly. Almost everyone on the team seemed to be decent sorts, too, even if they were all afraid of Theo. And what was up with that, anyway? Niklas set the book in his lap. Sure, Theo was closed off and didn't show much emotion, but he wasn't *mean*.

If he was being honest, though, he could at least see why people thought that. Theo rarely smiled first. He certainly never initiated conversation. He was quiet and introverted, and he didn't give good interviews. He didn't bother with long, thoughtful answers to questions, and when he thought a reporter wasn't worth his time, he made it clear with clipped responses and a quick brush-off.

And there was the time he'd lost his temper in a truly spectacular fashion. Niklas had seen it happen live, and he'd watched the replays, more than once. It was the year they'd gotten within a hair's breadth of the Final. Niklas had been a teenager, awkward and gangly and already obsessed with Theo. He'd been with the Sentinels for a while by then, fifth year on the team, and in the four years since he joined, they'd been trending steadily upward. Theo was hopeful, still. It was clear in his eyes, in the way he held himself, how he'd smiled more easily and moved with purpose.

They'd gotten through the first semifinal against the Riptide and it had gone better than everyone had hoped. They took the win in four games, with Theo recording two shutouts, and advanced with high hopes to the next round.

It had been a different story against the Ravens. Five games this time, exhausting and bloody and brutal. But they'd *won*, somehow, keeping it together by sheer grit and determination and somehow, *somehow*, coming out on top.

The last round was against the Otters. If they won, they'd take the Eastern Conference Finals and be in the Stanley Cup Final. But it had cost them all seven games, and it was a struggle from the beginning. They were already worn out, dealing with multiple injuries, and the cracks were showing at the seams. They'd lost their star forward in the sixth game to a separated shoulder when he was knocked hard into the boards, their best defenseman in the game before to a dirty hit.

They went to overtime. Not once, not even twice, but *four* times with no score. Niklas still remembered, viscerally, the exhaustion that had plagued both teams, slowing their plays and dragging their bodies down in exhausted drooping curves.

He'd watched on the living room floor of his parents' house, knees hugged to his chest in breathless anticipation and hand pressed to his mouth to keep from waking them up.

In the end, it had been a stupid, awful, gutting mistake that had finished things. Theo had ducked behind the net to play the puck out with an Otter bearing down on him. He'd dealt it to a rookie who was still in front and Niklas had known exactly what he was doing. The rookie was farther away from the Otter. All he had to do was catch the puck and make a run for the offensive zone. Even if he lifted it out, it would at least give them breathing room to regroup.

Instead he'd fumbled the puck off his skate, and in his desperate attempt to retrieve it before the Otter could get there, he'd lunged with his stick and knocked it right into his own empty net.

The Otter threw up his arms.

The rookie crumpled to his knees.

And Theo had taken his stick to the net, battering it until the stick cracked and splintered, screaming his fury and heartbreak in an unguarded display of emotion that made tears spill down Niklas's face as he watched. Then he'd thrown the pieces across the ice and left without looking back.

He'd refused to take any interviews. Refused to even acknowledge it happened, disappearing completely for the summer to parts unknown until just before the next season started. Then he'd sat down with a reporter, quiet and apologetic for how he'd reacted and determined to do better. To *be* better.

But it had never happened. The team made it to the playoffs the next year but were swept in the first round. They never recovered and instead slid slowly back into obscurity, relegated to a laughingstock or an object of pity. And Niklas had watched Theo's dreams slip between his fingers, year after year after year. He'd put up barriers, refused to let anyone in, growing quieter and less approachable as time wound on.

It made sense that almost everyone gave him a wide berth, that everyone thought he was just a prickly asshole. But Niklas knew better. He thought about the letter, tucked inside the pages of The Game, and shook his head. The man who'd written that letter had been kind, thoughtful. He'd taken the time out of a busy season to write by hand to a boy who adored him and not just give him advice but also tell him stories of time spent on the ice with legendary players. Those weren't the actions of an asshole. Theo Wallin was a good man. Maybe he tried to hide it, but Niklas wasn't fooled.

Eight

THEO WORKED until his phone went off and he blinked as he surfaced. *Fuck*, he had an interview and he'd forgotten all about it. He ran for the house, kicking off his shoes in the kitchen and washing his hands as quickly as he could as someone knocked on the front door.

"You okay?" Niklas asked, half off the couch as Theo dashed into the living room.

"I forgot, I *fucking* forgot I had an interview today." Theo shot him an apologetic glance. "It won't take long, okay?"

"Oh, I'll go in my room—"

"No, stay." Theo pulled the door open before Niklas could protest, giving a smile that felt almost genuine to the woman on the other side. "Julianna, welcome."

Julianna was a pretty redhead in her early thirties, a cameraman lurking behind her that she introduced as Victor. "Pretend he's not here," she said. "Means he can do a better job." As usual, she didn't quite meet Theo's gaze, a brisk smile on her face that didn't reach her eyes. She caught sight of Niklas as he shifted his weight. "And who's this?"

"This is the Sentinels' newest acquisition," Theo said.

"Niklas Stromberg, this is Julianna. Don't let her scare you. I've known her for years and she's actually quite nice for a reporter, plus she doesn't ask *too* many dumb questions. Nik is a goalie, Julianna."

Julianna held out her hand and Niklas accepted it, bobbing his head awkwardly.

"Can I offer you a drink or something to eat?" Theo asked.

"Water's fine for both of us," Julianna said.

"I'll get it," Niklas interjected, and he was gone immediately, leaving Theo staring after him bemusedly.

"He seems sweet," Julianna said, shifting her weight and flipping through her notes as if she needed something to do with her hands.

Theo made a noncommittal noise and showed Julianna to a seat, settling across from her as Victor fussed with his camera, muttering under his breath about the lighting.

When Niklas came back, he had three glasses of water on a tray and a platter of cookies, painstakingly arranged in careful rows. Theo accepted his glass, the ice clinking, and Niklas smiled at him, clearly anxious.

"Is this okay?" he asked quietly in Swedish.

"Yes, of course," Theo said, glancing at him. "Thank you."

Julianna took a glass and a cookie and leaned back in her chair. "So, Theo, how have you been?"

Niklas shifted his feet. "I'll just—" He took a step away, and Julianna put a hand out.

"Why don't you stay? Maybe I can ask you a few questions about Theo."

Niklas darted a look at Theo, who nodded. Why not? Maybe he'd deflect a little of the attention. Theo wasn't proud of himself but still honest enough to admit the prospect was enticing.

"Season's about to start," Julianna said to Theo as Niklas sank onto the cushion beside him. "This was your first day of camp, wasn't it? Why don't you take us through your thoughts on the team this year?"

Theo obliged, keeping his critical comments to himself and praising the players. He kept his comments short, a blatantly false smile on his face, and wondered if Niklas was taking note of how to do it. He'd have had his own share of interviews in Sweden, of course, but North American reporters were a different breed, even if the Canadian ones tended to be a little less aggressive than their United States counterparts.

"And what about Niklas here?" Julianna asked after a few minutes.

"He did well today," Theo said honestly, giving Niklas a quick glance. Niklas squirmed, cheeks blooming faintly pink. "He even survived Coach's bag skates. Not many manage that, especially not the goalies. I think he's going to be a valuable addition to the team."

"Not worried about him replacing you?" Julianna's eyes were sharp, and Theo stiffened briefly, keeping still with an effort.

"Well, time marches on, doesn't it?" He glanced at Niklas, who was rigid with clear distress. Theo shook his head, the smallest of motions, and Niklas relaxed a fraction, still watching him like a hawk. Theo looked back at Julianna and somehow brought up a smile that was more a grim twist of his lips. "We all know I'm not getting any younger. But I'm not ready to retire just yet. I'll be around awhile longer, and I'm looking forward to seeing how Nik finds his place on the team."

"Niklas," Julianna said, switching her focus to him. "How do you feel about playing with Theo?"

"Excited," Niklas answered. Theo wondered if Julianna

could hear the distaste in his voice. Probably not—he was hiding it well, and hopefully she'd write it off as him not being comfortable in English if she *did* catch it. "I watched Theo as boy—as *a* boy. You would say... I grew up with him."

Julianna's eyebrows went up.

"He means he grew up following my career," Theo added. He slanted a small smile at Niklas, who nodded. "We just met yesterday for the first time."

"How do you like Saskatoon?" Julianna asked Niklas, who looked like he was still fighting the urge to squirm.

"Very pretty," he said, enunciating his words carefully. "Everyone is... so nice."

Theo pushed back the urge to pat his knee. "You're doing great," he murmured in Swedish, and Niklas flashed a smile at him.

"Where are you staying, Niklas?" Julianna asked.

"Oh, here," Niklas said, turning the smile on her. "Theo is so nice. He ask me to stay, so I say yes, of course!"

Julianna's eyebrows were in her hairline. "Theo, you invited your rival to *live* with you?"

"He's not my rival," Theo said harshly, and took a breath, forcing himself to calm. "I realize that conflict sells stories, but Niklas is a rookie and a teammate and didn't have a place to stay. I offered him one of my bedrooms temporarily. That's all this is."

Niklas looked unhappy, mouth drooping.

Thankfully, Julianna took the not-very-subtle hint and changed the subject, asking Theo what he'd done that summer.

"I went to Japan," he said. "I studied at a temple in Sendai to help learn mindfulness and how to center myself."

"You're pretty mindful already, I'd say," Julianna commented.

"There's always room for improvement." Theo managed a tight smile.

"And how do you see this season going?"

"It's too soon to tell," Theo said. "But I'm hopeful. We have some real talent on our roster this year. The rookies are showing a lot of promise, and I can't wait to see what we can do."

"And what about your own life?" Julianna asked.

Theo sighed internally. Just like clockwork. "What about it?"

"You've been single for a while, haven't you? No potential love interests on the horizon?"

Niklas squirmed as if wishing he could leave. Theo sympathized.

"No," he said evenly. "I like being single. I can do things the way I like. At this stage of my life, whoever I meet would need to be extraordinary for me to want to rearrange my entire way of living to accommodate them. I'm just as happy alone."

Julianna made a note but thankfully, moved on to the next question.

The interview lasted another excruciating thirty minutes, but finally Theo and Niklas were alone again.

"Is it always that bad?" Niklas asked once the door was closed.

Theo raised an eyebrow. "That was pretty mild."

Niklas shuddered. "Are they going to ask me questions about my love life?"

"Some of them," Theo said. "Until you get a girlfriend, at least. Then they'll back off a bit."

Niklas made a face, surprising him. "No time to date. Who can date as a rookie in the NHL?"

Theo chuckled, low. "Are you really surprised by how many guys your age think with their dicks?"

Niklas muttered something under his breath. "Do you think I'll be sent down?"

Theo blinked at the abrupt change of topic and Niklas hunched his shoulders.

"Sorry. Been thinking about it for a while."

Theo nodded. Understandable. "You want my honest opinion?"

Niklas nodded, firming his jaw.

"It's what I would do, if I were your coach," Theo said.

Niklas stared at his lap.

"You're good, Nik," Theo said gruffly, and gentled his voice. "You're *really* good. But you need experience. Think about it. I'm the starting goalie right now. I'm still pretty close to the top of my game, which means I'm their best chance of making it to the playoffs. They're not going to risk putting you in net too often just yet, not when you're used to playing in Europe, on a bigger rink, with less pressure." He held up his hand before Niklas could protest. "I know, there was plenty of pressure then. But it's still different here. And there's Finn. He's every bit as good as you. He deserves a chance at the position too."

Niklas scowled, fists balling.

"That drive is what got you here," Theo said before he could speak. "So get out there and show Coach you deserve it more than Finn. *Earn* it."

"I will," Niklas said, lifting his chin. "I *will*."

"No one wants to be sent down," Theo said. "But if it happens, it'll be good for you. And hey, tell you what. Why don't you just leave your stuff here? *If* it happens."

Niklas looked up, eyes going wide. "Oh, but—"

"It makes more sense than you getting a place and having to pay the utilities and rent on a place you're only in for a few weeks at a time," Theo pointed out. "This way you have a place whenever you need it, and once you're up for good, whenever that may be, then you can think about finding something of your own."

Niklas's mouth worked. "Are you *sure*—I know you don't want—"

"I'm sure," Theo interrupted. "I wouldn't offer if I wasn't."

Niklas studied his face for a minute and finally nodded. "If you're sure. But if you regret it, if you change your mind and you want me to go, I promise I will, just tell me and—"

Theo held up a hand to forestall him, unable to stop the smile. "You really are a sweet kid. But it'll be fine."

"Can I ask you something?"

Theo lifted an inquiring brow.

"Why is everyone afraid of you?"

Theo's face shuttered. "It's really not that deep. I'm not very friendly."

"I know you're pretty private," Niklas said. His eyes were heartbreakingly earnest as he leaned forward, hands clutched in his lap. "But you're just... intense. I don't understand why people act like you'll knife them if they breathe wrong around you."

Theo stood so quickly Niklas flinched. "I have a lot of work to do. Dinner's at six." He strode away without looking back.

Safe in his workspace, he stared unseeingly at the maple plank in front of him. How did he make Niklas understand he simply wasn't easy to like? For that matter, why didn't Niklas already see that for himself? Why did he persist in this delusion that he was actually kind, deep down? The thought of watching Niklas's faith in him fade made his chest constrict, but it *would* happen. He knew that from bitter experience. It was better to rip the bandage off clean, get it over with. But how to do it without hurting him?

He needed someone else's perspective.

Anjali picked up on the second ring. "What's wrong?" Her light British accent was as crisp as ever but Theo could hear the distraction in her voice.

"Why do you assume something's wrong?" Theo deflected. He ran a hand over the maple—the grain was silky smooth. It was perfect for his purposes.

The silence from the other end of the line was pointed.

Theo sighed. "One of the goalie prospects is staying with me for training camp."

Anjali said something, her voice muffled like she was covering the phone's speaker. "Was that your idea?" she asked.

"If you're busy, it can wait."

Anjali snorted. "I'm always busy, darling. You know that. As long as you don't mind me doing a fitting at the same time, I can talk. No, I want the hem an inch lower."

"I'm assuming you're not talking about my hems," Theo said dryly.

"Don't deflect."

Theo gave up. "Fine. Yes. It was my idea."

"Uh-huh. Why?"

"Because... he's Swedish. His English isn't great. He's a good kid and I have plenty of room. It's no trouble."

"And that's it?"

Theo rolled his shoulders. Anjali's ability to cut through the bullshit was usually his favorite thing about her, but it could also be pretty uncomfortable in the moment. "He says I'm the reason he became a goalie."

"Ah."

"What does that mean?"

"Oh, Theo. You pretend you don't need people, don't *like* people—"

"I don't," Theo muttered.

"But even you have an ego. I'll wager hearing him talk about how much he admires you made you want to curl up and purr, didn't it?"

Theo scowled at the sandpaper on the bench. "It was horrifying."

"Of course it was. But it also felt good, didn't it?" Anjali paused for a reply but Theo didn't give her one. "You're human, darling. It feels good when people admire us, even when we don't think we deserve it."

"How do I make him see I'm not… the person he thinks I am?"

"If he lives with you for even a week and doesn't realize it by the third day, he's too stupid for you to waste your time on. And you wouldn't have offered him a place to stay if he was stupid."

Theo almost laughed. "No, I wouldn't have."

"So let him discover the truth on his own. Either he'll decide you're what *you* say you are—a horrible monster who deserves to be alone forever—"

"Hey!"

"Or he'll see you're human, with flaws, yes. But also with a huge heart and a generosity of spirit you can never truly hide."

Theo blew out a breath and rubbed his face. "I don't want him to… be disappointed."

"Is that so?" Anjali said, tone sharpening, and Theo cursed himself silently. "Is it like that?"

"It's like nothing," Theo snapped. "Don't get any ideas."

"I would never," Anjali purred. "Tell me more about this goalie."

"First of all, I'm over a decade older than him," Theo said.

"Some people like an experienced lover," Anjali pointed out.

"He's an *infant*!" Theo protested.

"If he's a prospect, he's a grown man," Anjali countered. "He might be young but he's not a child. And it sounds as if you like him."

"I don't *know* him," Theo said. He picked up a pencil and set the phone on the table beside him, putting it on speaker. "It's really not like that, and you have *got* to stop assuming anyone who's friendly to me wants in my bed."

Anjali's laugh rolled out, rich and delighted. "Oh, my darling, of course I don't assume that. But you have to admit this is not something you would do for just anyone."

Theo rolled his eyes. "I don't have to admit anything." He drew light, curving sketch lines on the maple, letting the woodgrain tell his pencil where to go.

"What are you working on?" Anjali asked.

"A screen for Inga," Theo said absently. "Her birthday's coming up and Sunny asked me for ideas. I'm going to do some lattice work on it, freehand, and see what happens."

"A lattice pattern would make a lovely design for a vest," Anjali mused. "Send me some pictures when you've made some progress. I must dash. I look forward to meeting your new pet soon."

"He's *not*—" But Anjali had already disconnected.

Theo thunked his forehead lightly against the wood and then straightened. Anjali was maddening but as usual, she'd been right. Niklas would figure it out for himself and if he couldn't, it wasn't Theo's problem.

Nine

CAMP SEEMED to last forever and nowhere near long enough. By the third day, Niklas was beginning to recognize faces. He still hadn't figured out who'd called Theo an asshole the first day, but he would have put money on it being Xander.

He had other things to worry about, in any case. Namely, proving to Coach that he was better than Finn. And Finn wasn't going to go quietly. He matched Niklas's energy, save after diving save and making it look easy as he fought off every assault without getting rattled.

Coach called a meeting on the last day of camp. "Roster's up," he said without preamble.

No one moved.

"Those who aren't on it," Coach continued, sweeping the room, "I want to thank you for your time and effort. This is never an easy decision to make, and you made it even harder than usual. Please come back next year."

With that, he nodded and left the room.

There was a breathless silence, and then the rookies broke

for the door, elbowing each other as if reaching the list first would ensure their name was on it.

Niklas forced himself to wait, standing and shaking his hair out of his eyes before heading for the hall and the group clustered around the huge cork board at the far end. Theo joined him, hands in the pockets of his sweater.

"Do you want me to look for you?" he asked under the clamor.

Niklas wanted nothing more. He shook his head and dove into the crowd, wriggling through until he was at the front. He ignored the lists of forwards and defense pairs, skipping to the bottom where the goalies were posted.

STARTING GOALIE: Theo Wallin

BACKUP: Finn Wilson

ASSIGNED TO BANDITS: Niklas Stromberg

That was it, then. Niklas turned away from the list, letting the others jostle and buffet him as they all crowded closer to see. He'd done his best, and it hadn't been good enough.

Theo was watching him, sympathy in his eyes. "I'm sorry," he said quietly.

From somewhere, Niklas dredged up a smile. "I'll be back." He squared his shoulders. "Can't get rid of me that easy."

* * *

"Car's here," Theo called from the living room.

Niklas zipped his last bag and slung it over his shoulder before grabbing the duffel with all his gear in it and hauling everything to the front door.

Theo met him there, looking warm and cozy in another

shawl-collared sweater, this one the color of his eyes, like gray mist on the prairie at dawn.

"Give 'em hell," he said.

Niklas wanted to hug him, thank him for opening his house to him, but Theo's hands were back in his pockets, his bearing closed off even though his eyes were soft.

"Thank you," Niklas said instead, hoisting his bag higher. "I mean—you know. For everything."

Theo almost smiled, just a flicker of his lips twitching, but Niklas treasured it anyway. "You'll be back before you know it."

Niklas nodded. "See you."

Theo watched from the door as Niklas loaded his bags in the trunk, and Niklas's last sight was him lifting one hand in farewell as the car left the driveway.

* * *

He'd been assigned to an apartment with three other rookies, and he knocked but no one answered, so finally he dragged his luggage through the unlocked front door, not knowing what to expect.

It was bland and nondescript, an open floor plan with a small foyer in front of him, living room beyond, and the kitchen to his left. There were dishes piled high in the sink and scattered carelessly across the counter amid the wreckage of frozen meal containers and takeout. Horrified, Niklas watched as a fly landed on the lip of one of the takeout containers and minced its way delicately inside.

"New guy!" someone yelled, and thundering footsteps came from overhead.

Three young men skidded into the foyer at the same time, falling over each other in a wild tangle of arms and legs. Two of them were shirtless, the dark-haired one in ratty sweats and the blond in a pair of basketball shorts that had seen better days. The third was wearing a T-shirt and jeans, neat and pressed, with pale hair falling in a shining wave over his forehead.

The two shirtless boys untangled themselves and the nearest one put out a huge hand. The other grabbed him and yanked, putting his own hand out.

"Joel Weaver," he said, beaming at Niklas, who hesitated but finally took his hand. "You're Niklas?"

Niklas nodded.

Joel shook his fair hair, a few shades darker than his roommate's, from his eyes. He had a round face and a mouth that smiled easily, acne still spotting his chin and cheeks. "Morgan Buckley," he said, indicating the dark-haired one, who scowled at him but put a hand out to Niklas. "*Not* a country music singer, despite the name."

Niklas blinked and Morgan rolled his eyes. Joel continued blithely.

"And this is Cam Spencer. He's got a stick up his ass but he's okay."

Niklas shook hands all around. "Uh. Room?"

"Right! You're next to me," Morgan said. He was tall, only a few inches shorter than Niklas, with eyebrows that slashed across his forehead and dark, striking eyes. When he smiled, his eyes lit up. "C'mon, I'll show you. You tired? We were gonna play some Chel before dinner."

Niklas shook his head, settling his bag again. "Not long drive."

Morgan grabbed the gear bag. "Fuckin' goalies," he complained as he swung it up over his shoulder. "Is that why you're all so jacked? Carting all this gear around?"

"You checking out their asses?" Joel asked, snickering.

Cam hadn't said a word, eyes missing nothing, but now he

punched Joel's shoulder, making him yelp. "Don't be an asshole."

"Ow! I *wasn't*!" Joel rubbed his shoulder, glaring at Cam aggrievedly. "I was just making a joke!"

Cam just rolled his eyes and turned away.

"Stick," Joel said to Niklas in a confidential tone. "Wedged *way* up there."

Niklas couldn't stop the snicker, which won him a delighted grin from Joel.

"Come on," Morgan called, already halfway up the stairs, and Niklas hurried after him.

There were four bedrooms, none of them huge, and Niklas set his bag on the floor in the one at the end of the hall.

Morgan lingered in the doorway. "You like sushi?"

"Yes, of course," Niklas said.

"Cool. I'm gonna place the order. You can cash app me." With that, Morgan disappeared, yelling something incomprehensible to Joel, who shouted back from downstairs.

Niklas sat on the bed, looking at the bare walls. He didn't want to be there. He *shouldn't* be there. But pouting about it wouldn't do any good. He just had to prove to everyone that he had what it took. He could do that.

"Strommer!"

He was pretty sure that was Morgan.

They were in the living room when Niklas came down the stairs, Joel and Morgan with controllers in their hands as they stared fixedly at the television, and Cam tucked neatly in an overstuffed armchair, long legs folded underneath himself and a book in his hands.

"Strommer, you gotta help," Joel said, not looking up.

"Terrible nickname," Niklas said. He settled himself on the arm of the couch. "What help you need?"

"You gotta make sure Morgan doesn't cheat." Joel shouldered the cheater in question and Morgan scowled, shoving him right back. "And you have to have a nickname!"

"So, I hear you're some kind of goalie legend?" Morgan said over Joel.

Niklas grimaced. "If legend, I'm with Sentinels, not here. Sorry."

Cam didn't look up from his book. "Gotta work your way up, right?"

"What would you know about that?" Joel sniped. "His dad is *rich* rich," he said to Niklas. "Like Richie Rich money-bags. Disgustingly loaded."

Cam threw his book at Joel, who ducked. It bounced off Morgan, who squawked.

"It's not my fault my dad's got money and I'm *sick* of hearing about it," Cam hissed. "Besides, I don't hear you complaining when I pick up the tab. Now give me my book back."

"Whoa, hey, Cammer, don't be like that," Joel said. He grabbed the book and held it out like a peace offering. "I was just helping Nik get to know us. Like, your dad's rich, Morgan's dad's an asshole, mine took off when I was a kid, that kind of thing."

"He's not an asshole," Morgan said. It sounded automatic, like he'd said it a thousand times. Sure enough, Joel and Cam mouthed the next sentence along with him. "He just cares about me."

Joel rolled his eyes at Niklas, who fought a smile. Maybe this wouldn't be so bad.

"So what about your dad?" Joel asked.

Niklas shrugged. "Works a lot," he said.

"That kind," Morgan said, nodding sympathetically. "Sucks."

"Paid for hockey," Niklas pointed out.

He learned more about everyone as they ate sushi. Cam

was a forward. Joel and Morgan were defensemen. Joel's stick-handling wasn't the best, at least according to Morgan and Cam, but he threw big hits and he didn't run from a fight. Morgan's stick-handling was excellent and his footwork was even better, according to Joel through a mouthful of sushi.

Cam punched his shoulder hard. "You're disgusting."

"But also right," Joel said, and ducked the next swing as he grabbed another piece of sushi and shoved it in his mouth.

Ten

IT *WASN'T* SO BAD, Niklas decided. For one thing, he was starting in net, as his coach told him. That alone was almost enough to ease the sting of being sent down.

For another, he liked his team. They skewed young, but there were a few veterans, men in their thirties who weren't going to make it to the show, knew it and had made their peace with it. John Alden was considered the team dad, bringing the rookies over for dinner almost every week.

"Helps that his wife is a total rocket," Morgan confided to Niklas, and got punched by Cam for his troubles.

"Don't objectify, it's rude."

"It was *respectful* objectifying!" Morgan protested, rubbing his arm.

Niklas's defense was solid, with Joel and Morgan making up one of the pairings. He was happy to see that for all their horsing around off the ice, once they were on it, they were all business. Morgan was a stay-at-home defenseman, preferring to keep to his own end, but Joel showed a lot of offensive talent.

"He's got the franchise record for most goals by a D-man," Morgan said. He sounded proud.

Cam was a forward, with quick feet and silky hands. A week into his stay, Niklas had realized most of his reserved behavior was simply shyness. He was always the first to offer to pay for anything, and even if it was because he wanted the others to accept him, Niklas could understand that.

Even the Bandits' goalie was welcoming, a reserved Finn named Joonas Ratia. He was in his late thirties, most of his career solidly behind him, and not threatened by Niklas's presence.

Still, Niklas missed Theo. He'd only known him for two weeks, but he wanted to be back in Saskatchewan with him, to be the one on the bench watching him play from the best seat in the house. To be in the *net*, with Theo watching *him* play.

It helped that Theo texted him, though, almost every day. He seemed to always appreciate the snaps Niklas sent, even if he rarely sent pictures back. A week in, as he and the others watched a movie, Niklas's phone buzzed.

How was your day?

Niklas perked up. He was only catching bits and pieces of the movie anyway. *Who is this and how did you get my number.* He grinned as he pressed Send.

Sure enough, the reply arrived in under a minute. *Very funny.*

Thanks, Niklas sent. Was Theo in bed already? Probably—two weeks with him had been enough to show Niklas that he liked his bedtimes early. *The guys are great. I like it here. But I'd rather be there.*

I know, Theo responded. *Keep working. It'll happen before you know it.*

Good luck tomorrow, Niklas wrote.

"Who're you talking to?" Joel asked, leaning over to peer at the phone. "You're always on that thing."

Niklas reflexively held it out of reach. "No one. And you no room to talk, shut the fuck up."

"Does no one have a name?" Morgan asked. He was slumped sideways, head on Cam's shoulder, and Niklas had assumed he was asleep until he spoke.

"Is it a girl?" Joel said. "Come on, Nik, spill. We're all single, we gotta live vicariously."

"How do you even know that word," Cam muttered, crossing his ankles on the coffee table.

"Fuck you, I've read a book," Joel retorted. "Nik? Ni-ik. Nikky baby. NikkyNikkyNikky—"

Niklas put a hand over his entire face to shut him up. "Is not a girl. Just Theo."

Joel pulled Niklas's hand away. "Theo as in... Wallin? As in the main reason I *don't* want to get called up?"

"You—what."

Joel shrugged. "He eats D-men for breakfast, man. He's terrifying. Like if you do something wrong, he'll rip your head off. He's mean. No one likes him."

"He's *not*."

Joel blinked, clearly taken aback by the vehement response, and Morgan sat up.

"We fighting? Already?"

"Shut up," Cam said with no heat. "No one's fighting."

"Theo is... good person," Niklas said, furious but struggling to contain it. English was hard enough when he was calm, dammit. "He's not mean."

"Then how come no one likes him?" Joel asked, one skeptical eyebrow raised.

Niklas shook his head hard. "I stay with him," he said. "He *invite* me. Ask me. Would a mean person be this way?"

"Maybe he just wants his competition where he can keep an eye on it," Cam suggested. He held up his hands when

Niklas switched his glare to him. "Just saying. I've never met him."

"I have," Morgan said.

All three of them turned to him and he fidgeted under the sudden attention.

"I played a couple of games last year when Sundstrom was out. It was before your time, Cam, but Joel, you remember."

"Oh yeah. I'd just gotten here. So what'd you think of him?"

Morgan lifted a shoulder. "He's not as bad as everyone thinks. But—" he said hurriedly as Niklas straightened in triumph, "I can see *why* people think that. He got mad at a forward who made a stupid decision, tore strips off him—"

"Yelled at him," Joel said, catching sight of Niklas's visible confusion.

"Sorry, yeah," Morgan continued. "The guy had turned over the puck and couldn't catch up to the player who got it. They had a two on one and Theo didn't stand a chance. When the guy tried to apologize, after the game, Theo just *looked* at him. Icy cold. Like the dude wasn't even worth speaking to. Walked away without a word. The guy was put on the fourth line the next day." Morgan shrugged again. "I dunno. He's a good goalie but he's pretty scary if you get on his bad side."

Niklas shook his head again. He didn't even know where to *start*.

Joel took pity on him, patting his knee. "S'cool, dude. You got a thing for him. Happens to everyone. He *is* pretty hot, even if he's old as balls."

"A... thing," Niklas echoed.

"Crush," Joel said helpfully. "You want to kiss him. Call him daddy—*ow*! Stop *punching* me, Cam!"

"Stop saying stupid things then," Cam said. "And leave Nik alone. I want to watch the movie."

Joel grumbled but settled back down as Morgan made

himself comfortable against Cam's shoulder again and Niklas stared at the screen without seeing it.

"I do," he said suddenly.

Joel startled. "Huh?"

Morgan didn't move, eyes closed again.

Cam quietly paused the movie, saying nothing.

Niklas lifted his chin, chest tight. "I have... *thing* for Theo. Is problem for you?"

Joel blinked rapidly, glancing between Niklas and the others, who still hadn't spoken.

"It's fine," Cam said. His voice was as even as ever. "Jojo?"

"Why are you asking me?" Joel complained. "Why not Morgan?"

"Because he knows I don't have a problem with it either," Morgan said. His eyes were still closed, arms crossed over his chest.

Joel's eyes nearly bugged out of his head and he scrambled off the couch.

"Aw, there it is," Cam said, amusement threading his tone.

Morgan sighed and sat up. "Joel, can you get the freakout over with already so we can finish this damn movie or what?"

"You guys?" Joel demanded, voice high with shock. "*And* him?" Gesturing at Niklas. "Did you know he—"

"Gaydar isn't a thing," Morgan said.

"Yes it is," Cam said instantly.

Morgan glared at him. "No, we didn't know until Nik said something. The *point* is we don't have a problem with it. Do you?"

"Well of course not!" Joel spluttered, and the tightness in Niklas's chest eased. "You guys could have just *told* me, though! What, you didn't trust me?"

Cam sighed. "Can you blame us?" He glanced at Niklas, sitting very still. "You've got balls, man. Coming out when you didn't know how we'd react?"

Niklas lifted a shoulder, wishing he was anywhere else. Wishing he was back in Theo's house, sitting at his counter and eating his food.

"We've got your back," Morgan added unexpectedly.

Niklas glanced at Joel, unable to stop himself. So did the other two.

"Why are you all *looking* at me?" Joel said plaintively.

"You know why." Cam, his voice implacable.

Joel fidgeted. "Nik, you're my boy. O-of course I've got your back. But like... you're not gonna hit on me, are you?"

"Joel Alexander Weaver," Cam snapped, voice so hard Joel physically flinched back a step. "That was the *stupidest* fucking thing you've ever said and you've said some incredibly stupid shit around me. Apologize. Right now."

"Sorry," Joel mumbled, eyes on the floor. He looked up suddenly, shame on his face. "I *am*, Strommer, really. You're my *goalie*. And like... my friend. I care about you or whatever."

Niklas stood and crossed the room to pull him into a rough hug. "So stupid," he said against Joel's hair.

Joel laughed, the sound a little wet. "Yeah, well. Are we good?"

Niklas released him to poke him in the ribs, making Joel squawk inelegantly. Niklas used the distraction to get him in a headlock. Joel squawked again, flailing wildly, but Niklas had a good hold and tickled him mercilessly with his free hand until Joel was begging for mercy, breathless and hiccuping with laughter as Cam and Morgan watched, grinning.

"Don't worry," Nik said, Joel's head still trapped under his arm. "You too ugly for me, Jojo."

Morgan hooted a laugh. "We've already established he likes them hot and mean. You're neither, buddy."

Joel flailed and Niklas poked him in the ribs again. When he finally let him go, Joel made a vain attempt to straighten his hair and regain his dignity, although his bright red face gave it the lie.

"So, like," he said, flopping on the couch next to Morgan and beckoning until Niklas sat again too. "We gotta find you a boyfriend, huh?"

"*No*," Niklas spluttered.

"Sure we do," Joel insisted. "S'not right you're alone. Do you *want* a boyfriend?"

Unbidden, an image of Theo smiling at him sprang to Niklas's mind.

"No," he said, sliding down on the cushions.

"You know Wallin's like *super* old, right?" Joel asked.

"He's not!" Niklas protested, sitting bolt upright again.

Joel snickered, holding out a palm that Morgan immediately smacked.

"Fuck off," Niklas muttered, slouching again.

Joel leaned in, eyes innocent. "I know what you want."

Niklas watched him warily.

"Daddy," Joel crooned, and Niklas tackled him off the couch.

Eleven

THE HOUSE WAS TOO EMPTY. Theo hated it. Niklas had only been with him for two weeks. What right did he have to come in and turn everything Theo liked on its head, make him *miss* the sound of Niklas singing along, tuneless and full of joy, to the song on his phone?

He scowled at the pan in his hand. He'd made too much food and now he'd have leftovers for a week. And no one there to eat them but him.

He was busy putting the quesadillas into several containers when his phone rang.

Was it Nik, maybe? They hadn't spoken on the phone since Niklas had been sent down, but they texted every day. Niklas seemed content with Theo's short answers, sending pictures of his roommates playing Twister or wrestling—Theo couldn't always tell which—or descriptions of his dinner. Apparently, said roommates were also appalling slobs, so Niklas complained about washing a lot of dishes too.

Theo wiped his hands on the towel tucked into his pocket and scooped up the phone. It was Coach.

"Finn twisted his ankle playing basketball, the stupid fuck," he said by way of greeting.

"Is he okay?" Theo asked.

Coach made an irritated noise. "He's fine. Probably won't even need much recovery time. But he can't back you up tomorrow."

Which meant Nik would be called up. Theo fought the smile. "Okay," he said as neutrally as possible.

"I want Nik to start tomorrow," Coach said abruptly. "Okay with you?"

"We're playing the Otters," Theo said. "It'll be a good test."

"Yep." Coach hung up and Theo nearly laughed as he set the phone down.

A text popped up on the screen.

Tell him for me, Coach had sent.

He could do that.

Niklas answered on the fifth ring, sounding startled.

"Theo? Everything okay?"

"Yes, of course," Theo said hurriedly. "Why would you think otherwise?"

"You don't call me," Niklas said. "I mean—we just don't talk on the phone. I know you're busy. What's going on?"

"I don't mind talking on the phone sometimes," Theo said. "At least when I like the person I'm talking *to*."

He could hear the smile in Niklas's voice when he replied. "Then maybe I'll call you sometimes. Get your feedback after games."

"I'd like that," Theo said, knowing he was smiling too but unable to stop himself. "But I did have a reason for calling today. You're being called up."

Niklas caught his breath. "Really?"

"You're starting against the Otters tomorrow. Think you're up for it?"

"*Yes*," Niklas said instantly. "Joel! Cam!"

"What?" someone yelled in the distance.

"I'm called up!" Niklas shouted back, and the other person—Joel or Cam, Theo had no idea—whooped like a banshee.

"Get packed," Theo said over the noise of them celebrating. "Be up here tonight so you can practice with the team tomorrow. You have someone who can drive you?"

"Yes! I'll see you soon!" Niklas shouted, and hung up as Theo winced.

He arrived two hours later, gear bag over his shoulder and a huge grin on his face as he waved goodbye to the person who had driven him.

"Your friend doesn't want to come in?" Theo asked as the driver put his car in reverse and hurriedly backed out of the driveway.

"He's terrified of you," Niklas said cheerfully. "Hi! You look good."

Theo peered over his shoulder, but the car was already on the road. He swallowed and looked up at Niklas, who was still smiling.

"You too," he said. It shouldn't hurt, that someone he'd never even met was so afraid of him. It was what he'd wanted for so long—to be left alone. He was being stupid. Again.

Niklas dropped his bag in the hall and reached for him. Theo found himself pulled into a hug before he could even react, tucked in under Niklas's chin with his nose pressed to Niklas's collarbone. He smelled good, like cedar and some kind of flower Theo couldn't identify.

Niklas released him almost immediately, looking embarrassed. "Sorry," he said, rubbing the back of his neck. "Didn't mean to make you uncomfortable."

"You didn't," Theo said. He smiled up at him and Niklas's face lit with his returning smile.

"I missed you. Is that silly? I know it's only been a few weeks."

Theo bent to grab Niklas's bag, mostly to hide his face. "It's not silly," he said as he straightened. "What would you like for dinner? I have quesadillas I can warm up."

* * *

Niklas was awake before Theo for once, tiptoeing into the kitchen to turn on the coffee Theo couldn't function without and then padding into the living room. The sky was gray through the huge bay windows, pale sunlight creeping across the prairie and setting the tips of the grass aflame with flickers of rose and gold.

He rolled up on his toes and stretched for the ceiling, then bent double to press his face to his knees, arms around his legs as the muscles in his back loosened by degrees.

As he worked through his stretches, he thought about the stricken look on Theo's face when Joel hadn't wanted to meet him. He'd hid it quickly, but Niklas had still seen it, and it hurt him, somewhere deep in his chest. Theo deserved to be loved. No matter how much he said he liked being alone, Niklas knew it wasn't the truth.

But how to make others see Theo the way *he* saw him?

He dropped into the splits and folded face down onto the floor, arms over his head, as a plan began to form.

He was greeted with rowdy hugs and back-slaps in the dressing room, emerging from the crush with his hair in his eyes and a grin he couldn't smother.

"We missed you," Cole informed him.

"Theo's grumpy when you're not here," Sunny added.

"I am not," Theo said without looking up from his equipment bag.

Niklas tried to ignore the pleased warmth in his chest. "I missed you too." He caught a glimpse of Xander scowling at him. "Theo always tell me how hard it is, playing with you. He says he has to do all by himself. So sad!"

"I do *not*!"

Niklas made an exaggerated pouting face at Sunny, whose grin was spreading. "I tell you secret. What works best for him."

"Tell me," Sunny said, looking delighted.

Niklas leaned in, pitching his voice loud enough for Theo to hear. "Put him to bed, give him bottle when he's grumpy. Work every time."

"*Hey*!"

Sunny laughed out loud over Theo's indignant sputtering. "Oh yeah, we definitely missed you." He slung an arm around Niklas's neck. "You're coming to dinner tomorrow." He pointed at Theo. "Both of you."

Theo glanced between them, studying their faces. Niklas waited for him to push back, object to being teased in front of the team, but instead Theo shrugged.

"I'm guessing I don't have much of a choice. Nik, get changed, we have drills to run."

Niklas followed him to the ice, wondering if he'd gone too far, but Theo's smile was easy when he turned to face him.

"Long t-pushes first, I think."

Niklas followed his lead and they warmed up in silence, moving in unison. The familiar repetitive motions helped, but he couldn't stop thinking about the upcoming game. His first NHL game. He was playing *in the NHL*, in an arena with thousands watching. Oh God, he was going to throw up.

"Race you," Theo said abruptly, and took off without

waiting for a response. He was almost to the blue line before Niklas managed to get himself going, moving faster than should have been possible in all that gear.

Niklas swore and scrambled after him. He caught up by the face-off dot but before he could pull ahead, Theo neatly tripped him.

Niklas went sprawling, air driven from his lungs, as Theo crowed in triumph and whipped around the net to race back up the ice.

Son of a—Niklas rolled onto his back and stared at the rafters high above him, wondering when Theo had grown a devious streak.

Theo appeared over him, still grinning. He'd taken off his helmet and was holding a water bottle. "Did you die?"

Niklas pushed at one of his skates. "Attempted murder isn't nice, Theo."

Theo laughed and held out the bottle. Niklas accepted it, made a show of tightening the lid that won him another laugh, and took a long drink. Then he clambered to his feet and upended the bottle over Theo's head.

The squawk was satisfying. So was the laughter from the rest of the team, which had trickled onto the ice somewhere in between their impromptu race and Theo's cheating.

Niklas tousled Theo's soaked hair, making it stand on end in outraged little spikes, and skated back to the bench to applause from the players.

"He cheats," he said loudly, pointing at Theo behind him. The hurricane of butterflies in his gut had slowed their wings. He could do this.

The confidence lasted until it was time to take the ice for warmups.

Theo appeared as if out of nowhere and sat down on the

locker beside him. Niklas didn't look up, focused on getting his pads in place. The strap refused to thread through the buckle, maybe because his hands were shaking so much.

"Let me," Theo said, and gently batted Niklas's hands away. He bent and deftly fed the strap through the buckle and pulled it tight. "Good?" he asked, glancing up.

Niklas nodded mutely. He'd thank him, he thought distantly, just as soon as he could figure out words again.

Theo's eyes softened and he straightened. "First game in the show," he said, pressing his shoulder to Niklas's briefly. "It's okay to be nervous."

"I'm not nervous," Niklas's mouth said without his input.

Theo laughed at him, brown eyes bright and amused. "Sure, kid, if you say so."

Niklas looked away, swallowing hard. "What, um—anything I should know about the Otters?"

"Coach covered most of it," Theo said. "But they're known for their speed. They're fast and they use it. Plus they'll get right up on top of you, try to take away your eyes. Don't let them fluster you. Push them out of your crease if they get too close. Our D-men will help, especially Sunny."

"I got you, kid!" Sunny yelled from a few stalls over, flashing him a grin.

"I'm help you too," Kasha put in.

"You're a forward," Niklas pointed out.

Kasha scowled. "Does this mean I can't defend you? I'm strong, see?" He flexed, and someone wolf-whistled.

"They're all going to take care of you," Theo said under the hooting and cheering, and Niklas glanced at him. "Don't worry."

I want to make you proud. Niklas managed to keep the words from slipping out. Instead he just nodded.

Theo patted his knee and went back to his stall to get dressed.

. . .

It didn't seem real until Niklas stepped out on the ice for warmups. The arena was already filling up, people with signs plastering the glass and pounding on it with their fists, trying to get the players' attention over the pounding bass of the warmup music.

Niklas dropped to the ice and stretched, watching the players on the far end as they swirled around, lining up to take shots on their goalie. It wasn't that different from the games he'd played with the Spirit, he told himself. More fans filling the arena, maybe, but it was still just hockey, still the beautiful game he'd grown up loving. This was where everything made sense. He wondered, distantly, if Cam and Joel and Morgan were watching.

He finished his stretches and took up position in the net. That was easier, he discovered immediately. Now he could focus on shaving down his crease, running through his rituals to get himself in the right headspace, and settling into the crouch that signified to his team that he was ready for shots.

They obliged, peppering him with everything they could think of. Niklas stopped what he could and ignored the ones he couldn't, losing himself to the thump of the music and the scrape of blades against ice, the crisp *crack* of a puck hitting a stick, the dull thud when one smacked into his glove.

He was sweating when warmups were over, muscles loose and ready, most of the nerves dissipated.

Theo skated over as the last players left the ice and leaned in until their helmets were almost touching. "Better?"

Niklas smiled at him, and something relaxed around Theo's eyes. "Better," he said.

"Let's win a hockey game, then!"

* * *

He forgot his nerves at the first puck drop. Red jerseys with white trim flung themselves into action against white, maroon, and gray jerseys, chasing after the puck so far away Niklas could barely even see it. Play was swirling at center ice, the Sentinels trying to push it into the offensive zone, but a white jersey flicked it past them and into Niklas's end.

Niklas kept himself loose, crouched in his crease and tracking the puck as skaters hurtled toward him. He had no idea who had the puck or who was chasing him. It didn't matter. All that mattered was stopping the puck.

Two Sentinels were hassling the player driving forward but he ducked back and around. Wrist shot. Niklas moved on instinct. The puck smacked into his glove hard enough to sting and the whistle blew.

Niklas straightened and held out his glove to the ref who swept in to collect the puck. Without meaning to, he glanced toward the bench. Theo was watching him, face expressionless, but somehow Niklas could read the approval in his eyes.

Niklas didn't smile, even though he wanted to. He just rolled his shoulders and readied himself again as the players got in position for the next drop.

It wasn't easy. The Otters weren't going to give them the win just because Niklas was a rookie and this was his first NHL game. They fought hard, both metaphorically and then, twice, physically. The first was a big defenseman squaring up against Sunny after a big hit on a forward. The second was an Otter—Lebedev, Niklas saw on his jersey—who went after Tanaka for tripping someone. Niklas didn't see who. Didn't really care. He waited for them to be separated and sent to their respective boxes.

Their special team needed work, he already knew. He'd seen them in practice, and Theo had spent plenty of time complaining about how they didn't connect with each other and passed *too* much instead of taking shots.

It was no different in a real game. The Otters were faster and more tenacious, less likely to fall apart at the first sign of adversity. Someone drove hard to the net and sank the puck just past Niklas's toe, barely avoiding a collision with him. Sunny yanked him off and the player laughed, brown eyes sparkling, and spun to hug his teammates. His jersey said O'Brien. Any other time, Niklas might have thought he was attractive.

Not that it mattered, he realized, as Lebedev reached O'Brien and pulled him into a hug, touch possessive and eyes soft, and O'Brien melted into it eagerly.

Niklas looked for Theo again. He was watching him again, still no expression on his face. Niklas gave him a rueful tilt of one eyebrow, and the corner of Theo's lips flickered briefly with a smile.

Niklas rolled his shoulders again. Tapped his goalposts. Right, left, right. Elbows on the cross bar, feet off the ice. One hard breath blown out to erase what just happened. Then he dropped back into his easy crouch and waited.

Orsher scored two minutes later on a breakaway and Niklas cheered with the crowd, smacking his stick against the ice in approval.

They went into the third still tied at one. Niklas was more tired than he'd expected. He'd had to face over thirty shots so far and he wasn't sure how he'd managed to keep some of them out. Blind luck and tenacity, maybe. But he kept his angles clean, remembered his positioning, and they hit the ten minute mark of the third period with the score still even.

Niklas's surroundings had long since faded around him. He watched the puck, watched the plays as they developed, lunged to make a save and another and then another. Sweat dripped from his scalp and he blinked it away. He loved when he hit this moment, and he'd savor the memory of it later. Right now, he was only purpose, letting nothing past him. He lunged for the puck, slapped another away with his blocker, kicked a shot away and fell into a desperate windmill to stop the rebound. Somehow, *somehow*, he made contact, and he rolled back to his feet to see Sunny bolting for the other end of the ice with the puck on his stick.

Two seconds later, the goal-horn went off and Niklas threw his arms in the air as the crowd roared.

I can *do this*. The thought was almost startling. He could win this game. He'd watched the Otters' top line for long enough that he was beginning to predict plays, could anticipate a shot and be in position before it happened.

The minutes ticked down. Turned into the final fifty-nine seconds. The Otters pulled their goalie, increasingly desperate, but Sunny had given the Sentinels the edge and they were determined to keep it. They clustered in front of Niklas, breaking up shots and forcing the play away from his net no matter how hard the Otters tried to bring it back.

Tanaka put the nail in the coffin with fifteen seconds left on the clock, a hard slapshot from his own zone. The puck hurtled down the ice. The arena sucked in a breath. The puck hit the back of the net, the goal-horn went off, and the arena erupted in cheers as lights flashed and Tanaka's goal song blared over the speakers.

It was over and the Otters knew it, but they didn't stop trying for the last fourteen seconds. Niklas had no time to track the clock, too busy scrambling to block every desperation shot they took, and the final buzzer startled him when it blew. Everyone was jumping the boards, charging down the ice toward him as the team on the ice engulfed him.

Niklas couldn't stop his smile. His eyes stung from sweat

and his muscles were burning, but it didn't matter. None of it mattered. They'd *won*. The players formed a sloppy line and congratulated him, their own smiles huge as they patted his helmet or hugged him.

Theo was the last in line and Niklas straightened unconsciously as he approached.

He'd never seen Theo smile that widely, he realized, and it plucked at something in his chest even as Theo reached up and wrapped his arms around Niklas's shoulders and hauled him into a hug.

Niklas couldn't hear what he was saying, and it didn't really matter. They'd won. *He'd* won. He thought he could float to the ceiling, he was so buoyed by happiness.

He was named first star and took a quick circle with his stick held up to the fans who cheered, still grinning so hard his face hurt.

Then it was back to the locker room, for cool-downs, showers, and finally the part Niklas always dreaded—interviews.

Theo sat with him for those, but he let Niklas get through them on his own, only stepping in when Niklas was visibly struggling. Thankfully, the reporters were patient, and they asked softball questions. How is it different, playing here versus in Sweden? How do you like your teammates? What's the biggest adjustment?

Niklas answered honestly, happiness still tumbling in his chest, and didn't even care when he tripped over his words.

Then finally they were free and Theo was smiling at him in the hall, a small and private thing.

"Ready to go out and celebrate?" he asked.

"*Yes*," Niklas said. He was buoyed on air, barely feeling the concrete floor under his feet. Every ache from the game had been forgotten. He wanted to go out, get drunk, and kiss someone. Theo for preference, but since that wasn't an option, he'd take whoever caught his eye. "You're coming, right?"

Theo hesitated.

"Oh come on," Niklas said, and Theo cut his eyes away.

"I'm not—you know I don't like to party."

"You don't have to party," Niklas said. "Theo, please—I wouldn't.... I'm here because of you. Please come out and help me enjoy this properly."

Theo sighed.

"You don't have to party," Niklas said, knowing he was pleading. "Just sit in the booth and have a beer or whatever you like. It won't be the same if you're not there."

"Has anyone ever told you your puppy eyes are really effective?" Theo asked, sounding resigned, and Niklas could *feel* the way he lit up with his answering grin.

"Does that mean you'll come?"

"Yes, dammit." A small smile tugged over Theo's mouth. "I'll come. Might even enjoy myself."

"Don't make promises you can't keep," Niklas warned, and Theo laughed, bumping him with a shoulder.

"Get dressed. Team's waiting."

Twelve

"WHERE THE HELL IS NIK?" Sunny shouted. "It's his night, why isn't he celebrating with us?"

Theo craned his neck to look over the dance floor, but he didn't see Niklas's lanky frame anywhere. By the bar, maybe? He scooted to the edge of the cracked vinyl seat and peered through the smoke. Niklas was hard to miss, but Theo still couldn't see him anywhere.

"I'll check the bathroom, make sure he's not throwing up from all the shots you forced down him," he said, which for some reason prompted a cheer from the rest of the table. Theo rolled his eyes and slid out of the booth.

There were several men in the bathroom lined up at the urinals, and one occupied stall. As Theo dithered, trying to figure out the best way to go about it, the toilet flushed and a stranger came out of the stall, blinking at Theo as if trying to place him.

Theo turned and ducked back out before he found himself having to sign autographs in a dirty public bathroom. In the narrow hall, he dug out his phone just in case Niklas had texted him, but there were no messages from him. Where the fuck *was* he?

The emergency exit sign above the back door caught his eye and Theo headed that direction without really thinking about it. If Nik had found some girl for a hookup, that was one thing, but there were still disreputable types even in a sleepy city like Saskatoon, and Nik wasn't exactly experienced. He'd end up getting his wallet stolen if he was *lucky*, and much worse if he wasn't.

Theo stepped out into the alley and nearly sighed with relief at the sight of Niklas's broad shoulders. His back was to Theo, head lowered, and he was very clearly kissing someone who was just as enthusiastically kissing him back, judging from the hands roaming over Niklas's back and up under his shirt.

Good for him, Theo told himself, and ignored the spike of... something that twisted through his gut. It was none of his business if Niklas hooked up. He was young and single and attractive and he'd just posted his first NHL win. Of course he was celebrating. As long as he wasn't getting mugged, Theo could leave him to it.

Niklas lifted his head and said something too low to be heard. Theo shook himself. Standing there like a peeping Tom, perving on Niklas's private business—what was wrong with him? He turned to duck back inside.

"Theo?" Niklas said, and he sounded startled and a little... guilty.

Theo turned back, pulling up his media smile. "Sorry, just making sure everything was, um... okay."

Niklas's partner peeked over his bicep, pushing shaggy hair out of his eyes. *His* eyes. Theo's world stuttered to a stop, narrowing down to the view in front of him as Niklas stepped back and fully revealed the man he'd been kissing. The *man*. He'd been *kissing*.

"No," Theo said through numb lips.

Something like hurt flickered over Niklas's face. "Theo—"

"No," Theo said louder. "*No*. I can't—*you* can't—oh my God." There was an anvil on his lungs, and he couldn't get a full breath. He braced himself with a hand on the wall, fighting the panic clouding the edges of his vision.

Niklas said something to his partner, who sighed but nodded, shooting Theo a vicious look as he slipped past him back into the building.

Theo barely registered it, still trying to hold back the panic. Niklas was queer. Niklas was out *in public* kissing another man. Niklas was going to—

"You *can't*," he said again.

"You know what?" Niklas said, and his tone was equal parts fury and disappointment. "I can do whatever the fuck I want, Theo. You're not my father or my boss, and you have *no right* to tell me what I can and can't do. You hear me?"

Theo shook his head, trying to clear it. "Nik—"

"No," Niklas spat. "*Fuck* you, Theo, I thought you of all people would be okay with—" His breath hitched. "Fuck you," he repeated. "If you can't accept me for who I am, then I don't need you."

He brushed past and Theo grabbed his sleeve, hauling him to a stop. Niklas jerked his arm away, lips tight.

"Me of all people?"

"Fuck off," Niklas snarled.

"What do you mean, me of all people?"

"I mean you're the only one I've ever trusted," Niklas flung at him, and Theo flinched like he'd been hit. "You wrap your stick, you march in the parade even though I *know* you hate every second of being in public like that, you volunteer with that one shelter for queer kids. I thought you didn't care about—" His breath hitched.

"*Wait*," Theo said desperately. He felt like he was

drowning in quicksand, unable to breathe or move, but he had to wipe that stricken look off Niklas's face. "It's not—you think I care that you're gay?"

"What the fuck else is it?" Niklas snapped, but he didn't move.

"It's not that," Theo said. The panic receded a fraction and he took a deep breath. "Nik. I'm—promise you won't tell anyone what I'm about to tell you. Please."

"Why should I promise you anything after you had a freakout over me kissing a guy?" Niklas shot back, and that was definitely deep hurt in his blue eyes.

"I'm so sorry," Theo said. "Nik, please, you have to believe me. You can kiss anyone you want. But—" He swallowed hard. "This is not the place to have this conversation. Will you—will you come home with me and let me explain?"

Niklas looked at him for a minute, big hands hanging loose by his sides. Finally he nodded sharply.

The ride home was silent. Theo had barely touched the beer Sunny had shoved at him, which meant he was distressingly sober and far too aware of the way Niklas slouched in the seat beside him, staring out the window with his hands in his lap.

Inside the house, Theo took his shoes off, still trying to figure out what to say. Niklas stood in the middle of the living room, a challenging tilt to his chin.

"Get it over with," he said. "Tell me I'm sick, perverse, whatever it is you're thinking. Get it all out, so I can pack my stuff and ask for a trade, because I won't play with a homophobe, I *won't*, I—"

"*Stop*," Theo said, throwing out his hand, and Niklas's mouth snapped shut. "Nik, goddammit—" He rubbed his face and sat down on the couch. After a minute, Niklas moved to the chair opposite and sank onto the edge of it, poised as if ready to flee.

"You said, that first day—" Theo hesitated. "You mentioned a girlfriend. I thought—"

"It took me awhile to figure shit out," Niklas snapped. His mouth was tight, eyes colder than Theo had ever seen them. "Not that it's any of your business."

Theo absorbed that without flinching. He deserved it, probably. "I have to ask you for something, and it's going to be the hardest thing you've ever done," he said after a minute. He was going to be sick. What was he thinking? He barely knew this young man. He *couldn't* risk everything he'd spent his life fighting for. It was unthinkable.

Niklas stared at him. "Ask it, then." His voice was hard, unwavering.

"I need you to promise that you will never tell anyone what we discussed tonight," Theo insisted.

Niklas sneered. "You're that afraid of being associated with the gay kid? You're a lot of things, Theo, but I never thought you were a coward."

"*Enough.*" Theo's voice was a whip crack of fury, and Niklas shut his mouth abruptly again. Theo glared at him. "Don't say another word you'll end up regretting, do you understand me?"

Niklas dropped his eyes, chin jutting mulishly, and Theo sighed.

"So dramatic. I remember being that young and tempestuous once. Everything was life and death, every decision the end of the world. Just promise me, Nik. Please."

"Fine," Niklas flung at him. "I promise. Happy?"

"Not remotely." Theo studied Niklas's face, the planes and angles of it, the remains of puppy fat clinging to his cheeks. "I'm gay, Nik."

Niklas's mouth fell open. "You—you're—"

"I honestly don't know how you didn't see that one coming," Theo said, almost amused in spite of everything.

"You really thought I freaked out because you were kissing a boy? And *that's* the only reason?"

"Then why *did* you freak out?" Niklas demanded. "If you—why do you care? Are you—are you jealous?"

"No," Theo said sharply. *Liar*, a tiny voice whispered in his ear. Theo ignored it. "You can kiss anyone you want. I have absolutely nothing to say about that. But in *public*? Nik, we play in one of the most homophobic sports in the country. It's not just what your teammates might do, it's what your *fans* might do."

"Saint—"

"Saint is the captain of his team, a hockey prodigy in his own right. What applies to him doesn't apply to us. Besides, he has Karma. You think anyone's going to try to be homophobic to Saint when Carmine Quinn is around?"

Niklas shook his head. "That's not true. That can't be true. What about Adam Caron?"

"Adam is a grown man and he'd just signed with the Wolverines. He was safe. And he and his boyfriend are still plenty careful not to be too demonstrative in public. I've seen some of the hate he gets—that they both get—and it's... ugly."

Niklas wrung his hands. "Why are you telling me this?"

"Because I don't want to see you get *hurt*," Theo said sharply. He slid off the couch onto his knees in front of Niklas, who gazed down at him with anguish in his eyes. "Nik, you're... you've got so far to go. You're going to be incredible. I couldn't bear it if—please, you have to *promise* me you won't do anything like that again, not until you're safer. Not until your career is safe. No kissing boys when you could still be sent down and left to rot in the minors, or risk angry fans who feel their manliness is threatened by you not being straight." He clutched Niklas's knees, desperate for him to understand. "All I want is for you to be okay," he whispered. "Please understand."

Niklas touched Theo's hand, then covered it with his own. "You're worried about me."

Theo nodded mutely.

"You don't think I'm disgusting."

Theo twisted his wrist and caught Niklas's hand, squeezing it fiercely. "I think you're the most amazing young man I've ever met, and *anyone* would be lucky to be with you."

Niklas blinked rapidly several times. "I have to... to be true to myself," he said, but he didn't pull away from Theo's hand.

"I'm not asking you *not* to be," Theo said. God, Niklas's hands were so lovely, so long and broad, with deceptively delicate fingers. Theo couldn't help tracing the knuckles with a fingertip, and Niklas shivered but still didn't pull back. "I'm asking you to be careful," Theo said, looking up at him. "Because if something happened to you—"

"But things are better," Niklas said. "I know they're not perfect, they're *not*. But they're better. We have Pride Night, and You Can Play, and Hockey is for Everyone—"

Theo sat back on his heels. "And 'gay panic' is still a viable defense in court when someone beats you up. I've seen first-hand the damage homophobia can do, Nik."

"You?" Niklas asked, swallowing hard.

Theo shook his head. His stomach churned. "My billet mate. We were... we were sixteen. And someone on our team caught him messing around with his boyfriend after a game. He—they—" He pressed a hand to his mouth, willing the nausea to recede. "His boyfriend got away. My teammate wasn't so lucky. He regained most of the sight in his left eye, but he never played hockey again."

There was horror in Niklas's eyes. "Were you there?"

"I was in the dressing room. I didn't know it was happening until it was almost over." *Liar*, that same voice whispered. Theo drew a ragged breath and pushed himself to his feet. Niklas gazed up at him, beautiful face so open and trusting, and Theo ached to kiss him.

There were so many reasons why that was a bad idea. He turned away. "I found some adults, they broke it up," he said over his shoulder. He spun back. "Do you see, though, Nik? Do you understand?"

Niklas stood. "I understand," he said quietly. The heat, the temper, the *hurt*—it was all gone, replaced by calm understanding. "I won't say anything, or risk your career in any way."

"*My*—Nik, *no*. I'm worried about *you*. I've *had* my career. You think I care what people say about me now?"

"Yes," Niklas said, watching him steadily. "And I won't put you in that position. But I won't stay in the closet long. Once I've signed permanently with the Sentinels, if I do, I won't hide any more. Can you live with that?"

"Do I have a choice?" Theo asked.

"No," Niklas said calmly. "Because like it or not, I'm an adult, and I can make my own decisions. But because I trust and respect you and want you to be happy, I will abide by your request for now. So you can sleep at night."

"It's not about me," Theo protested, but Niklas just cocked his head and looked at him.

"I'm going to bed. Sleep well, Theo."

* * *

Theo stayed in the living room by himself a while longer, looking at the picture of Jacques Plante on the wall but not really seeing it. He'd never seen Niklas so confident, so determined to do what he felt was right. It felt like... like he was growing up, even though intellectually, Theo knew he'd been an adult for years.

And the worst part was, he *was* right. Theo was a coward.

A craven thing, hiding who he was, pretending to be what he *wasn't.*

He rubbed his face. He couldn't do it. He couldn't be brave like Niklas, proud of who he was. It was safe in the closet, and if it felt a little stifled sometimes, a little choking, well... it was better than the loathing, the disgust he'd face by admitting the truth. He'd heard the talk in the locker room, on the ice. If he came out and no one could stand to be around him anymore, he didn't think he could bear it. He *did* care what other people said about him, despite what he'd told Niklas. But what could he do? He wasn't strong enough. Not like Niklas. He couldn't do it.

Finally, he went to bed, mind still in turmoil.

It took a very long time to fall asleep.

Thirteen

"ARE YOU READY?" Theo called. He sounded like he was at the door already.

Niklas rolled his eyes and grabbed his cufflinks and tie. "Almost!" he shouted, and shoved a foot into his shoe, hopping to pull the other on as he hurried down the hall.

Theo was indeed waiting at the door, one hand resting on the handle. He looked dapper and sleek in a dark red suit, the slim lines of his body accented by the drape of the material, and Niklas made an approving noise.

"*Very* nice, who is that?"

"The suit? Oh, it's Anjali. A gift for my last birthday." Theo smoothed a palm over his chest, looking self-conscious. "I wouldn't have gone with this color, but she insisted."

"Never argue with her again," Niklas said, looping his tie around his neck and dropping to one knee at Theo's feet to tie his shoe. "You look incredible."

Nothing but silence met that, and Niklas glanced up to see Theo's eyes firmly turned away, studiously examining the ceiling as if looking for cracks in the plaster, and it struck him that he was eye-level with Theo's crotch in this position.

"Uh, thanks," Theo said belatedly, as if he'd just processed what Niklas had said.

Niklas hid the amusement and finished the knot, then switched quickly to the other foot. "Sorry," he said, "almost done. You were rushing me."

"Take your time," Theo said, not moving.

"I know you don't like to be late." Niklas stood and grabbed his overcoat from the hook. Theo did the same and pulled the door open for him.

"We're not, I just don't want to be," Theo admitted, following him out and turning back to lock up. "And you look nice too."

"Think Anjali would dress me?" Niklas asked as he slid into the car.

"Sure, if you're willing to spend five thousand dollars," Theo said dryly.

Niklas blanched. "That's—holy shit."

"Mmhmm. She's good at what she does and she knows it."

The engine fired to life and settled into a steady purr, barely audible as Theo put it into gear and they rolled out of the driveway.

"So, the Seabirds," Theo said after a few minutes. "How much do you know about them?"

"The usual. Saint's a badass, Carmine will fuck up anyone who looks at him wrong, and Butterfly's the youngest goalie to reach fifty shutouts in NHL history so far."

A smile flickered across Theo's mouth. "Planning on beating that record, kid?"

I'm not a kid. Niklas suppressed the now-familiar retort. "What if I am?"

Theo laughed out loud. "That fire of yours is the whole reason you're here," he said. "Don't let go of it. Just be glad you're getting a chance to see them playing up close without having to face them yourself. Watch everything Saint does, especially when he's got a scoring chance, okay?"

Niklas nodded. "I'll take notes," he promised.

Kasha was at his stall getting changed when they arrived. He shot Niklas a smile but he looked nervous, lips bitten red as he pulled his chest protector into place.

"Hey," Niklas said, leaning over. "You okay?"

"Yes," Kasha said automatically, then winced. "No? I dunno. You know Birds were first NHL team for me?"

"Yes, I remember," Niklas said, stripping out of his suit coat and hanging it up.

"Is first game against them now. Against Saint. I'm... nervous."

"Why is that make you nervous?" Niklas asked.

Kasha shrugged, jerky and uncoordinated. "He's best. You know? I want him always to win. To *be* best. But also I want us to win, yes?"

"You think he make it easy on you?" Niklas said, unbuttoning his shirt. "Think maybe he say 'oh, Kasha has new team, I'll play bad, let him win, make him feel good'?"

That startled Kasha into a bark of laughter. "Saint *never* go easy on anyone," he said, eyes dancing.

Niklas grinned back at him. "So you play best game too. Simple."

Kasha thumped him on the shoulder. "Simple," he said, and firmed his jaw.

Niklas turned to his locker and caught Theo's eyes. There was approval there, mixed with a warm affection that stole Niklas's breath. He couldn't think of anything to say, so he just flashed him a smile and concentrated on getting changed.

* * *

The building was packed. While the Seabirds weren't technically rivals, games against them tended to be entertaining at the very least, according to Theo.

Niklas warmed up near the blue line, watching the white and teal jerseys on the other side of the ice. One of the goalies peeled off and headed for him. He was tall and rangy, not quite Niklas's height but close. Niklas couldn't see much behind his mask except for dark skin and pitch-black eyes that sparkled with mischief.

"You're new," he greeted Niklas, dropping to his knees to stretch next to him.

"You're Butterfly," Niklas blurted, and Felix grinned at him.

"I suppose I am. Are you in net tonight then?"

"No," Niklas said, forcing down the awe. *Butterfly*. Talking to *him*. "You're facing Theo."

"How do you like it here?"

"It's good," Niklas said, glancing involuntarily toward Theo, down ice. "Good team, good city."

"Well, good city, maybe," Felix said, smile widening.

The wonder evaporated immediately and Niklas bristled. "Good team too," he said, holding Felix's eyes.

Felix laughed and rocked to his feet. "I like you, *mon ami*."

"Not your friend," Niklas said.

Felix laughed again and tapped Niklas's pads with his stick before he skated away. Niklas glowered after him briefly and then returned his attention to his stretches.

Fourteen

LOSING TO THE SEABIRDS, whether at home or on the road, was a normal enough feeling. It stung more with Niklas watching, though. Theo got through the cooldowns on autopilot, still smarting from giving up four goals, and dressed without paying much attention to what he was doing.

Niklas nudged him. "Ready?" he asked quietly.

Theo nodded and followed him out.

They both stopped at the sight of Saint, Carmine, and Felix leaning against the wall, talking quietly.

"Hi," Saint offered.

"Good game," Theo said, the words sticking in his throat.

Saint's smile was sweet. "You made us work for it." The lie sounded almost believable in his husky voice. "Is Kasha still in there?"

"I'll get him," Niklas said, and ducked back into the locker room.

Felix raised an eyebrow at Theo. "That him?"

Theo just shrugged.

"Dinner," Felix said. "I'll even pay this time."

"I have to take Niklas home," Theo protested.

Felix's other eyebrow went up. "Home?"

Theo hunched his shoulders, acutely aware of the way Saint and Carmine were listening to their conversation with clear interest. "He stays with me some," he said, working to keep his tone casual. "He's not here full-time right now, it just... made more sense."

"For him to *live* with you." Felix sounded disbelieving. "We're definitely having dinner."

"I'm tired," Theo protested. "I don't want to go out."

"So I'll go home with you then," Felix said cheerfully, slinging an arm over Theo's shoulders. "There seems to be a lot to talk about."

"Ugh, get off."

That, of course, made Felix tighten his grip, plastering himself against Theo's body and bending to plant a noisy kiss on his cheek as the door swung open and Kasha stepped into the hall, Niklas right behind him.

Felix let go of Theo and pounced before he was all the way through it, wrestling Kasha into a headlock and ruffling his hair as Kasha squawked and flailed, clearly not trying very hard to get free. Felix finally let him go and dragged him into a rough hug as Saint and Carmine looked on, smiling.

"Missed you, kid," Felix said against his hair, and Kasha squeezed his eyes shut, burying his face in his shoulder briefly. "Listen, Saint and Caz are gonna take you out to dinner, catch up with you. I need to talk to Theo, though. When you come to Portland, plan on coming to see me and Fisher, yes?"

"How is Fisher?" Kasha asked, lifting his head.

Felix's smile was soft. "He's good. How's Wren?"

Kasha colored. "She's good too."

"Is she here? Bring her with us," Saint said.

Theo cleared his throat. "Niklas, have you met Felix?"

Niklas nodded once, his eyes cool. "In warmups."

Felix smiled at him but Niklas didn't return it. Felix

glanced at Theo, one eyebrow going up a fraction. Theo just shrugged. He wasn't sure why Niklas didn't seem to like Felix, but it was none of his business.

"Nik, I hope you don't mind, but Felix and I are old friends and he's going to come home with us tonight. We don't get to see each other often."

"It's your house," Niklas said, tone clipped.

Theo narrowed his eyes, but Niklas turned away, hands shoved deep in his pants pockets.

"Can we go?" he asked over his shoulder.

Theo sighed, nodded at Saint and Carmine, jerked his head at Felix to follow, and went after him.

Niklas spent the ride home staring out the window as Felix and Theo made polite conversation in the front seat, discussing the upgrades to the arena, the differing styles between their coaches, the weather, and anything else Theo could think of to fill the silence. Felix played along, the tilt of his mouth saying he knew what Theo was doing. Niklas didn't join in, even when Theo tried to pull him into the conversation, replying in monosyllables until Theo took the hint and stopped trying.

When they arrived, Niklas was out before the other two had unbuckled, striding for the door. Theo sighed, turning the engine off and watching as he disappeared inside.

"Sorry," he offered after a minute.

"He's not your son," Felix said. He sounded amused. "Any idea what's going on there?"

"No fucking clue." Theo rubbed his face. "I thought he was a fan of yours. I don't know why he's acting like this."

Felix opened his door. "I have a few theories. Come on, it's cold."

Inside, Theo took Felix's coat and hung it in the closet before ushering him through into the kitchen. Niklas appeared as Theo was handing Felix a beer, stopped dead in the doorway and turned on his heel to head back in the direction of his room.

"That's it," Theo said under his breath. He set the beer down hard on the counter. "I'll be right back."

Niklas's door was closed. Theo knocked and shoved it open without waiting for a reply.

Niklas was cross-legged on the bed, phone in his hand. His eyes went wide as Theo stepped inside and shut the door behind him.

"Theo—"

"What the *fuck* is wrong with you?" Theo hissed.

Niklas's mouth worked but nothing came out.

"You're being rude to my *friend*," Theo continued, clutching the door handle. "You are a guest in *my* house, and you don't have to like him but you *do* have to be polite to him."

Niklas stared at his hands.

The age difference between them had never seemed greater.

"Why don't you like him?" Theo asked abruptly. "Felix is a good person. One of the best."

"He—"

"He what?"

Niklas flattened his mouth and didn't answer.

Theo wanted to shake him. Instead he took a deep breath, and when Niklas still didn't speak, he opened the door and left, leaving Niklas glowering at his lap.

Felix wasn't in the kitchen when Theo got back, but there was a light on in the living room, so Theo headed that way. He found Felix stretched out on the couch, long legs crossed at the ankle, one arm behind his head, smiling at his phone.

"Fisher, huh?" Theo asked. He pushed Felix's feet out of the way and sat on the end of the couch, crossing his legs. "Is he why you didn't take me up on my offer last time you were in town?"

Felix sat up, looking suddenly guilty. "Ah—possibly. I should have told you. I'm sorry, Brick, I didn't—"

Theo waved a hand, cutting off the apology. "Tell me about him."

Felix held out his phone instead. Theo admired the picture of a dark-eyed man smiling at the camera, a lanky Siamese cat draped over his shoulders, before handing it back.

"He's gorgeous. And Henry likes him, I see."

"Henry knows a keeper when he meets one." Felix tucked the phone in his pocket and nudged Theo's calf with his toe. "You played a hard game tonight."

"Wasn't enough. It's never enough." Theo hunched over, resting his elbows on his thighs and letting his head hang. "They're all either scared of me or they actually hate me. It's the only thing they can agree on—that I'm an asshole."

"That's not true," Felix said softly.

"I took Nik in for training camp and one of the rookies referred to me as the Asshole of Saskatchewan," Theo said.

Felix nudged Theo's thigh with a toe. "I know how much you hate that."

"It's fine," Theo said automatically.

"Is it?"

Theo took a deep breath. "No. You know it's not." He looked up. "Nik heard him. I think... I think that's what I hated most."

Felix's smile was wry. "You really like him." It wasn't a question.

"More than I should," Theo admitted. He rested a hand on Felix's ankle absently. "How do you do it? You smile, and people just... love you. How do you manage it? You'd have my team eating out of your hand inside three days."

Felix snorted. "Assuming I'd *want* to. I don't know what

to tell you, Theo. If I knew how to make people see you how I do, and how I think Niklas does, I'd do it in a heartbeat. You deserve love, my friend." He sat up. "Speaking of Niklas."

"Can we not?" Theo asked, knowing it was futile.

Felix's grin was wide. "You have a crush on him."

"I *don't*."

"I have eyes," Felix said. He nudged Theo's shin. "Who can blame you, really? He's... very nice to look at. A little young but that's nothing time won't fix. And a blind man could see he absolutely worships you."

Theo folded forward, burying his face in his hands. "He's a *kid*," he said into his palms, then lifted his head to glare at Felix, who looked impishly curious. "I'm over a *decade* older than him. I'm—God, I'm a dirty old man for even *considering* it."

Felix cocked his head. "Why?"

"I just *told* you why."

"No, you didn't. You just feel like you're doing something wrong, but you're not. First of all, I'm sure he'd be more than willing, considering the way he looks at you. Honestly, I'm surprised he hasn't already propositioned you. Second, he's of age, Theo. He's a grown man. Maybe he's younger than you, but he's an adult. Don't you think you should let him make up his own mind?"

"It's not that," Theo protested, knowing it sounded feeble. "I know he's an adult. Believe me, I've noticed. But he's still so *young*. He deserves someone his own age, who speaks his language. He keeps showing me these pictures, they're called 'memes'? And most of the time I don't get the joke anyway. Why does he put up with me at all?"

Felix didn't even bother to try stifling the laughter. It bubbled up, bright and merry, as Theo glared at him.

"Forgive me, my friend," Felix gasped after a minute. "But you're telling me you don't know what memes are?"

"Of course I know what they *are*," Theo snapped, nettled. "I just don't *get* them."

"You don't have to," Felix said. He still looked amused but there was sympathy in his dark eyes. "You get *him*, do you not?"

Theo opened and closed his mouth as a memory rose unbidden. They'd been washing dishes after dinner one night as music they'd been able to agree on played on Niklas's phone, hooked up to Theo's speakers. Niklas had looked at Theo, his hands buried to the wrist in soapy water, and a calculating look had flickered through his eyes. Before Theo could react, Niklas had scooped up a handful of suds and dropped them on his head.

"Perfect," he'd declared, clearly very pleased with himself.

Theo had just rolled his eyes and tipped his head forward to let the bubbles slide off back into the water, but the minute Niklas was distracted, he'd pulled the collar of Niklas's shirt away from his neck and dropped a handful of suds down it.

Watching Niklas squirm and yelp and wriggle, trying to get away from the feel of the bubbles sliding down his spine, Theo had laughed harder than he had in a very long time.

Felix was watching him keenly.

"I—suppose," Theo said.

"You do," Felix said firmly. "You'll figure it out."

"Tell me about Fisher."

Felix's face lit up. "Oh, Fisher. He's too good for me. He teaches *kindergarten*, Theo."

"And he fell for *you*?" Theo teased. He settled in to listen as Felix told the story of how they'd met, brown eyes alight with a happiness that had been missing all too often lately.

* * *

Niklas found him the next morning, curled up in his favorite seat to watch the sun rising over the prairie, a mug of coffee cradled in both hands and feet tucked underneath him.

There were dark circles under Niklas's eyes, hair on end like he hadn't slept well.

"I'm sorry," he said before Theo could even speak.

Theo took a sip of coffee, watching him over the rim.

Niklas shifted his weight. "I'm—I shouldn't have acted that way. It was rude and ungracious of me. A-and I'm sorry." He looked so young, suddenly, scared and vulnerable as he asked forgiveness, and Theo ached with the need to kiss him into the smiles that were far more his natural state.

Instead he took another measured sip of coffee before speaking. "Why did you? Act that way, I mean."

Niklas looked at the floor and mumbled something.

"Can't hear you," Theo said.

"It's stupid," Niklas said, looking up. "I'm not... proud of it."

"Will you tell me anyway?"

Niklas sighed. "When I was warming up, Felix came over and he—he was rude about our team, implied we're terrible."

"Well, we are," Theo said gently.

"But *he* doesn't get to say that!" Niklas said, eyes blazing. "A-and then, when I came out of the dressing room with Kasha, he was... and you were *smiling*. Like you smile at me."

The light dawned. "You were jealous," Theo said softly.

"I didn't want to share you," Niklas said in a rush. Surprise dried up any response Theo might have made as Niklas forged on, a determined set to his chin. Color crept up his throat and stained his cheeks. "I just—you're so... you don't let anyone in. But you... you smile at me. You *talk* to me. You seem like... you like me. Like you like having me around." He shrugged one shoulder. "I don't—I didn't want to share you," he repeated. "And especially not with Felix, who thinks we're shit to scrape off his shoe."

"First of all, he doesn't think that," Theo said instantly. "Felix and I were in juniors together. He's a dear friend and I love him very much. He teases because that's who he is. He loves to joke and play pranks. There is *nothing* mean-spirited about him, though. You have to understand that." He put the coffee cup on the windowsill and studied Niklas's face. "Just like you have to understand that I can have more than one friend."

"I never meant—"

"Felix and I have been friends a very long time," Theo interrupted. "I hope you and I are also friends for just as long, if not longer. But I'm not an object to fight over. There's room for both of you. Can you accept that?"

Shame flickered across Niklas's face. "Yes," he said, his voice low. "I'm really sorry, Theo."

"It's forgotten," Theo said. "Go get some coffee and come watch the sun rise with me."

Fifteen

"SO HOW'S NIK?" Sunny asked one day during practice, several weeks later.

Xander fired a puck and Theo missed it by a mile, turning to glare at Sunny, who raised one eyebrow.

"How would I know?" Theo said tightly. "Shouldn't you be running drills?"

If anything, Sunny looked more intrigued. "You telling me you don't talk to him?"

Theo had to stop another puck, which gave him a chance to gather his thoughts. "Of course I do."

"Then you know how he is," Sunny pointed out. "Which is all I was asking, but now I feel like something's going on."

"Seriously," Theo said, a little desperately. "Drills."

"Nah, this is more interesting," Sunny said. He leaned on his stick and inspected Theo's face. "Something's definitely going on."

Theo was too busy deflecting the next few shots to pay attention to him, but Sunny was still there when the last shooter had taken his turn and headed back to Coach for instructions.

"Look," Theo said, lifting his helmet and wiping away the sweat. "Nothing's going on. Nik is fine. We text some but not a lot, he's pretty busy. Did you catch his last game? He's tearing it up down there."

Sunny's eyes creased with his smile. "Lightning in a bottle, that kid. Can't wait to see what he can do when he really hits his stride." He bumped Theo's shoulder. "Reminds me of you."

Theo snorted and dropped his helmet back into place. "Go run drills with the rookies, you're setting a bad example."

The truth was, no matter how off-balance Theo *still* felt, Niklas didn't seem to be bothered at all by what had happened. He texted Theo multiple times a day, pictures of his teammates or blurry views of the road from his seat on the bus. He also sent selfies sometimes, which Theo surreptitiously saved in a folder he labeled Tax Documents, just in case anyone snooped through his phone.

Theo answered almost every text, even though sometimes he had no idea what to say. It was a harsh reminder of the generation gap between them—Niklas so comfortable with using technology as an extension of himself, and Theo struggling to remember how to text. He really didn't get the point of emojis, but Niklas didn't seem to mind. He still sent him countless messages, whether or not Theo responded. He even somehow got Theo to download TikTok. Niklas was the only person in his contact list there, but it was worth it for the short videos he sent Theo, the selfies with silly captions or just endless stretches of prairie.

Niklas found so much *joy* in life, and Theo desperately wanted to know what that was like. How did he do it? How did he always have a smile, that unflagging energy and kindness that seemed to radiate from him no matter what happened? Theo thought about him playing for the Sentinels for years, never even getting close to the playoffs, let alone winning a Cup, and he wanted to be sick.

Niklas deserved to be on a team that had a *chance*. He deserved to know what it felt like to lift the Cup as the fans cheered. But for some reason, he wanted to be with the Sentinels. It wasn't right, and Theo didn't know how to fix it.

His phone chimed next to him in the stall and he glanced at it. It was another snap from Niklas, this one of some baby sunflowers planted in fresh black dirt. The caption read, *they said these will be taller than me when they're full grown, can u believe it??*

Someone snatched the phone from Theo's hand, making him protest sharply. It was Cole, a young forward Theo didn't know well yet, but who was already good friends with Niklas.

"You talking to a pretty girl, Brick?" Cole asked.

Theo stood. "Give it back, idiot."

Cole held the phone out of reach, grinning at him. "Nah. I think we need to know who you're dating. C'mon, spill."

Theo narrowed his eyes, but Cole didn't seem fazed. He handed the phone to Tyler, one of Theo's favorite defensemen. *Formerly* favorite, he amended as Tyler tossed the phone to Xander, who caught it easily and handed it off to Foz.

"You even *think* about going through that and you won't walk out the door," Theo said flatly, and Foz gulped.

Cole slung an arm around Theo's shoulders. "Who is she, man? Tell us about her. Look, I'll show you my girl." He dug in his pocket and produced his phone. His lock screen was a very pretty brown-haired girl, holding a small wire-haired terrier and smiling at the camera. "Isn't she something?" Cole sounded almost awed, and Theo softened a fraction even as he held out a hand for his own phone, which Foz immediately gave him.

"What's her name?" Theo asked.

"Layla," Cole said. He unlocked the phone and opened the pictures, flipping through them. "I think I'm gonna ask her to marry me."

Theo's brows climbed. "That's a big step. How long have you been together?" *Keep him talking about his girlfriend, maybe he'll forget about me.*

"Since high school," Cole said. "But you still haven't told us about *your* little secret."

Dammit.

"Not much to tell," Theo said carefully. "Just a friend."

"Sure," Tyler said, coming up beside Cole. "I always smile like that at texts from *friends*."

Theo sighed, and they both beamed at him.

"So?" Cole prompted.

"I thought you were supposed to be afraid of me," Theo said.

Cole grinned at him. "Ever since Nik sprayed you with water after you cheated to win that race, you've been a little less scary."

"Man, that was great," Tyler said, sighing happily. "He looked like a pissed off baby duckling."

"Technically a duckling *is* a baby," Joshua chimed in. "It would either be a baby duck or a duckling."

"*Technically* you should suck my dick," Tyler said, giving Joshua the finger.

"You wish, bitch," Joshua tossed back.

"Get a fucking room," Xander called. "I don't need to hear that gay shit."

Theo tensed but Tyler laughed and danced across the room to where Joshua was stripping out of his gear. He pressed a hand to his heart, batting his eyes, and put his head on Joshua's bare chest.

"It's okay to finally admit our love, baby," he said.

"Get *off*," Joshua said, shoving him away. "You stink."

"You love it," Tyler said, and blew him a kiss.

"Fucking disgusting," Xander muttered, and turned his back.

Theo's stomach turned over and he swallowed hard, but Cole was already swiveling back to him as Tyler and Joshua kept bickering.

"So?"

"You're really not going to let this go," Theo said.

Cole's smile was wide and sweet. "I want to know more about you. So tell us about this girl who makes you smile like that."

Theo glanced around the room but no help was coming for him. Several other players were watching them, clearly curious to hear what he said. He clutched his phone in his suddenly sweaty palm and tried to find words.

"I—it's new," he said carefully. "I, uh... don't want to jinx it."

"Come on, you can tell us a *little* bit, can't you?" Cole wheedled.

Cole was charming, funny, and personable. Everyone on the team liked him. And at that moment, Theo would have happily fed him through a wood chipper.

"She's a little younger than me," Theo said, fatality settling over him. He was really doing this, then. "But it's not a sugar daddy situation, before you say it."

Cole deflated. "If you say so."

"She makes good money," Theo said, glaring at him, but Cole didn't seem too worried, motioning for him to continue. How far was he going to take this, Theo wondered briefly.

"What's she look like?" Cole prompted.

"Dark hair, blue eyes, perfect cheekbones, and a killer dimple," Theo said, and promptly wanted to crawl in a hole. Had he really just described Niklas as his fictitious girlfriend?

No one seemed to have noticed the similarity.

"She sounds *hot*," Cole said appreciatively. "Got a picture?"

Theo's brain screeched to a halt. "Uh, no."

"None at all?"

"None that I'm showing you," Theo shot back, and several players laughed.

"I think you've tortured our introvert goalie enough," Sunny said, appearing out of nowhere. He slapped Cole on the back. "Go shower, Tyler's not the only one who stinks."

"It's my manly musk," Cole said, putting on an offended air. "Girls love it."

"I don't know who's been lying to you," Sunny said, turning him toward the showers, "but I'd love to know how you actually managed to *get* a girlfriend." He shoved him and Cole grumbled but headed for the adjoining room as Sunny turned back to Theo. "Sorry," he said in Swedish. "I should have stopped it sooner. I was talking to Coach."

"I didn't—stopped what?" Theo still felt slightly dizzy, like he was floating just above his body. "He was just being friendly."

Sunny examined his face. "Come for dinner tonight," he said abruptly. "Inga misses you and so do the kids."

Theo worked moisture into his mouth. "Okay," he said. "Usual time?"

Sunny nodded, and Theo mustered something like a smile and headed for the showers, making sure his phone was securely locked before leaving it in his stall.

Thankfully, most of the team seemed to have not even noticed what had happened. There was the usual raucous shouting over the sound of the water, everyone in good spirits from a solid practice.

Scuffling erupted two shower heads over, and Theo glanced over to see Tyler pinning Joshua in a headlock as Joshua flailed wildly.

“Fucking—let go!” he squawked, but Tyler just tightened his grip.

“Not until you admit I’m sexy.”

Joshua managed to nail him in the ribs and Tyler grunted but didn’t let go, grinning maniacally.

“Say it,” he said.

“Fuck off!”

“Boys,” Sunny said mildly, and Tyler let go like he’d been burned, springing away from Joshua and turning to slip under the nearest shower head.

“Don’t drop the soap,” Xander taunted Joshua, who flushed bright red and spun on his heel. Xander snickered and went back to his own shower, utterly unaware of Theo silently watching.

How could Niklas want to come out in an atmosphere like this? Maybe Xander was the only one being overly homophobic, but no one was stopping him. No one was standing up and telling him it wasn’t okay to say those things. They just accepted his hatred as part of him, like the fact that he had green eyes.

Theo’s stomach turned over again. He could still Petr’s face in vivid, shocking color, the scarlet of the blood dripping down his ruined cheek, the flash of white bone where the skin had been peeled back, the purple and angry crimson creeping in around the edges as he cupped his cheekbone in both hands as if trying to hold his face together while Theo stood frozen in horror in the background, unseen and forgotten in the chaos.

He was going to be sick. He slapped the water off and headed for the locker room as fast as his shaky legs would carry him. Only a few players were in there, all absorbed in getting dressed to go home, and no one paid any attention to Theo as he dropped onto his locker and braced his elbows on his knees, breathing deep and slow through his nose and willing back the urge to vomit.

Don't think about it don't think about it don't think about it. Just another thing to shove under the rug, to hide. Theo swallowed nausea and misery and squeezed his eyes shut.

"Brick?" Cole sounded worried.

Theo lifted his head, making an attempt to school his face.

"You okay?" Cole asked. "You look—" He gestured. "—Not okay."

"Must have eaten something funny," Theo said.

"You sure?" Cole shifted his weight. "Because like, Sunny's mad at me. He said I shouldn't have pushed you so hard, that I was being rude?" He looked miserable. "I didn't mean to make you uncomfortable. I just wanted to—"

"You were being friendly," Theo said, taking pity in spite of himself. "When you're in love, you want everyone else to feel it too, don't you?"

Cole's face lit up. "Yeah, yeah that's it! I just—Layla's so great, and *you're* great, even though you pretend you're not, and you should be happy, and you *looked* so happy smiling at whatever your girl sent you, and I just...." He shuffled his feet. "I just wanted to know who could make you smile like that, because she must be pretty special." He looked at Theo again. "So are you *sure* I didn't—"

"I'm sure," Theo said, standing to slap him lightly on the shoulder. "Just something I ate."

Cole relaxed into a relieved smile. "So what's her name, anyway?"

Theo swore silently. He groped for words as every single girl's name that had ever existed suddenly vanished from his brain. "Oh," he said, turning away to reach for his pants. "It's—Ebba." First Swedish name he could think of, and of course it was his mother's. But Cole didn't know that.

"Cool name," Cole said, smile widening. "I'll let you get

dressed, but we should go out together sometime, the four of us."

Theo could have laughed, but nothing about the situation was funny. "I'd like that," he told Cole, who bobbed his head and headed for his own stall.

He waited to check his phone until he was home, sitting in the car and unlocking it to find a handful of messages from Niklas.

They didn't say much, but Theo read them slowly, savoring each one.

We're done with practice. Couple of the guys and I are going for lunch at this little place they say is great. Although I think it's because Joel has a crush on one of the waitresses.

Theo half-smiled.

Okay, she's pretty, the next text read. *But I'm not sure she's pretty enough for whatever this is.*

There was a picture attached, of limp fries and a very pallid burger.

Theo grimaced in sympathy.

Rescue me, Niklas wrote. *Why aren't you answering? Isn't practice over for you?*

There was another picture then, this one of Niklas himself, one long arm slung around Joel's neck as they both mugged for the camera.

Theo stroked his phone case with a thumb, memorizing the details of Niklas's face yet again. His blue eyes were bright with happiness, dimples flashing as he grinned. The light was behind him, making a halo spring up around him. He was too beautiful to be real, Theo thought absently. He was like a fever dream made real, the personification of everything Theo had ever wanted and could never have.

Nik could never know Theo was attracted to him. *Never.*

His stomach turned over at the thought, at the way Nik would be flattered, of course he would, Theo was his childhood idol, but then there'd be pity, and fumbling attempts to let him down gently, to make sure Theo understood Nik simply didn't see him the same way. Or *worse*, he might even offer Theo sex out of some horribly misguided effort to make Theo feel better about himself.

It made the nausea come surging back, and he locked the phone and shoved the car door open in a sharp, vicious motion. Enough. He had work to do until it was time to go over to Sunny's for dinner. He still wanted to draw that chest of drawers that was tickling the back of his mind. He couldn't quite see it yet, but he thought he had a few vague ideas how he could bring it to life.

Woodworking always made him feel better. It was almost as good as hockey that way.

Sixteen

INGA GREETED Theo at the door with a warm hug and a kiss to both his cheeks, cupping his face in her warm hands and beaming at him.

"What does it take to get you to visit?" she scolded, pulling him over the threshold. "You're only five minutes away but we never see you!" She towed him into the living room, where Sunny was sprawled on the floor with several blond children on top of him. They caught sight of Theo and tumbled off their father with shrieks of glee, rushing to greet him. Theo laughed, bending to catch them both and hoist them up.

"Lilly, Oscar, you're so *big*!" he said, and set them back on the ground, pretending he'd hurt his back as he straightened.

Lilly giggled and threw her arms around his waist. "We're *eight* now. We're super big!"

"I'm bigger," Oscar said, puffing his chest out, and Theo ruffled his hair.

"Rainer, get up and greet our guest," Inga chided, but Sunny just flipped a hand from his spot on the floor.

"I saw him this morning, my love," he said mildly. "Come sit, Theo."

The twins dogged Theo's path to the armchair he chose, and Lilly was in his lap the minute he sat down, Oscar leaning against his arm.

"How's school?" Theo asked them.

He listened to the flood of stories about friends and teachers and terribly boring schoolwork for several minutes, as Inga appeared and handed him a glass of ice water with a smile and Sunny relaxed on the floor, apparently quite content to stay where he was.

Finally, though, he dragged himself to his feet. "Grill should be hot by now. Brick, come help me?" He caught Oscar around the waist as he tried to follow, swinging him up into the air effortlessly. "Not yet, you," he said, poking him in the ribs as Oscar squirmed and giggled. "You stay here and help your mother. You too, Lilly. You can both talk to Uncle Theo more later."

It was cool but not cold outside on Sunny's big patio. Theo settled into a chair beside the grill as Sunny raised the hood and began layering steaks on the rack.

Theo smoothed his palm over the arm of the chair. "These holding up okay?"

"Your work always does," Sunny said, not looking at him, and Theo smiled to himself.

A companionable silence fell between them until Sunny was satisfied with the positioning of the meat and turned to sit in the chair beside Theo. He rummaged in the cooler beside him and tossed a bottle of beer across.

Theo took a long pull, sighing after he swallowed. Creamy malt mingled with caramel and toffee on his tongue, followed by the sharp tang of hops.

"New one?" he asked idly.

"Playing with the recipe," Sunny said. "But I think it's pretty good."

The sun was dipping below the horizon, bathing them in

warm, golden light. Theo closed his eyes and let the peace settle into his bones. There wasn't much he could think of that would make the moment better. Except maybe for Nik being there with him, he thought, and smiled at himself for being foolish.

"What's funny?" Sunny inquired idly.

"Nothing," Theo said, opening his eyes. Sunny was watching him, blue eyes sharp and curious. When he said nothing, Theo frowned. "Really, I was just lost in my head."

"What were you thinking about?" Sunny asked, and Theo's frown deepened.

"Why are you pushing?"

"Just curious what's going on with you." Sunny didn't look away, concern in the pinch of his eyebrows.

"Absolutely nothing," Theo snapped.

"Uh huh."

Theo sighed. "Sunny."

"Theo." Sunny's tone was identical. He leaned forward. "You're distracted. Moody. Something's eating at you. If you can't tell your best friend, who *can* you tell?"

"Why do you think I need to tell you anything?" Theo countered.

"Because you need to tell *someone*," Sunny said evenly. "That's what friends are for, Brick. To carry each other's burdens."

Theo rubbed his eyes. "I hate that you're right," he muttered.

"Also what friends are for."

Theo glowered at him and Sunny beamed.

"When I was with Brynäs, a kid got attacked," Theo said abruptly.

Sunny's eyes went wide. "What happened? Did you know him?"

"Yeah," Theo said. His throat threatened to close at the

memory rising unbidden yet again. "I—we were billeted together. Good friends. There was—" He leaned forward to brace his elbows on his knees, staring at the deck. "He was gay." He paused. "Is, I guess, he didn't die."

"Thank God," Sunny said. "What happened? Can you talk about it?"

Theo shook his head, but it wasn't denial. "He had a boyfriend. I knew about them, he'd come out to me a few months before. I never said anything, I wouldn't have, Petr knew that. He brought his boyfriend to practice once. I think they thought they were safe, and a couple of our teammates found them kissing in the hall."

"They hurt him?" Sunny asked, sounding horrified, and Theo nodded, swallowing the nausea trying to rise again.

"His boyfriend got away. But Petr—" He set his beer down abruptly and dug the heels of his hands into his eyes. "He went back to his parents' after he got out of the hospital. I never saw him again."

"Did he leave the league?"

"He lost most of the sight in one eye," Theo said harshly, and Sunny sucked in a breath. "So yeah. He left."

"Jesus, Theo." Sunny leaned across the space and put a hand on Theo's forearm. "What's got you thinking about this now?"

"There's this kid," Theo said, grateful for the warmth of Sunny's hand anchoring him. "Friend of mine, new to the league still. He wants—" He stopped briefly. "He wants to come out publicly. Says he can't do anything but live his truth."

"And you're scared for him," Sunny said.

"I'm fucking *terrified*," Theo spat. He shoved himself to his feet and took several steps away and then back as Sunny watched, eyes sympathetic. "I saw," Theo managed around the rock in his throat, "I saw what they did to Petr. He could have died. He lost *everything*."

"Not everything, surely," Sunny said. "Or did his parents disown him?"

Theo paused. "No," he said after a minute. "No, they were... supportive, I think. But he lost *hockey*. He lost what he wanted so much, and what he could have been. He had his entire future ripped from him in the space of ten minutes."

"It's awful," Sunny said. He was still watching Theo as he paced. "But *was* it his future?"

"What do you mean?" Theo asked.

"I mean... sometimes kids join the league to keep their parents happy, or because they love the game but not necessarily enough to pursue a professional career later in life. There are any number of reasons why it might not have been everything to him the way it is to—" He stopped and Theo narrowed his eyes.

"To me," he said. "Go ahead and say it."

"I know how much it means to you," Sunny said, holding his eyes. "It's understandable you'd think Petr's life was ruined. But not everyone lives and breathes it like you do. I'm just saying, it's possible he could have found happiness in something else, isn't it?"

"It's possible," Theo said slowly. "But my friend—it *is* everything to him. And if he comes out, then it gets taken from him?" He pressed his hand against his stomach, phantom pain lingering in his core. He caught Sunny's eye again and dropped his hand. "It would kill him," he said simply.

"You think it's a possibility?"

"I think people full of hatred are everywhere," Theo snapped. "And maybe he's not famous yet, but he's good. He will be. People will know his name. He'll be recognized on the street. *Anything* could happen to him, and I can't protect him,

I can't keep the darkness from touching him, I can't keep him *safe*." He doubled over, bracing his hands on his knees as he fought for air.

The chair creaked as Sunny stood. He put one big hand on Theo's back, rubbing it in slow, easy circles.

"You care a lot about him," he said, voice completely neutral.

Theo straightened. Sunny kept rubbing his back, eyes warm.

"He's a good friend," Theo said. "Sorry, I didn't mean to —"

"Don't even say it," Sunny said, tone sharp. "I told you, that's a friend's job. So you're afraid for this kid, because you don't want something like what happened to Petr happen to him. Come on, sit down." He guided Theo back to the chairs and Theo sat as Sunny turned to the grill to flip the steaks. When he was done, he joined him, picking up his beer and draining it with a satisfied sigh.

Theo turned his own half-empty beer in his hands, looking unseeingly at the label. "What do I do?" he asked after a few minutes.

"Why do you think there's anything for you *to* do?" Sunny asked gently. "This is his decision."

"I just—"

"You don't want him to be hurt, I get it. If Oscar realizes he's gay and joins the NHL anyway, I'll be fucking terrified. I'm not going to lie to you. But it will be his decision to do it. And if he comes out, then Inga and I will be there supporting him every step of the way."

"*Is* he—" Theo asked, curious in spite of everything.

"A little too early to tell," Sunny said, eyes creasing with amusement. "But he'll have my support if that's how it unfolds, that's all I'm saying. And that's all you can do for your friend. Support him."

"He's not—I asked him to wait a little while, get more established before he comes out," Theo said, feeling the shame of it rising again. "I know it's cowardly, but you know how people are. They'll say he's not good enough, or if he *is* good enough—and he is, Suns, he's *so* good—they'll say he's getting special treatment, players going easy on him or something. His entire identity will revolve around his sexual orientation. He'll never be anything but 'the gay hockey player'. How can he even *think*—" He cut himself off. "He deserves to be recognized for his skill, his talent," he went on more moderately. "If he wins awards, they'll say he's getting them as some sort of 'affirmative action bullshit'. It'll never be because *he's* so talented. They'll never see *him*."

"And what do you think should be done about that?" Sunny asked.

That pulled Theo up short. "What do you mean?"

"You think staying quiet will help him, at least with his career. Okay. You're probably right."

Theo blinked, and Sunny's smile was wry, no amusement in it.

"I know the league, the fans, as well as you do. And you're right. It'll be hard for him. So fucking hard, and I understand why you're scared. But if he keeps his mouth shut, that doesn't really solve the problem, does it? It might keep him safe, but what about kids like Oscar, ten, fifteen years from now? If your friend says nothing, then nothing changes. And everyone continues to steep in their hatred of the unknown, because of ignorance and fear and bigotry."

Theo squeezed his eyes shut. "But why does *he* have to be the one to say something?" he whispered, hating the way his voice caught.

"He's not the first," Sunny pointed out. "There's Caron. And yeah, if you venture into the comments in any article about him, you'll read stupid shit. Which is why you *never*—"

"Never read the comments," Theo finished, almost smiling. "Yeah."

"And there's Saint. He won almost every single award before he came out. Where was the preferential treatment? And you know that kid's going to hoist the Cup, sooner rather than later. He's done that on his own, *proven* he belongs here."

"So I'm the problem," Theo said, and Sunny's eyebrows lifted.

"I never said that."

"But it's true," Theo said bitterly. "Because I'm too much of a coward to let him be himself."

"Oh Theo," Sunny said. "You have every reason to be afraid. This is bigger than you and your friend. It's bigger than all of us. And it's going to take all of us to fight it. It's okay if you're not ready to do that. It's okay if you're *never* ready to do that. But you can't live your friend's life for him, and I think you know that."

"I don't want to," Theo managed. "I just want him to be safe."

"I know. Let's talk about something happier. What are you working on right now?"

"Chest of drawers," Theo said gratefully. "It's still telling me what it wants to be, but I've got some sketches. I think I'll use maplewood, with birch accents."

Sunny took his phone when he handed it over, flipping through the sketches as the door opened and the twins came tumbling out.

"Mama said to tell you she's almost ready," Oscar said, small chest inflated with the importance of being the one chosen to bear the news.

Sunny ruffled his hair. "Alright, my love. I think we're nearly there too."

Lilly clambered into Theo's lap. "You look sad, Uncle

Theo," she said, and put her head on his shoulder. "Why are you sad?"

Theo settled her more firmly and wrapped his arms around her. "How could I be sad with you around, sweetheart? How's hockey? Who's faster now, you or Oscar?"

"Me," Lilly said, sounding pleased with herself. "But Oscar's a better stick-handler."

"You'll get there." Theo's phone chimed and Sunny handed it back immediately. It was Nik, he saw, and guilt swamped him again. He hadn't spoken to him all day. He had to be worried sick—this wasn't like Theo.

The message was short. *Are you okay, or are you trying to tell me something?*

Of course he'd jump to that conclusion. Theo would have too.

I'm having dinner with Sunny's family, he sent back. *Can I call you tonight before bed?*

Nik's reply was immediate. *Yes.*

Theo locked his phone and put it away. He had a lot to think about, but right now, Lilly was prattling on about the goal she'd scored in practice, and Oscar was piping up at regular intervals to tell him more details, and he could put everything away, lock it up tight and just be in the moment with these people he loved.

Seventeen

THEO DIDN'T CALL until Niklas was actually in bed, reading on his phone when it rang, startling him into nearly dropping it.

"Hey," Niklas said when he'd recovered it.

"Hi." Theo sounded tired.

"*Are* you okay?" Niklas asked before he thought better of it.

"Other than being an asshole, I'm fine," Theo said.

"You're... what? You're not an asshole."

"I've ignored you all day because I was upset about something. I made you worry. I'm an asshole."

"Theo...." Niklas stared at the wall of his tiny bedroom, barely eight feet away. "Was it—" He closed his mouth. He couldn't ask.

"It wasn't you, if that's what you were going to say," Theo said. "Just... the rookies horsing around, Xander being homophobic."

"About you?" Niklas asked sharply.

"No. No, he doesn't know. But Tyler and Josh were

pretending to flirt and he didn't like it. Kept saying shit, and no one called him on it." Theo heaved a sigh. "*I* didn't call him on it. And I don't like that about myself."

"It's not your fault he's a dickhead," Niklas said. "And it's not your job to call him out."

"I'm one of the leaders in the room," Theo said. He sounded resigned. "Just because I don't have a letter doesn't mean they don't look to me. I should have said *something*." He took another breath and blew it out. "Enough of me moping. How are you? I guess you survived the diner."

"It was a near thing," Niklas said. "How can food be cold *and* hot at the same time?"

Theo laughed, just a little, but it was something. "How are you feeling on the ice?"

"Good, yeah. Have you been watching?"

"Of course. That last game was something else. Your glove-hand's getting better, too." Theo's voice sounded just like always, warm and smooth. It was deeper when he spoke Swedish, and it melted Niklas's bones, more than a bit, to listen to him talk. He rolled onto his back and stared up at the ceiling as arousal curled warm in his belly.

God, he wanted so much to know what Theo sounded like breathless and begging. He wanted to press him into the mattress until they were both panting, wanted to inscribe his brand into Theo's skin with teeth and tongue, mark him up and make him *beg*.

He pressed the heel of his hand to his erection, willing it away. He was *not* jerking off while Theo was literally talking to him, but the longer he had to listen to Theo's *voice*, the more he felt like a coiled spring, wound too tight and about to explode.

"Nik?"

Niklas flinched, brought back to earth with a thump. "Sorry," he managed.

"Someday you'll tell me where you go when you zone out on me like that," Theo said, sounding amused. "Good thing I'm not insecure."

I'm thinking about you. Niklas didn't say it. "Guess I'm more tired than I thought."

"I'll let you go," Theo said immediately.

"No!" Niklas draped an arm over his eyes, grateful Theo wasn't there to see the blush burning its way up his throat. "I mean—not unless you *want* to. Don't you have a game tomorrow? You should rest."

"Are you trying to imply I'm old?" Theo said, and he was definitely teasing now, Niklas could hear the laughter in his voice, and it made something ease in his chest and the arousal less of a chore to push away.

He huffed, sounding more put-upon than he felt. "You said it, not me. I can go all night and still play a full sixty minutes."

Theo's laugh cut off and he coughed. "Well, I definitely can't, not anymore." And just like that, the arousal came surging back and Niklas caught his breath.

"Well, just remember to hydrate," he said, managing to keep his voice even with an almighty effort. "Plenty of rest breaks. You can probably make it longer than you think."

"We're, uh—" Theo's voice was just slightly unsteady and it made Niklas want to crow with triumph. "We're talking about hockey, aren't we?"

"Of course," Niklas said, putting as much innocence into his tone as he could. "What else would we be talking about?"

"Nothing," Theo said way too quickly, and Niklas smiled up at the ceiling.

"So what's your latest project?" he asked, mostly so Theo would keep talking.

Theo launched into a description of a chest of drawers he

was designing, and Niklas listened, making appropriate noises and asking the occasional question to keep him going.

It needed more investigating, some more evidence, but he was fairly sure Theo was attracted to him. Maybe it was simple flirting and nothing more, a reaction to being celibate and touch-starved, but if it *was* more... well. That warranted further investigation and he couldn't *wait* to get started.

For now, though, he was content to listen to Theo talk and think about what it would be like.

It took him a scant handful of minutes after they'd hung up to come, biting the inside of his cheek to stifle the noise as he spilled helplessly into a tissue, toes curling with the force of it. After, he lay quietly, breathing still a little ragged but his mind blessedly blank.

Finally, he dropped the tissue into the trash and rolled onto his side. "Goodnight, Theo," he whispered, and fell asleep.

Theo lay on his back, staring up at the ceiling. *Don't*, that tiny voice in his head whispered. *It'll be so much harder if you do.*

He draped an arm over his eyes, but the arousal simmering under his skin refused to abate. If anything, it surged, stronger than ever. *Niklas, crawling onto the bed, purpose clear in his eyes and lip caught between his teeth. His long, lovely fingers teasing over Theo's abdomen, a soft promise of things to come before he lowers himself to kiss him.*

No one had to know. Theo knew he was the worst cliche in the world even as he had the thought, but he was already pushing his pants down just enough to pull himself out and groping for a tissue with his other hand.

He could do this. He could think about how Niklas would feel, how he would taste, and keep the fantasies locked away in the deepest reaches of himself, where no one would ever know how he felt.

He came on a stifled moan, breath harsh in his throat, but after the first rush of bliss, guilt followed hot and stinging, flooding his lungs until he thought he'd choke on it.

Rolling onto his side, he let the tissue fall and buried his face in the pillow.

Eighteen

"MY OFFICE!" Benson shouted when Theo came through the door.

Theo went through his mental laundry list of potential sins but couldn't come up with anything bad enough to make Benson look so thunderous as he followed him down the hall and into the small office.

Benson spun to face him. "What the fuck is going on with Finn?"

Not the direction Theo had expected. He recalibrated. "How do you mean?"

"I mean, he's *off*. Ever since he sprained his ankle, he hasn't been as sharp. He's letting shit through that he used to be able to stop in his sleep. And *you* haven't even noticed. Why haven't you noticed?"

"Maybe because I'm not actually your goddamn goalie coach?" Theo snapped, but Benson matched his snarl.

"Like it or not, you're the best we've fucking got. So figure out what's wrong with your backup, because right now I've got colanders less leaky than him."

. . .

Theo took Finn out for lunch after practice. Watching him pick at his food, head down, guilt stabbed through Theo. Something *was* wrong, and from the looks of it, had been for a while. And Theo hadn't even noticed, too wrapped up in moping about a boy too young for him and feeling sorry for himself.

"You need to eat," he said, as gently as possible.

Finn took a bite of his burger, chewing and swallowing as if he couldn't taste it, and then set it down again.

"What's going on?" Theo asked.

Finn hunched his shoulders and looked away.

"Finn," Theo prompted.

"I don't want to do this anymore," Finn blurted, and covered his face.

Theo sat back. "Do what, exactly?"

Finn dropped his hands. "Hockey. *This.* I can't—it's so much pressure, Theo, how do you do it? I don't—everyone's watching me, talking shit about me. Saying horrible things when I make a post on Instagram, like—" His breath hitched. "I'm not a person to the fans, I'm just something there to stop pucks, and when I don't, they—"

"The worst ones are always the loudest," Theo agreed quietly. "Set your account to private if they're bothering you that much."

"It's not just that. It's—it's everything. Everyone I talk to wants to talk about our chances for the Cup this year, or pick apart my latest game and tell me everything I did wrong. I can't keep *doing* it, Theo, I hate it, I miss my girlfriend and my family and I just—" He broke off, covering his mouth with a shaking hand. "I want to go home," he whispered. A tear slid down his cheek.

"I'm so sorry," Theo said helplessly, hating the inadequacy. "I didn't—I didn't realize. I didn't know you were dealing with this. I should have. I should have seen it sooner and said something. Finn, I'm so *sorry.*"

Finn shook his head and then covered his face again. His shoulders shook. "I want—I need...." He hiccupped. "Can I go home? Please?"

"I don't know," Theo admitted, but he leaned across the table and took one of Finn's hands. "I'll do everything I can to help you, okay?"

Nineteen

"FINN'S OUT," Benson announced when Theo picked up his phone the next morning. "His agent pulled some strings, called his parents, and he's going home. Temporary for now, to see if he can get his head on straight. If he wants another chance, he'll have to start with the Bandits and earn it."

"Is he okay?" Theo asked.

"His parents just got here and he smiled for the first time in a month when his mom hugged him," Benson said. "He's in a bad place but he's got support. He'll make it."

Theo nodded silently, even though Benson couldn't see him.

"I'm bringing Stromberg up today," Benson continued. "He'll be your backup until further notice. Oh, and Spencer is coming too, he's ready."

"Okay," Theo said. Guilt and happiness clashed in his chest. How could he be glad about this when Finn was so clearly struggling? He was a terrible person.

"Tell him for me," Benson said, and hung up.

* * *

"So, the Ravens. Tell me what you know." Theo wasn't looking at him, eyes on the road, but Niklas knew by now that he didn't miss a thing.

"They win but they play ugly," Niklas said, grimacing. "Lots of hits. Very physical game."

"Yes. Now in English."

Niklas groaned, throwing his head back against the seat. "Do I have to?"

"English." Theo's voice left no room for arguing. "Like you're talking to a journalist."

Niklas sighed noisily. "The Ravens are a strong team. Aggressive. They will use their strength to try and in—inti—intimate us?"

"Intimidate," Theo said, lips twitching.

"That. But as long as we don't take stupid penalties, we will be okay."

"Good. You're getting much better. Tell me, Nik, do you have a girlfriend?"

"I have never time to date," Niklas said. "Too busy. Hockey is my girlfriend right now."

"No time," Theo corrected. He continued in Swedish. "That's good, make them laugh, they'll like that. The Ravens will rush you. They'll crash your net. Make you afraid to make stops because you'll be worried about them hitting you."

"Fuckers," Niklas muttered.

"Indeed. *Are* you worried?"

"Should I be?"

"Depends how afraid you are of getting hurt."

Niklas rolled his head on the seat to look at him, admiring Theo's perfect profile yet again. "I'm twenty-two. I think that means I'm immortal right now."

Theo's lips tightened the way they always did when Niklas mentioned his age. "You're not immortal," he said, words clipped. "You can get hurt. You should take care of yourself, be more careful."

"I'm careful, Theo," Niklas said. "But I also heal fast. I'm not afraid of the Ravens. They can't scare me out of stopping their shots."

Theo slanted a look at him. "If they hurt you, I'll kill them," he said.

Warmth spread through Niklas's core and he hid his smile.

"No murder necessary," he said. "I'll be fine."

* * *

The Ravens weren't all that, Niklas thought scornfully as he picked himself up off the ice. It was obvious they were trying to intimidate him, taking every opportunity to trip or jostle him as they swept by in their battles for the puck. Well, it wasn't that fucking easy. He glanced at the bench. Theo was leaning forward, yelling something at the player who'd just collided with Niklas and was currently trying to skate away like it hadn't happened.

He didn't get very far, though. Kasha launched himself at the player and they went down in a tangle of limbs and flying fists. Several others skidded into the fray and Niklas turned to take a drink. The bottle was empty, he realized as he pulled it from the pocket, and he scowled and skated for the bench.

Theo still looked ready to come over the boards, fury clouding his gray eyes as he watched the fight. His gaze snapped to Niklas, but he didn't relax, looking him over like Niklas was hiding an injury from him.

"Did he hurt you?" he asked in Swedish as he handed another water bottle to him.

Niklas took a long drink and poured some water over his hair, shaking his head and letting the droplets spray before answering.

"I'm fine," he finally said. He smiled at Theo, who didn't look appeased.

"You hit the ice hard. Are you sure?"

"I'm *fine*," Niklas repeated. "You can inspect me in the shower later if you don't believe me."

He savored the sputtering noise that got him as he skated back for his net and settled in. The referees were dragging the fighters apart, and Kasha headed for the box, shaking his hair out of his eyes.

Niklas shook it off, put it all away, and readied himself for the next puck drop.

* * *

"Your first shutout!" Sunny yelled over the noise of the bar, slinging an arm around Niklas's neck and hauling him close. "How are you feeling?"

Niklas beamed at him. "I feel good!" he shouted back. He was pleasantly tingly, warm and flushed from the alcohol but not drunk.

"Gonna pick up?" Sunny asked. He nodded in the direction of the bar. "Coupla rockets over there been giving you the eye all night."

Niklas looked where Sunny was indicating. A curvy blonde girl was sitting next to a tall brunette, both of them watching him. The blonde waved and Niklas waved back, making both girls giggle.

"Go talk to 'em!" Sunny said.

Theo slid into the booth, setting two mugs of beer on the table and shoving one toward Niklas. "Talk to who?"

"Sunny's trying to get me laid," Niklas yelled.

Theo's eyebrows went up and he took a sip of his beer.

Sunny turned to talk to Josh and Niklas scooted closer to Theo.

"You think I should go for it?"

Theo gave him a cool look. "You tell me. Is that something you're interested in doing?"

Niklas glanced around the table. No one was watching them, the music so loud they couldn't be heard unless their heads were pressed together. Still, Niklas kept his voice low, his lips to Theo's ear, and spoke Swedish.

"You know it's not. But how do I get out of it?"

Theo sighed. "I don't know, Nik. Fake it?"

"Well, how do *you* do it?"

"I don't pick up," Theo said simply. "The guys are used to it. They tease me about being a monk, but they don't expect me to actually do anything."

"And you're okay with that? Do you not like sex?"

Theo shot a look at him. "How is that your business?"

Niklas tried his most winning smile. "I'm just curious. I got a shutout, did you hear?"

Theo's lips twitched and he tried to cover by taking another swallow of beer. "Yes, I was there." His tone was dry but Niklas could hear the amusement underneath. "I like sex. But I also have a perfectly good right hand, and getting laid is just... too complicated."

Heat flashed through Niklas at the mental image of Theo touching himself. Was he noisy? Probably not, he decided. He was too self-contained for that. But could Niklas *get* him to make noise? He very much wanted to find out. But how to broach the subject? If he just asked—offered himself up the way he so desperately wanted to, Theo would turn him down without a second thought. So how could he get Theo to admit he wanted him too? He watched Theo take another sip of beer and a plan began to form.

When Sunny glanced back, eyebrows raised, Niklas just smiled at him. "Later," he yelled over the music. "I wanna stay here and get drunk first. I got a shutout!"

"Shots!" Sunny roared, and everyone at the table cheered.

* * *

"Step," Theo said, out of breath. "Come on, careful—" He gripped Niklas's waist like a vise, carrying almost all his weight as Niklas felt for the step and slid his foot onto it.

Theo had only had a single beer, mindful of driving home, but he'd watched as Niklas put back shot after shot, his whole body getting looser, smile getting wider and movements more expansive as the alcohol flooded his system. He'd leaned against Theo more and more, until he was basically draped over him, and Theo had hated it and loved it and never wanted it to end, the feeling of Niklas's body pressed to his, the scent of his woodsy aftershave and the shampoo he used that smelled like flowers because Niklas was many things, but fragile in his masculinity was not one of them.

Niklas tightened the arm he had around Theo's shoulders. "S'cold," he mumbled.

Fighting with his keys to get the right one, Theo just hummed in acknowledgment.

"Warm me up, Theo," Niklas whined, and Theo dropped the keys.

"Dammit." It took a minute to figure out how to keep Niklas upright and stoop swiftly to snatch the keys, but he managed it before Niklas's knees buckled. He had the door open a minute later and bodily hauled Niklas over the threshold.

Niklas giggled, arm back around Theo's shoulders. "Smell so nice," he said, and put his nose in Theo's hair, taking a huge breath.

Theo kicked the door closed with gritted teeth. Niklas didn't move at first, breath warm against Theo's scalp, and Theo shut his eyes and prayed for strength.

"Bed," he finally said, and turned them down the hall.

"Mm, bed. Will y'be in it?"

Theo somehow kept his voice steady. "No, Nik, I won't be in it."

"But I want you to be." He sounded sad, as if confused, and Theo's heart clutched.

"I'd like that too," he said before he could stop himself. "But it's not a good idea. Come on." He pushed the door open and eased Niklas onto the bed, where he immediately flopped over on his back. Theo knelt to take his shoes off as Niklas stared up at the framework of the iron canopy.

"S'not fair, you know."

Theo looked up. "Hm? What's not?"

Niklas propped himself on his elbows and peered down his long body at him. "You. This. The—" He flopped a hand. "You won't let me have sex."

"I—what?"

"I got a *shutout*," Niklas continued, sounding faintly accusing. "'An' I can't even *celebrate*. I can't get laid for my first shutout. Not fair." He collapsed backward onto the bed, leaving Theo kneeling on the floor and feeling like he'd been kicked in the stomach.

There was silence for a minute and then Niklas jolted upright.

"We should have sex."

"*What*?"

Niklas beamed delightedly at him. "S'perfect! I can celebrate with *you*!"

Theo shot to his feet. "That's—no. You're drunk. You don't know what you're saying. We're *not* doing that."

Niklas's face fell. "Oh." He plucked at the seam of his jeans. "You don't want me." His voice was sad and small, and Theo clutched at his hair.

"That's not the *point*."

"But you don't." Niklas looked up. "S'okay, Theo. I know I'm not—I'm sorry for—" He waved a hand again.

"I want you so much I can't bear it," Theo whispered, and snapped his mouth shut, horrified at himself. But it was too late. A smile broke on Niklas's face like the dawn.

"You do?"

Theo did his best to make his expression stern. "We're not discussing this. You're drunk off your ass, and you need to sleep."

Niklas grabbed his wrist as Theo tried to help him get comfortable on the bed. "C'n we talk 'bout it tomorrow?"

Their faces were close together. It would be so easy to lean down and take a kiss. Instead Theo brushed the hair off Niklas's forehead.

"*If* you remember this conversation," he murmured. "Yeah, we can talk about it tomorrow."

Niklas's smile returned. "Okay. Will you kiss me goodnight?"

"Sure," Theo said, and pressed a swift kiss to Niklas's forehead.

Niklas scowled. "Thass not—you know what I meant, Theo!"

Theo smiled at him. "Don't lie down yet." He went to the bathroom, Niklas still huffing in outrage behind him, and got a glass of water and the aspirin from the cupboard, then padded back out.

Niklas had lain down and was already asleep, mouth open just slightly. Theo smoothed the hair off his forehead again, unable to stop the rush of affection.

"Nik, honey, wake up."

Niklas moaned and rolled away. Theo gently pulled him back.

"Come on, you need to drink this. Sit up for me."

Niklas squeezed his eyes tightly shut and turned his head away. "Sleepin'."

"Trust me, your head will thank me in the morning," Theo said, and tugged until Niklas was half-up, propped on an elbow. He had to hold the glass to Niklas's lips, but Niklas obediently drained the whole thing before collapsing back onto his pillows again.

Theo went to the bathroom and refilled the glass. Setting it on the bedside table, he gave himself a minute to look down at Niklas, already asleep again.

"Goodnight, beautiful boy," he whispered, and let himself out the door.

He didn't sleep. How could he? He tossed and turned, thinking about what Niklas had said. Had he meant it? Was Theo just a convenient warm body or did Niklas actually *want* him? How could he, though? Theo was old enough to be his father—well, maybe not. Still, he couldn't wrap his head around the idea that Niklas wanted *him*. Nik was young, he was horny. He'd made a promise to Theo, and he was going to keep it because that was the kind of person he was, but that didn't mean he didn't still want and *need* that physical release.

Theo wasn't an idiot. He knew Niklas going without sex wouldn't kill him. Wouldn't even hurt him. But would it affect his play? They'd been winning more than they'd been losing lately, something Theo wasn't used to, and if sleeping with Niklas would improve his performance between the pipes even more, well.... This might be Theo's last chance at winning the Cup, and he was just selfish enough to admit that not only did he want Niklas, but he wanted to lift that damned Cup.

He could do this. He could keep it from getting complicated. He'd hooked up with Felix for *years* without either of them developing feelings. As long as he made sure Niklas understood that it was *just* sex, that there would never be anything between them, it was doable. He'd find out what Niklas tasted like, be able to touch that beautiful, lean body and draw responses from him, and maybe, *maybe*, even win the dream he'd been chasing his whole life.

Theo rolled onto his side and pulled the blankets up over his shoulder. It was going to be a moot point if Niklas didn't mention it in any case, because there was no way Theo was bringing it up if Niklas had been too drunk to remember. He didn't need that kind of humiliation. It was a very long time before he was even able to doze.

Twenty

NIKLAS WOKE with a horrible taste in his mouth, a faint lingering headache, and a sense of triumph blooming under his ribs. It took him a minute to remember why, but then he grinned up at the ceiling, rolled out of bed and stumbled to the bathroom, where he used liberal amounts of Listerine and stared at himself in the mirror. There were dark, puffy circles under his eyes and lines around his mouth that he didn't remember. Somehow he'd escaped the worst of the hangover he'd expected after drinking so much, but he'd looked better. Still, he was on a mission.

He turned to his dresser for clothes. He could smell eggs frying, which made his stomach growl loudly, and he hurried to pull on jeans and a Sentinels T-shirt, then a cozy sweater over it. Theo liked to keep it cool in the house, and Niklas had learned early to dress in layers.

Theo was at the stove, in the middle of flipping an egg. He smiled over his shoulder at Niklas.

"Good morning."

Niklas returned the greeting automatically even as he looked closer. There was tension around Theo's normally serene eyes, a tightness to his smile that wouldn't have been visible to a casual observer. So he definitely remembered their discussion too.

"What's wrong?" Niklas asked.

"Nothing," Theo said automatically. He gestured with his chin to the counter opposite. "There's coffee."

Niklas poured himself a cup, watching Theo out of the corner of his eye. They didn't speak as Niklas made his coffee, then reached into the refrigerator for a yogurt.

"You don't have to feed me, you know," he said as he sat at the table.

"I'm already cooking for me," Theo said without looking at him. "Might as well make enough for both of us. It's no trouble."

Niklas admired the view for a minute. Theo's shoulders were deceptively broad for his height, moving smoothly under his long-sleeved T-shirt. His waist tapered to a narrow pair of hips that were nevertheless no match for his perfect ass, toned and shaped by all the skating he did.

Theo glanced over his shoulder and Niklas hastily turned his attention to his yogurt.

"How's your head?" Theo asked.

"S'fine," Niklas said through his mouthful, and laughed at Theo's grimace.

"Didn't anyone teach you manners?" Theo muttered, sliding an egg onto the plate beside him and reaching for another one.

"They tried but it didn't take," Niklas said cheerfully. He took another bite of yogurt and went back to appreciating Theo's ass. There were definitely worse things to wake up to. "So what'd we talk about last night?"

He wasn't expecting Theo to drop the egg on the floor. Surprised, Niklas sat up and leaned over in his chair so he could watch as Theo mopped it up on hands and knees.

"You're *blushing*," Niklas observed, fascinated.

"No, I'm not." Theo dropped the paper towels in the trash and rocked back to his feet. "We didn't talk about anything important."

"Now why don't I believe you?" Niklas said. He stood and sauntered into the kitchen, resting a hip against the counter a few feet away from where Theo was very determinedly not looking at him as he cracked another egg into the skillet. "The-oo," Niklas wheedled, and Theo hunched his shoulders.

"If you don't remember, then it wasn't important." His tone was flat, forbidding further discussion, but that hadn't intimidated Niklas for a long time.

He reached out and bracketed Theo's wrist with his fingers. Theo went still, but his pulse was jackhammering under Niklas's thumb. Niklas watched, entranced, as he swallowed hard and looked up at him. His pupils were blown, lips parted slightly.

"Can I tell you a secret?" Niklas asked.

Theo looked wary but nodded.

Niklas stroked his pulse point, savoring the satin feel of Theo's soft skin. "I wasn't that drunk last night."

Theo jolted but didn't pull away. His eyes were wide, breath coming rapidly. "You—"

"I didn't know how to just come out and say what I wanted without you shooting me down immediately. Because you would have. So I figured... give us both plausible deniability, right? But I remember what you said."

Theo shook his head, brief and jerky. "It's a bad idea, Nik."

"Why? Because I'm so young I don't know what I want?"

Theo scowled. "You *don't*, Nik, you're—"

Niklas's finger against his lips stopped the rest of the sentence.

"Do me the courtesy," Niklas said, low and dangerous, "of trusting me to know my own mind."

Theo's mouth was soft under his finger. He looked up at Niklas mutely, his eyes pleading with him to understand.

"I'm not a kid," Niklas said. He dropped his hand. "You know that, right? I'm an adult. I may be younger than you but I'm not a child. I've bought a car, been in a relationship, had my own place. I don't have the experience you do but that doesn't mean I don't know what I want."

Theo closed his eyes briefly. "I know you *think* you want it, but—"

Niklas wanted to shake him. "Theo." He waited until Theo looked up at him again. "Do you want *me*, Theo?"

Theo shivered.

"Tell me the truth."

"I've wanted you for months," Theo whispered. His voice was hoarse, scraped raw with honesty, and Niklas's heart banged painfully against his ribs. "I can't—I shouldn't—"

Niklas bent and stopped him with a kiss. Theo drew a shocked breath as Niklas cupped his face and licked gently across his lips, asking to be let in. The moment stretched out, Theo seemingly frozen in place, and then his lips parted and he went up on his tiptoes, snaking his arms around Niklas's neck.

Niklas met him halfway, Theo's mouth hot and hungry and desperate under his. He tasted like coffee and smelled like wintergreen, his breath coming shaky and helpless as Niklas memorized his mouth.

This was what he'd been waiting for. Dreaming about. He was kissing the man he'd been half in love with since puberty, but it wasn't just that. He was kissing *Theo*, his friend, his goalie partner, a man he genuinely liked and respected, who giggled when he was drunk or very tired, who dumped soap suds down Niklas's shirt, who hated showing vulnerability but had opened his home and his life to Niklas.

The rush of tenderness made Niklas dizzy. He bent and caught Theo's hips, lifting him up and onto the counter. Theo's breath hitched but Niklas didn't give him a chance to say anything, stepping between Theo's spread knees and tugging him closer so he could go back to devouring his mouth.

They kissed for several long minutes, until Niklas's lips were pleasantly tingling, warmth growing in the pit of his stomach.

"Nik," Theo said suddenly, tearing away and struggling to control his breathing. "You know this—us—whatever we're doing—it wouldn't be a relationship, right?"

Niklas groaned, dropping his forehead to Theo's shoulder. "You really know how to kill the moment," he mumbled.

Theo cupped the back of his head. "Sorry," he said, voice low. "I just... need you to understand."

"Just sex," Niklas said, looking up. His heart twisted but he kept his face smooth.

"It's better this way," Theo said, touching his face. "Safer. For you."

As if Niklas gave a shit about *safe*.

He leaned in and pressed a kiss to the bolt of Theo's jaw. "I don't want to talk right now," he breathed, and Theo shivered again. Niklas sealed their mouths together again, savoring the taste and feel of Theo's lips and tongue, the way he arched into the kiss, wrapping a leg around Niklas's hips to pull him closer.

Niklas caught one of Theo's hands and brought it between them, pressing Theo's palm to his cock, already throbbing painfully with his arousal. Theo caught his breath and rotated his wrist to cup Niklas's length properly, fingers tracing along the outline of it. When he got to the tip, he ran one finger through the wet patch spreading and then lifted his finger to his mouth.

"*Fuck*," Niklas managed as Theo licked it clean and then reached down again. He worked his hand under the waistband this time and Niklas let his head fall to Theo's shoulder, hips rocking into the touch as Theo grasped him.

The angle was awkward and Theo couldn't get much leverage, but it didn't matter to Niklas. It was *Theo*, one arm around Niklas's shoulders and the other down his pants, and it felt so good it threatened to drown Niklas with the gathering sensations. But after a minute, Theo made a frustrated noise and pulled away.

Niklas protested wordlessly, blinking his eyes open—when had he closed them?

Theo kissed him, quick and soft, and then pushed him gently away so he could slide off the counter. His hair was rumpled from Niklas's hands in it, his pupils blown dark with desire. For *him*, for Niklas. Theo *wanted* him. The thought shook Niklas to his core.

"Bedroom," Theo said. He turned the burner off, then wrapped his long fingers around Niklas's wrist to pull him down the hall.

Niklas cooperated, but he couldn't help teasing him as Theo led him to the master bedroom. "Are you one of those people who only has sex in a bed?"

Theo shoved the door open and gave him a stern look that was belied by his twitching lips. "Do I *seem* like one of those people?"

Niklas pretended to look him over thoroughly. Theo crossed his arms, arching one eyebrow. "Kinda, yeah," Niklas finally said, fighting his own smile. "All buttoned-down and neat, not a hair out of place—usually." He flicked the strand of hair currently falling into Theo's face and Theo wrinkled his nose as Niklas continued. "You like things to be done in the proper order. Beds are for sleeping and sex, couches are for watching movies or reading books. Kitchen is for eating."

"That's it, let's go," Theo said, and pushed Niklas back out into the hall.

Startled, Niklas grabbed at him. "What—"

"We're fucking in the living room," Theo announced, and tried to drag Niklas in that direction.

Niklas set his heels as laughter caught in his chest. When Theo yanked on his arm, Niklas pulled back just as hard and Theo overbalanced and toppled into his chest with a startled *oof*.

"You've made your point," Niklas said, letting his hands wander down the planes of Theo's muscled back. "And while I am *enthusiastically* in favor of you bending me over your couch at some point—" He didn't miss the way Theo's breath hitched at that. "—I do think our first time would be better in a bed."

"*First* time?" Theo said, righting himself. He looked faintly ridiculous, hair standing on end and lips kiss-swollen and pink, and Niklas wanted him so much he couldn't breathe. "What makes you think there'll be a *next* time?"

Niklas was a goalie. He knew how to read people. Lust radiated off Theo in waves, showing in his shortened breaths, his blown pupils, the way he couldn't stop looking at Niklas's mouth.

"You tell me," Niklas said, and pulled his shirt and sweater up over his head and off in one smooth motion. When he surfaced, Theo was staring at him, mouth slightly ajar. Niklas gave him a challenging look and took a step back, into the bedroom. "You saying you only want to do this once, Theo?"

Theo swallowed hard, hovering on the other side of the door.

Niklas turned his back and pushed his pants down, bending to pull them off his feet. Theo made a noise and Niklas looked back to see him clinging to the doorframe, watching him with naked hunger in his eyes.

"It's just sex," Niklas said. "Are you up for it?"

He'd never met a professional hockey player capable of backing away from a challenge, and Theo was no different. His mouth tightened and he stepped into the room instantly, closing the distance between them to muscle Niklas onto the bed.

Niklas hit the mattress with a bounce and laughter he didn't bother trying to stifle. Answering humor lit up Theo's face but he didn't immediately follow. Instead he straightened, holding Niklas's eyes as he unbuttoned his cardigan and let it fall. He was wearing a soft T-shirt underneath, and he skinned out of it in a quick, economical motion.

"No striptease?" Niklas managed with a suddenly dry mouth, propping himself on his elbows to get a better view.

"Not this time," Theo said, and his lips curved as their eyes met, soft and amused, a secret smile for Niklas only. His hair fell over his forehead as he untied the waistband of his pants and pushed them down. He was fully hard, cock hanging thick and heavy between his legs, and Niklas couldn't stop the groan that ripped from him.

"Theo, *please—*"

Theo slid onto the bed. His dark eyebrows were drawn, all his considerable focus on Niklas spread out in front of him. He looked like a bird of prey, intent on his target, and it was Niklas's turn to shiver as Theo crawled across the mattress to kneel between Niklas's thighs. He smoothed a palm over the muscle.

"What do you want?" he asked, looking up.

"God, anything," Niklas managed. It was taking every ounce of willpower he possessed to not touch himself.

A smile flickered across Theo's face, there and gone almost immediately. "Careful," he said, letting his hand rest on Niklas's knee. "There's an awful lot that can go into 'anything'."

"I don't think there's anything you could do to me that I wouldn't *want* you to do," Niklas whispered, and Theo's eyes widened.

"*Christ*, you—" He reached for him and Niklas was already sitting up to reach his mouth, desperate to taste it again. They collided in a hungry gasping tangle and Niklas pulled until Theo was following him down to the mattress. He twisted, rolling them so he was on top, still kissing him so hard he was dizzy from it but he couldn't stop. Theo was warm and solid beneath him, hands roaming restlessly over Niklas's shoulders and back as if he couldn't get enough either.

Niklas ducked his head and Theo tilted his chin obligingly so he could kiss down the soft line of his throat, lips dragging over stubble. Niklas thought briefly about sucking a mark into the skin, but reluctantly discarded the idea. Theo wasn't the kind to parade around a locker room flaunting love-bites, and he wouldn't want to field the inevitable questions that followed.

Theo tangled a hand in Niklas's hair. He didn't try to move him, seeming content to let Niklas work his way over the broad expanse of his chest, lightly furred with softly curling golden blond hair that darkened to tawny on his abdomen as it thickened, leading Niklas down, over the ridges of muscle—it took longer and longer lately for him to maintain a six pack, Niklas knew, more and more effort necessary, keeping away from sweets and adhering to a rigorous diet.

Filled with a sudden tenderness for the stubborn man beneath him, Niklas kissed his belly button and Theo twitched. He kept his mouth shut, though, even when Niklas raised his head to look at him inquiringly.

Satisfied, Niklas went back to exploring the dips and valleys of Theo's ribs, tasting the skin and cataloging the micro reactions Theo was giving him.

Understated as ever, Theo was barely making noise. If it

weren't for how hard he was, Niklas would have thought him disinterested, flat on his back and not even watching him. Instead he was staring at the ceiling as if there was something fascinating on it.

Something fierce and possessive pulsed in Niklas's chest. Theo *would* make noise, because Niklas was going to make him feel so good he forgot everything else, all his vaunted self-control.

He licked a wet stripe up the underside of Theo's cock and Theo made a quietly strangled noise, abs jumping.

More like it. Nikas didn't go for the prize immediately, though. Instead he moved back down, until he was crouching between Theo's spread legs. Never in his wildest dreams had he ever let himself imagine he'd be here, with Theo allowing him—*inviting* him—into this most intimate of moments. He wanted to savor it, commit every single sensation to memory in case this really was the only time he was going to get to do this.

The hair on Theo's inner thigh was sparse and fine, softer than silk against Niklas's cheek. The skin there smelled faintly of his soap, traced with faint blue lines. It would bruise so easily, Niklas thought, running a thumb over it and pressing in just enough to feel the heavy muscle.

Theo twitched again but kept his mouth shut. Niklas lifted his head to see him staring down his body at him. Theo's eyes were dark and hungry, lips bitten red.

"Tell me if I do something you don't want me to do," Niklas said.

Theo's eyes softened. He stretched out a hand, cupped Niklas's cheek and smoothed a thumb over his cheekbone, but still he didn't speak.

Niklas turned and pressed a quick kiss to the inside of Theo's wrist, then lowered his head again and set his mouth to Theo's inner thigh, up high where no one would see it.

Theo sighed, above him, and lifted his leg to give him better access.

That was all the permission Niklas needed. He set to work in earnest sucking on the spot he'd chosen, drawing the blood to the surface in long, rhythmic sucks, pausing to scrape briefly over the sensitive area with his teeth and savoring the way Theo was shuddering all over now. It took a while to get the mark as dark as he wanted, but he'd always been one to put his whole heart into whatever job was in front of him.

At some point, Theo reached down and tangled both hands in Niklas's hair. Niklas made a pleased noise when Theo inadvertently jerked and pulled. He lifted his head.

"Do that again," he rasped, and didn't wait for a response before going back to work.

Theo half-laughed, sounding despairing, and pulled his hair again. Niklas's eyes slid shut at the burst of fireworks in his scalp, the heat spreading out under his skin. *God*, it felt good, arousal turning his blood to lava as it pumped heat through his veins until he was burning up from the inside out. He ached with the need to come, balls heavy and full already, but he pushed it away to focus on Theo.

He was getting close, Niklas thought, if the way he was steadily leaking pre-come onto his belly was any indication. He still hadn't touched himself, though, still staring up at the ceiling with a stubborn set to his jaw like this was a battle he was determined to win.

Niklas hated losing. He went to his elbows and sucked Theo down in one quick motion. Bitter salt exploded on his tongue as Theo jolted, a ragged noise falling from his mouth. This was a trick Niklas hadn't practiced in a while, but he was hoping he still had the knack.

He relaxed his jaw and slid down until the head of Theo's cock was nudging the back of his throat. His eyes watered but he focused on keeping every muscle loose so his throat would open, working his way down another millimeter, then another.

He didn't stop until his nose was brushing the soft curls at Theo's groin. He breathed shallowly through his nose, reaching up blindly for Theo's hand. When Theo gave him to him, Niklas guided it back down, pressing Theo's fingers to his throat. Theo traced wondering fingers over the bulge of his own cock there, touch soft and reverent.

"Nik," he whispered. "Fuck, Nik, you look so good—"

Niklas hummed and Theo's hips jerked, catching him off guard. He choked, tears spilling down his cheeks, and pulled off, coughing into his elbow.

"I'm so sorry," Theo said, and he sounded *horrified*. "Christ, Nik, I'm so fucking sorry, that was awful of me—"

Niklas wiped his face. His throat was sore but not unbearably so. "Shut up," he said, his voice gravelly and rough, and dove back down.

He went slower this time, but he didn't stop until Theo's cock was buried in his throat again. Theo was waiting when Niklas reached for his hand, gently pressing on the bulge until Niklas's eyes were watering again. His brain was sending up warning signals, *not enough air not enough air*, but Niklas ignored them, breathing slow and shallow through his nose. It *was* enough, if he didn't panic, and he'd had practice at this.

When he began to bob his head, Theo swore out loud, thick and vicious, and slapped the mattress with his free hand. His thighs were trembling, his whole body rigid as he fought the need to thrust harder, deeper, into Niklas's willing mouth, and yet another wave of tenderness washed through Niklas. He sped up, using his free hand to nudge up between Theo's spread legs.

Theo made a noise like a sob when Niklas found his hole, tightly furled, hot and dry, and pressed against it with his index finger. He didn't have lube, and he wasn't going to break his rhythm to even use spit, not when every drop of his head elicited a string of swearing from Theo, every pass of his tongue, every convulsive swallow around his cock made Theo tense and tremble beneath him, clearly clinging to the edge of reason by his fingernails.

Niklas didn't want reason. He didn't want logic or facts. He wanted Theo to come so hard he forgot his own name, wanted him to spill down his throat and let Niklas take it all.

He squeezed Theo's hand encouragingly, pushing again with his other hand until the tip of his finger breached Theo's body up to the knuckle.

"Fuck, *fuck*, I'm gonna—*Nik*—"

Niklas squeezed his hand again, sinking down all the way and swallowing.

Theo curled up off the bed as he came, every muscle rigid with it. Niklas wanted to watch him but he couldn't keep his eyes open, too many sensations threatening to pull him apart if his focus slipped for even an instant. Instead he memorized Theo's harsh breathing as he collapsed back to the pillows, the heave of his lungs laboring for air, the way his cock still throbbed weakly as Niklas drew off, stopping to hold just the head in his mouth. He ran his tongue along the underside, delighting in the bitter taste and the way Theo swore, going tense again with the overstimulation.

He didn't want to stop. He needed to come, quite desperately, but he wanted to savor the aftershocks still rippling through Theo's body, tongue along his cock again just to hear the names Theo called him.

"Get up here," Theo managed after a minute. He tugged at Niklas's shoulder, no force or coordination behind it, and Niklas let go of his cock reluctantly, allowing himself to be pulled up until he was straddling Theo's hips.

Theo's eyes were hooded with exhaustion, but he was smiling as he drew Niklas down into their softest kiss yet.

There was no need behind it, no driving urge to chase his pleasure, and Theo took his time, dipping inside with his tongue more and more, hand clasped over the nape of Niklas's neck to keep him where he wanted him.

Niklas jolted as Theo's other hand closed over his cock and he made an embarrassingly needy noise that Theo swallowed, humming soothing noises as he spread Niklas's pre-come over his shaft. After a minute, he pushed on Niklas's shoulder and let go.

"Spit," he said, holding his hand under Niklas's mouth.

"That's disgusting," Niklas rasped, and did as he was told. He didn't wait to see what happened, pressing their mouths together again. He groaned as Theo's hand found him, slick and wet now, and couldn't stop the way his hips rolled, thrusting into it.

"Is that good?" Theo murmured as Niklas broke the kiss to gasp for air, burying his face in the warm skin of Theo's throat.

"A little tighter," Niklas managed. "There—oh *fuck*, Theo, yeah, that's—"

"Let me take care of you," Theo whispered. "Can I give you this, sweetheart?"

Niklas nodded blindly, helpless against the sensations gathering in the pit of his stomach, the scalding hot waves of pleasure that pushed him higher every time they washed through him. His skin felt hot and too tight, every pass of Theo's hand too much and nowhere near enough.

He mouthed at the jut of Theo's collarbone, hips working helplessly. Theo was still talking, whispering endearments and nonsense phrases against Niklas's ear as Niklas writhed, a sob caught in his throat.

God, he wanted this to be real so badly he thought he'd choke on it. He wanted *Theo*, not just his body but all of him. His heart, his fascinating mind; Niklas wanted every piece of him, wanted to wrap himself up in all of his oddities and rituals, unlock his secrets and strip him truly bare. He wanted Theo to want *him* that way too, wanted to be as irresistible to Theo as Theo was to him, wanted Theo to not be able to keep his hands off him.

"Beautiful boy," Theo whispered, and Niklas swallowed the noise, hips stuttering. "That's it," Theo continued. "God, you're so beautiful. Come for me, sweetheart. Please, I want to see it. *Nik—*"

Niklas cried out as he let go, the pleasure lighting up the inside of his skull in white-hot molten pulses. Theo worked him through it, whispering words Niklas was too exhausted to decipher against his ear, and didn't stop until the bliss edged into overstimulation and Niklas squirmed, whining softly but not wanting to pull away. He wanted Theo to touch him forever, to hold him like something precious and breakable and look at him with awe in his eyes.

Theo stopped stroking but he didn't let go. Instead he planted a foot on the mattress and pushed, rolling Niklas off him so they were on their sides facing each other and slinging one leg over his thighs once they were comfortable.

Niklas's eyelids weighed a thousand pounds. He tried to blink, to open his eyes, but he was overtaken by a yawn instead.

Theo laughed softly and placed a featherlight kiss on Niklas's nose. "Sleep," he said. "I'll be here when you wake up."

Twenty-One

THEO WAITED until Niklas was sleeping soundly before sliding quietly from the bed. He pulled on pants, then stopped to look at the picture Niklas made, one long arm stretched out and the other tucked to his chest. His brown hair, in need of a trim, fanned out over Theo's pillow, straight and silky-fine. Theo wanted to run his fingers through it again but instead he slipped from the room and tiptoed down the hall to the kitchen.

Scooping up his phone, he stepped out into the backyard. The air was cool, nipping at his skin, but he ignored it, staring out over the prairie that stretched for miles beyond his house.

Was he panicking? He honestly couldn't tell. Physically he felt incredible, ready to run for miles. Mentally? He took stock. He wasn't sure the panic wouldn't still show up, but instead of freaking out, he just felt... sated. Happy. He'd made it clear to Niklas that there'd be no relationship and Niklas had accepted it without argument.

There was no danger of either of them falling in love. They were just two consenting adults in a physical arrangement that suited them both.

He had a message from Anjali, he saw when he glanced at his phone.

I'm in the area in two weeks. Got room for me?

Always, Theo sent back. *Send me the details.*

When he got back to the bedroom, Niklas was stirring, lifting his head to knuckle sleep from his eyes. His hair was rumpled, creases in his cheek from the pillow, and he smiled when he saw Theo, slow and sweet.

"Hi," he said, putting his head back down. "Why are you all the way over there?"

Theo slid onto the mattress and Niklas wrapped an arm around his hips, tugging him closer with a satisfied noise. He pressed his nose to Theo's shoulder and took a deep breath.

"You're cold," he murmured. "Did you go outside?"

He slung a thigh over Theo's, pressed against him in a long line of heat from shoulder to ankle, and Theo shivered.

It took him a minute to remember Niklas had asked a question.

"Yeah," he said. "Just wanted some fresh air."

Niklas kissed his shoulder, then opened his mouth and set his teeth in the muscle, scraping gently over Theo's skin.

"Ah—fuck," Theo managed. "Nik—"

Niklas hummed. He was already hard against Theo's thigh, hips rolling in fractional movements, but he lifted his head and there was nothing but sincerity in his eyes as he gazed down at him.

"We don't have to," he said quietly. "I'll be fine. I just... always want you."

Theo cupped the back of Niklas's head and drew him into a kiss, savoring the taste of his mouth. Niklas kissed like there was nothing else he'd rather be doing, not as if it was a means to an end, even as he crowded closer, slipping his tongue deeper into Theo's mouth.

They didn't speak for several minutes, intent on learning each other. Niklas liked it when Theo nipped his lower lip, and he liked it even more when Theo rolled them so Niklas was under him, pinned by Theo's weight so he could lean down and take his time, deepening the kiss until Niklas was writhing, breath ragged in his throat.

His reactions were so beautiful, Theo felt drunk on them. Everything about him was beautiful, from his seaglass blue eyes to the elegant swoop of his collarbones, his long fingers, the sinews in his thighs—Theo wanted to spend hours discovering everything about him, everything that made him tick, and especially what drew those delicious noises from his throat.

He nosed along Niklas's abs, breathing in the salt tang of sweat and dried come. Objectively, it should have been gross, and it *was*, but it was also *Nik*, a hand in Theo's hair as Theo licked a wet stripe over one nipple and then closed his mouth to suck. Niklas curled up off the bed with a strangled noise and Theo let go and laughed.

"Sensitive?"

"Do that again," Niklas panted.

Theo obeyed, teasing the nipple into a stiff nub, rolling it between his teeth as Niklas's ribs heaved. When he bit down, Niklas *shouted*, heels scrabbling against the sheets, and his hand in Theo's hair tightened to the point of pain.

Theo let go and licked it soothingly, eyes closed and concentrating on the way Niklas shivered at every pass of his tongue.

"W-will you fuck me?" Niklas managed, and Theo jerked his head up.

"*Now*?"

There was color high on Niklas's cheeks, but he met Theo's eyes, firming his jaw.

"Doesn't have to be now," he said, running a finger along Theo's shoulder and down over his collarbone. "But at some point?"

Theo sat up. "Nik—"

"This isn't a relationship," Niklas said immediately. "I know, Theo. But for now, we can count on each other for sex, at least. Can't we?"

Theo leaned forward and kissed him.

"And for friendship," he murmured.

Niklas sighed and curved a hand around the nape of Theo's neck. "You're so—you. Better than I ever imagined you would be."

"Thought about me in bed a lot, have you?" Theo teased, sitting up and nudging Niklas's legs apart so he could settle between them.

"I'm twenty-two," Niklas pointed out, eyes hungry as Theo got comfortable. "Sometimes it's *all* I think about."

Theo rubbed his nose along the soft skin of Niklas's inner thigh. "You said you were too busy to think about... this kind of thing," he mused.

Niklas laughed, chest vibrating. "I lied, Theo. You look like every wet dream I've ever had right now." He propped himself on his elbows. "You don't have to—do this, you know."

Theo didn't bother answering. He just closed his mouth over Niklas's cock and delighted in the way Niklas curled forward, stifling a noise.

"Fuck, that's—oh God, Theo, you look—" Niklas's voice was ragged, breath short. He was clearly working hard to keep from thrusting up into Theo's mouth, and Theo patted his thigh, sinking as far down as he could.

Niklas's fair skin was blotched pink, his chest heaving. He'd dropped his head back to the pillow, an arm over his eyes as if he couldn't handle the sight of Theo with Niklas's cock in his mouth.

After a few minutes of testing just how unsteady he could make Niklas's breathing, Theo looked up. "How am I measuring up to the fantasy?" he asked, and Niklas jerked his head up.

"Are you *kidding* me?"

Theo laughed and went back to it, enjoying Niklas's strangled moan as he closed his lips around the head again. He was getting hard too, drunk on the way Niklas squirmed and twitched and panted, clearly close to begging.

It didn't take long after that. Theo decided this might be his favorite version of Niklas yet, fucked out and pliant, a sweet smile curving his lips as he reached for him.

"Do you want my hand or my mouth?" he asked once Theo had crawled up the bed to lie alongside him.

Theo kissed his shoulder. "I'm fine."

"But you didn't—"

"We have a game," Theo reminded him. "And I'm not twenty-two and immortal. Another orgasm would slow me down too much."

Niklas *pouted*, lower lip pushed out and eyes big.

Theo laughed and leaned in to kiss him. "This was fun. And if you want, we can do it again. But you have to take it easy on me."

"You act like you're so old," Niklas grumbled, pushing Theo onto his back. "If I *want*? So I guess you haven't figured out yet that I want to keep you in this bed for the foreseeable future?" He bent to kiss him and Theo cupped the back of his neck, opening willingly. Finally, though, he put both hands on Niklas's shoulders and pushed until Niklas growled but let himself be moved away.

It was heady, being wanted so desperately. But Theo

hadn't gotten where he was in life by giving in to his baser desires.

So he patted Niklas on the thigh and rolled out of the bed.

"Showers. *Not* together."

Niklas sighed, and Theo took a minute to admire the sight he made, sprawled on Theo's bed gloriously unselfconscious in his nudity. His hair was rumpled, mouth pink from Theo's kisses, and Theo turned away before he did something stupid, like crawl back into the bed with him.

At the door to the bathroom, he turned back briefly. "Nik —"

Niklas propped himself on one elbow. "Hm?"

"You can't... tell anyone."

Niklas's eyebrows drew together. "Theo—"

Theo hurried on before he could finish. "I just—I'm sorry. But I can't risk it. *You* can't risk it. You can't tell anyone you even got laid, let alone the gender or *who*."

Niklas slid off the bed and stalked around it to loom over Theo, who stood his ground and looked up at him, heart thudding painfully against his ribs.

"I'm a grown fucking man," Niklas growled. They were so close Theo could feel his body heat. "I'm not going to *out* you, Theo, not when you're so fucking ashamed of who you are. But you can't tell me what to do. Hear me? If I want to tell my friends I got laid, that's *my* business. I won't name names, I'm not an asshole. But you can't *muzzle* me, either. At least no more than you already have."

Guilt lanced through Theo, sharp and sickening, but Niklas spun before he could apologize, striding from the room without looking back.

He'd fucked up. Again.

Theo showered on autopilot, mind spinning. He *hadn't* muzzled Niklas, he wanted to protest. But that wasn't strictly true, was it? He'd asked Niklas to hide himself, to deny who he was. Theo could say it was for his own good all he wanted, but the stark truth remained—Niklas was staying silent when he didn't want to, for Theo. And Theo had just twisted the knife.

He had to apologize. He had to somehow find the words to show Niklas that he was only trying to keep him safe. Niklas was angry, and rightfully so, and Theo couldn't bear that.

But when he emerged from his bedroom in his game-day suit, Niklas greeted him in the living room with a sunny smile, slipping his phone in his pocket and standing.

"You look nice," he said.

Theo worked saliva into his mouth. "Nik—"

"Don't." Niklas's tone was sharp and he stopped to take a steadying breath. "I don't want to fight," he said more gently. "You have your reasons and I'm trying to respect them. But I don't want to get into yet another argument. Okay?"

Theo swallowed misery and nodded.

Niklas smiled down at him and took a step closer. "Let's go play hockey."

Theo nodded again and reached out, bracketing Niklas's wrist and drawing it to his mouth. He kissed his knuckles as Niklas watched him. *I'm sorry*, he said silently, and Niklas's eyes softened.

"I know how we can celebrate if you get a shutout."

Theo groaned and Niklas laughed as he turned him for the door.

Twenty-Two

THREE HOURS **Later**

Coach stepped into the room, looking as neat and composed as ever in his perfect suit. The players quieted, turning to him. He rarely said much after a win, although he sometimes gave Sunny his credit card to buy rounds for everyone.

"You realize what this means?" he asked.

A few of the rookies looked baffled, glancing at each other in confusion. Sunny was smiling, arms folded across his chest, but he didn't speak. Several of the other vets were grinning too.

Theo was baffled too, although he hoped he didn't show it.

"Six points," Coach said, "We're six points out of the play-offs. All you need to do is win the next three games and we clinch."

Dead silence fell, broken by a sudden whoop from one of the rookies. The dam gave way and the rest of the players added their voices, crowding around Coach, who was grinning wider than Theo had ever seen.

Theo hadn't even *realized*, so caught up in his own head and with his own worries. He looked for Niklas and found him staring at him from across the room where he'd been talking to one of his friends. When their eyes met, Niklas broke into a huge smile and Theo couldn't help smiling back.

"We're going out!" someone shouted, and more cheering went up as Theo hid instant dismay. He didn't *want* to go out. He wanted to go home and fuck Niklas through the mattress, and judging by the amusement in Niklas's eyes, he knew it. Theo managed to summon a smile as Sunny threw an arm around his shoulders.

"We gonna celebrate our brick wall!" he yelled, and Theo winced at the din but managed to keep the smile in place.

"One drink," he said, mostly to keep up appearances. This got him roundly booed, of course, and Sunny tightened his grip.

"Nope," he said firmly. "We're gonna show the youngsters how it's done. Get your clothes on, what's taking so long?"

Theo was bullied into getting dressed and dragged out the door, Niklas somewhere in the throng behind him. Theo resolutely didn't look for him.

At the bar, Theo ended up pinned between Sunny and Niklas, who'd somehow maneuvered his way to his side. Elbows might have been thrown, Theo wasn't sure. Either way, he welcomed Niklas's solid warmth against him as the first round of beers arrived.

Sunny grimaced as he tossed his back, and Theo laughed.

"Snob," he said, poking him in the ribs. He glanced at Niklas, watching them curiously. "Sunny brews his own beer."

Niklas's eyebrows went up.

"He brings us some sometimes," Foz put in from across the table. "My favorite's the mango beer. When are you gonna make that again, Sunny?"

"When you score," Sunny shot back.

"Guess we're never having that one again," Josh said under his breath, and Foz whirled.

"Who said that? Fucking—I'll score on *you*, asshole!" He got Josh in a headlock and they grappled as everyone lifted their beers out of the danger zone.

Theo sipped his.

"You think we can do it?" Niklas asked, leaning in and keeping his voice low. His hair was damp, falling in his eyes, and Theo's fingers itched with the desire to brush it away.

"Yeah," he said. "I—yeah, I think we can."

Niklas grinned at him. "You ready to admit we're good this year?"

"No," Theo retorted. "But maybe we're not as awful as we have been in the past."

Niklas's eyes were very bright in the dim bar. "Playoffs, Theo."

"We're not there yet. Don't get cocky."

"I'm not, it's just—*playoffs*. Maybe—"

Theo got a hand over Niklas's mouth just in time. "Whatever you were about to say, swallow it. Better yet, bury it. Don't even *think* it."

"But—"

"He's right," Sunny said, leaning in, and Theo jerked his hand away.

"You're superstitious too?" Niklas asked.

"That's what this sport does to you," Sunny said. "Don't tempt fate, kid."

Niklas made a show of zipping his mouth shut.

"We're not drunk yet," Sunny continued. "And this beer

may be shit but it's still beer, so—" He shoved another mug at Theo, who grimaced but accepted it. "Let's get shitfaced!"

"To Brick!" Cole yelled, and Theo groaned as the others took up the cheer, mugs held high.

Under the table, Niklas tangled their fingers together and squeezed once before letting go and lifting his drink.

Theo laughed helplessly and held up his mug too.

Twenty-Three

NIKLAS WOKE before Theo and managed to slide from the bed without disturbing him. He stood for a minute, just watching him. Theo's lashes were dark against his pale skin, beautiful mouth soft and unguarded in sleep. The hair he kept under control almost ruthlessly when he was awake fell over his forehead in rumpled waves, making him look ten years younger.

He was still tired, Niklas could tell. There were dark circles under his eyes, and he'd barely had the energy to reciprocate the blowjob Niklas had given him the night before.

He'd played like a madman the last two weeks, posting back to back wins, another shutout, and arguing with Benson when he insisted Niklas rotate in to help save his stamina.

They'd clinched a playoff spot in four games, and Niklas had nearly kissed Theo right there on the ice when the final buzzer sounded and it was official. Thankfully, Kasha had hurled himself into Theo's arms and nearly bowled him over as the rest of the team buzzed around him, hugging each other and yelling joyfully over the racket of the crowd's applause.

They'd made it. They were in the playoffs for the first time in nearly ten years, but Niklas was worried. He saw the way Theo favored his knee when he thought no one was looking, the frequent trips down the hall to their trainer for treatments, the ice-packs he strapped to it every chance he got.

Niklas padded out of the bedroom and down the hall to the kitchen. Theo would take it badly if he figured out Niklas was trying to take care of him, but surely there was nothing wrong with making breakfast for him, maybe waking him up with it and another blowjob.

Boiled eggs were easy, and Theo had put a muesli base in the refrigerator just two days ago. Niklas started the coffee and set a pot on the stove to boil water, humming to himself.

The bread was in the toaster and he'd just put the eggs in the pot when the doorbell rang.

Niklas straightened, startled. It was barely seven in the morning, and Theo hadn't mentioned expecting company.

The bell rang again and Niklas dropped the hot pad on the counter and hurried for the door. If it was someone needing directions or a salesman, he didn't want Theo disturbed.

He yanked the door open and found himself faced with a tiny woman with sleek hair and sunglasses so dark Niklas couldn't see her eyes. She was wearing a tracksuit several sizes too big for her—the cuffs puddled in folds around her slim wrists and ankles—but the diamonds around her neck and the designer label on the bags at her feet warned Niklas not to put her in a box. There was something vaguely familiar about her but Niklas couldn't put his finger on it.

"Hi?" he said cautiously.

The woman slid the sunglasses down her perfect nose and studied him. The second Niklas saw her eyes, recognition snapped into place.

"Anjali?" he blurted.

"Interesting," Anjali said. She removed the sunglasses completely, folding them without taking her sharp eyes off

Niklas's face. "I'm guessing you're Theo's replacement, the one he's so hung up on."

"The—I'm not—" Niklas snapped his mouth shut. He was. He knew that, but he didn't like thinking about it. He didn't *want* to take Theo's job, no matter how much he wanted to be starter.

"Where is he?" Anjali asked, peering past him down the hall. "He didn't tell you I was coming, did he?"

Something squirmed in Niklas's stomach.

"Thought so." Anjali picked up her handbag and stepped inside, ducking past him before Niklas could protest.

"*Wait,*" Niklas said desperately, but it was too late.

"Anjali?" Theo still sounded exhausted, standing in the doorway of his bedroom with no shirt on and soft linen pants slung low on his hips. "Fuck, that was today, wasn't it?"

Anjali stopped to look at him, hands on hips. "You forgot."

A timer in the kitchen went off and Niklas swore and ran. The eggs safely off the burner, he tiptoed back to the door to see if he could overhear the conversation.

"—Really sorry," Theo was saying softly. "I didn't mean to, I just—we made the playoffs, did you hear?"

"Of course I heard," Anjali snapped. "And you're not taking care of yourself, are you?"

"I'm trying," Theo protested. "The team needs me in top form."

"Which is why you look like you haven't slept in a week. Niklas!"

Niklas jumped and emerged sheepishly from the kitchen. From the sardonic tilt of Anjali's eyebrow, she'd known he was there the whole time.

"Is he skipping meals?" she demanded.

"Don't answer her," Theo said before Niklas could speak. "She's going to try to terrify you into doing what she wants, which will mostly consist of her ordering you around and telling you your opinions before you have a chance to form them on your own."

Anjali sniffed. "As if you can be trusted to think independently."

Theo rolled his eyes and reached for her, pulling her into a hard hug. Niklas watched as Anjali went on tiptoe to wrap her arms around his neck and Theo closed his eyes, tucking his face into her shoulder. Jealousy spiked in his gut, just like it had when Felix had hugged Theo, but this time Niklas pushed it down hard, stomped on it, and was able to summon a smile when they finally separated and turned to face him.

"Breakfast is almost ready," he said. "Are you hungry?"

Theo followed him into the hall when Niklas excused himself to change his clothes before they ate. Niklas didn't stop, heading for his own bedroom to dig out one of his favorite sweaters. It was the color of the winter sky outside his window in Sweden, a gray so pale it was almost white, like the clouds right before the snow fell, only a few shades lighter than Theo's eyes.

Theo was standing in the doorway, his arms wrapped around his midsection. He'd clearly dragged on the first shirt he'd found—one of his, Niklas realized. It was comically large on him, hanging in loose folds and exposing one collarbone. There was a faint bruise on it, a memento Niklas had dared give him the week before because it looked just like the other bruises Theo was currently wearing from the battle for their position in the standings.

"I meant to tell you," Theo said, his voice low. His eyes pleaded with Niklas not to be angry. "She told me weeks ago and I just—it slipped my mind. I'm sorry."

"Does she know?" Niklas asked, barely loud enough to be heard, and Theo shook his head.

"No one knows." Theo didn't meet his eyes.

Niklas nodded. "Alright." He took a step sideways to get to the door but Theo moved with him.

"Nik—"

"She's waiting," Niklas said.

Theo searched his face, mouth working, but finally he nodded jerkily and backed away.

Anjali was in the dining room, looking through a magazine about woodworking Theo had been reading the night before. She glanced up when Niklas entered, Theo close behind.

"Love that sweater," she said. "Where did you get it?"

"I made it," Niklas said evenly.

Anjali lifted an eyebrow. "Is it your design, too?"

"My mother's," Niklas said. "Not much time to design patterns these days."

Theo was staring at him.

"What?" Niklas said, suddenly defensive.

"You made that?" Theo asked. He looked stunned.

Niklas lifted a shoulder. "It's not a big deal."

"Actually, it's pretty impressive," Anjali interjected. "Some of those cables look really intricate, and you seamed the sleeves but made it look like part of the cabling. That's tricky. What kind of yarn did you use?"

"It's a wool and alpaca blend. How do you know so much about knitting? I thought you made suits."

Anjali leaned back in her chair. "I make anything I feel like making."

"Coffee?" Theo asked. "Looks like Nik got a pot started already."

"The toast is cold but there are boiled eggs," Niklas said. "I can—"

Theo put out a hand to stop him. "I've got it. Get some coffee and then sit."

Niklas obeyed, acutely aware of Theo beside him as he poured coffee into a mug and Theo peeled eggs in quick, deft movements. Niklas added sugar, then stepped around him just as Theo opened the refrigerator door so Niklas could take the creamer out.

Coffee prepared, Niklas sank into the chair across from Anjali, who was watching them without speaking.

"How long are you here, Anj?" Theo asked.

"I planned on a week, but that was before playoffs. I imagine you won't want me around too long now. Who are you facing in the first round?"

"Too early to tell." Theo pushed the sleeves of his too-big shirt up. "Still a few games to play to determine that."

"And will you be in net for all of them?"

"Most." Theo sounded calm but Niklas could hear the underlying tension, read it in the set of his shoulders as he flicked bits of eggshell into the bowl. "They may decide to rotate Niklas in occasionally to let me rest, but it's not likely."

"So, Niklas," Anjali said, switching her focus to him. "Tell me about yourself."

Theo's shoulders tightened more but he said nothing.

"Not exciting," Niklas said. "I grew up in Sweden watching Theo, always wanted to go pro. And here I am."

"Here you are," Anjali mused. Her chin was in her hand. Niklas had the feeling she was missing very little, from the state of his hair—that Theo had gotten his hands in during that blowjob—to the matching love bite on his collarbone from Theo, right down to the thick socks Theo had given him before they fell asleep because he knew Niklas's feet always got cold in the night. "Any family over here?" Anjali asked.

Niklas shook his head. "Father, mother back home." Her

scrutiny was unsettling. He tried not to show that it bothered him, sipping his coffee and not looking at Theo. He shook his head when Theo tried to give him some toast and boiled eggs, though.

"I'll let you catch up," he said in low Swedish, and nodded at Anjali. "Nice to meet you," he said in English, and stood.

He could hear Theo saying something to Anjali as he left, but he didn't look back. The door to his room was ajar, the afghan he was making for his mother on the end of the bed. Guilt prickled his skin. He hadn't touched it in a month—he hadn't even been in his room for more than a few minutes at a time in at least that long.

His phone was on Theo's bedside table, and there was no way he could sneak down the hall to get it without being heard.

Sighing, he settled himself cross-legged on the bed and pulled the afghan into his lap. Might as well get a few rows done while he waited.

He loved knitting. Something about the repetitive movement of the needles lulled his racing thoughts and calmed him when he was stressed. He loved watching the stitches taking shape under his hands, the way the cables twined and twisted around each other.

He lost himself in the swoop and dip of the needles, the wrap of the yarn, and nearly jumped out of his skin when Theo cleared his throat. He was leaning against the doorframe, watching, and Niklas put the needles down, faintly embarrassed.

"Why didn't you tell me you could knit?" Theo asked.

"Where's Anjali?" Niklas said instead.

"She doesn't know how to stop working," Theo said. He came into the bedroom. "She has a meeting with a young designer she says she's had her eye on for a while. She never would have come for a visit if it hadn't coincided with something else she had planned." He paused and winced, possibly realizing how that sounded. "She cares about me. I don't mean to suggest—"

"You don't have to explain yourself."

Theo took another step closer, then another, until he was right in front of Niklas. There was a pensive twist to his mouth as he reached down and touched the hem of the blanket.

"Why didn't you tell me you could knit?"

Niklas rubbed the back of his neck. "It's not—I didn't want to be teased, I guess."

"You think I would—"

"No," Niklas said hurriedly. "But... the others. They might. At least the Americans would."

Theo made a soft, scoffing noise. His eyes were on Niklas's, warm and searching.

"She doesn't know, does she?" Niklas asked.

Theo's mouth drooped and he shook his head. "About—me, yes. Of course she knows. But—us? I haven't—"

"And you don't want to."

"It's not that I don't want to," Theo said, his voice low. There was pain in his eyes. "I *do* want to. I want to tell everyone. But—"

"It's too important," Niklas finished. His heart ached but he just nodded. "I'll keep your secret, don't worry."

Theo cupped his face in both warm hands and bent to kiss him. His lips were soft, and he tasted like black coffee and lingonberry jam. Niklas closed his eyes and let Theo push him onto his back.

The fairy lights turned Theo's fair hair a glowing gold as he straddled Niklas and gazed down at him.

Niklas reached for him and Theo went willingly.

Just a few weeks, Niklas told himself as Theo kissed his way down his throat. He could do this.

Twenty-Four

THEO HAD NEVER SEEN SO many people in his arena. It was game five against the Wildfire and if they won, they advanced to the second round of playoffs, the battle for the division title. Elsewhere, the Seabirds were waging war against the Direwolves, and on the east coast, the Miami Spirit had swept the Racers and were waiting to find out if they would face the Atlanta Comets or the Toronto Wolverines.

The Birds wouldn't make it past the first round this year, Theo knew. Their offense was good, but their defensive core needed work and serious restructuring to close the holes. Deep down, he was quietly relieved he wouldn't have to go up against Felix. It made it a little easier to tighten the straps on his pads and face what was coming.

Niklas sat beside him, already dressed, a snapback backwards over his silky hair. There was a little bubble of silence around them even as the rest of the room shouted insults and bravado at each other, occasionally followed up by a ball of sock tape.

"How are you feeling?" Niklas asked quietly.

Theo checked his pads for the third time and glanced at

him. "I'm fine."

"Are you nervous?"

Theo almost laughed at that. "Of course I am. It'll go away when I'm between the posts, don't worry."

"There's so much pressure—"

Theo touched his hand and Niklas snapped his mouth shut.

"You can't think of it like that. It'll crush you if you let it."

"How do you *not*—"

"You approach it like every other game," Theo said. He squeezed Niklas's hand briefly and let go. "It's just a game. A game we love, that we play for the sheer joy of it. I don't think about what happens if we lose. I'm going out there to play my beautiful game, and win, because I know I can."

Niklas swallowed hard and nodded. "Do you think Coach will put me in, next round?"

"Only if something happens to me," Theo said. He stood and swung his arms forward, then back, testing the fit of the chest protector. He smiled down at Niklas, still watching him with a tiny furrow of worry carved into his forehead. "Nothing's going to happen to me, Nik. Sorry to disappoint you, but you probably won't play a single game."

"If it means we—" Niklas stopped before he said the word. "I *want* you to play. This is your team, your series."

Theo wished desperately he could kiss him, pull him down and sip from Niklas's sweet, willing mouth until the fear deep in his blue eyes faded. Maybe some of that want showed on his face, because a faint blush rose on Niklas's cheeks and he ducked his head, clearing his throat.

"I'm taking Anjali to the airport after the game," Theo said. "Do you want to come?"

Niklas shook his head. "I'll say goodbye to her before. You should have some time alone."

"Alright," Theo said softly. "Thank you."

Niklas smiled up at him. "Let's play some hockey."

Theo got another shutout that night, playing like a man possessed. His nerves felt electrified, blood singing in his veins. He stonewalled the Wildfire's increasingly desperate attempts to get even one past him with almost insulting ease, turning aside shot after shot. The fans cheered every time, holding up posters with his name and pictures of brick walls on them and pounding on the glass.

The team mobbed him when the buzzer went off, crowding close to slap him on the back and press their helmets to his and shout their congratulations over the frenzied crowd. Niklas fought his way through the players and grabbed him, and Theo laughed as he was dragged into a hug.

"I told you!" he half-shouted against Niklas's ear, and Niklas just shook his head and tightened his grip.

"Great job, Theo," Benson said in the locker room, and waited for the players' cheers to subside before continuing. "Can you do it again?"

Theo smiled at him, flush with victory. "I'll do it in four next time."

They swept the Calgary Riders, riding high on their previous success and never allowing the other team a chance to get a foothold.

Theo played all four games, grabbing sleep every chance he got and eating the food Niklas made for him with minimal protest. Every fiber of his body was focused on staying the course, no room for anything else, but Niklas just rubbed ointment into Theo's cramped, exhausted muscles, working him over with those long, clever fingers after each game until Theo fell asleep, Niklas a comforting weight on his hips. Even his knee didn't hurt too much. Or it did, Theo could admit that to himself, but it wasn't enough to stop him.

They faced the Miami Spirit in three days. Theo had watched so much game tape he thought he could predict plays with his eyes closed. The Spirit was a big team, faster than they should be for their size, and not afraid to get their hands dirty. They were hungry, too—they'd pulled themselves from obscurity and made the playoffs three times in a row, but they'd never gotten this far before.

But the Sentinels were hungrier. Theo knew it, could feel it in the air when he entered the locker room. It went bone-deep, the determination to win, to finally prove the entire hockey world wrong and show they had what it took.

Niklas's friends had been called up and were making the fourth line a force to be reckoned with. Theo's favorite was the big, dopey one, Joel. He was still a little afraid of Theo, but he never shrank from defending him, sacrificing himself to stop pucks before they could reach Theo over and over again without hesitating.

They dragged Niklas out with them when they won the Conference Final over his loud protests that he needed to take care of Theo, and returned him a loose, alcohol-soaked giggling heap, dumping him into Theo's arms at three A.M.

As exhausted as he was, Theo had enjoyed the chance to take care of him for once, guiding him through a shower and getting him clean while Niklas fell asleep on his feet and then gently bundling him into clean clothes. Niklas pulled him down on the bed and wrapped himself around him, tucking his nose against the nape of Theo's neck, and they'd fallen asleep like that. Theo dreamed about the Spirit, facing them over and over in his sleep until the alarm clock jarred them both awake.

Twenty-Five

THEY HAD a few days off before they had to face the Spirit. Theo and Niklas spent them at home. They watched video reels on Theo's flatscreen television, Niklas curled against Theo's side with his knitting in his hands and his feet tucked beneath him. It always baffled and delighted Theo, the way Niklas could pull himself into such a compact ball despite his height.

Niklas was knitting, watching the screen as his needles clicked, and Theo eventually paused the reel. The first time Niklas had brought out his knitting after Anjali left, he'd stared at the stitches the whole time, shoulders tight like he was braced for Theo to tease him, but Theo had pretended he didn't even see the needles as he cued up more game footage.

"How do you do that without looking?" he asked when Niklas glanced at him inquiringly.

Niklas shrugged. "I can feel the stitches, I guess?"

"Feel them how?"

Niklas took Theo's hand and guided it to the needle. "This is a knit stitch. See how this loop's... leg, I guess you could call it—see how it's on the left side of the needle in front?"

Theo looked where Niklas was pointing. "It all looks the same."

"Not at all!" Niklas said. He sat up and Theo let his arm drop, but Niklas was just trying to get into better position to make his point. "Look." He pointed again. "See how it sort of looks like a little vee there?"

Theo peered at the stitches. "Oh—yeah, okay, I see it." The knit stitches formed a ladder of vees that marched in orderly rows up the fabric. He pointed to the way the pattern changed next to it. "But these are bumps. What are they called?"

"Purl stitches. It's just the back side of a knit stitch. It makes the little bump on one side and the vee on the other side."

Theo nodded. "What about these?" He pointed at what looked like ropes or chains, twining up the fabric. "They're—twisted?"

"Cables," Niklas said, relaxing against him. "All the stitches are on my needle, right? And I work them in order as I come to them. But if I work one or two out of order—before or after I *should* have worked it, then you get cables."

Theo wrapped his arm around Niklas's shoulders again and pulled him closer. Niklas made a soft, satisfied noise.

"This isn't what you were working on when Anjali was here," Theo observed after a few minutes of silence.

Niklas hummed. "Ran out of yarn and had to order more. It's coming from Sweden."

"So what's this then?" Theo fingered the hem of the fabric pooled in Niklas's lap. It was a soft pearl gray that made Theo think of mist on the plains in the morning before the sun rose to burn it away. The yarn was so soft it felt like clouds against Theo's skin.

"A sweater," Niklas said. He turned his head and rubbed one cheek on Theo's shoulder.

"And you just... know how to do this, no pattern, no instructions?"

Niklas pressed a kiss to Theo's throat. "It's not hard." His lips tickled. "It's just math. I used to knit before games, back in Sweden." He planted another kiss on Theo's neck, lower down.

"Why haven't you, ah—done it here?" Theo asked. Niklas had dropped his hands to his lap and seemed content to lean against Theo's side and explore his throat with his lips.

The question made Niklas hunch his shoulders and press his face against Theo's shirt. "I dunno," he mumbled.

Theo stroked his silky hair, thinking about it. "Brand new to the team and a rookie on top of that," he mused. Niklas's shoulders tightened but he said nothing. "Probably didn't want to get laughed at, did you?"

"It's not... manly," Niklas said, so low Theo had to strain to hear him. "I mean, it's—*I* don't care, men used to knit as much or even more than women, but the team—"

"You were trying to find a place," Theo said, sliding his hand into Niklas's hair. Niklas shivered but didn't move. "Wanted to fit in."

Niklas nodded silently.

"You have to be yourself," Theo murmured. He tightened his grip and tilted Niklas's head back until their eyes met. Niklas's were wide, only a thin ring of blue visible. His throat bobbed as he swallowed. "You're perfect," Theo whispered, cupping Niklas's jaw with his free hand. "You shouldn't have to hide any part of what makes you who you are."

Niklas opened his mouth to speak but Theo kissed him before he could, tongues tangling together hot and wanting until Niklas groaned and tore away.

"Wait, just—" His lips were red, hair mussed, and Theo

wanted to mark him all over, lay claim to every inch of his beautiful body until there was no question who he belonged to. Niklas was fumbling with the needles and yarn, swearing under his breath as he lifted it out of his lap and dropped the entire jumble of yarn, sweater, and needles in an unceremonious heap on the coffee table. "If I dropped any stitches, I'm blaming you," he said as he went to his knees and swung a leg over Theo's lap.

Theo grinned up at him, smoothing his palms over Niklas's heavily muscled thighs. "I have no idea what that means," he said.

Niklas rolled his eyes and looped his arms around Theo's neck. "It means," he said, and bent to kiss him. "That you're unfairly sexy, and—mm—" He deepened the kiss, arms tightening, and then tried to lift his head. "You should—" Theo tugged him back down and Niklas laughed, rolling his hips.

The friction made Theo shudder and he pushed into it wordlessly, unwilling to break the kiss but desperate for more.

"Theo," Niklas mumbled against his mouth.

"Hmm?" Theo managed. He slipped a hand between them and cupped Niklas's length, hard and leaking in his shorts.

"I want—"

Theo thumbed the head of his cock and Niklas swore and caught at his hand. Theo let his head fall languidly against the couch and smiled up at him. Arousal curled thick and sweet through his blood. His limbs were heavy, his movements slow, but his head was clear.

"What do you want, *älskling*?" he whispered, and ran a thumbnail over Niklas's trapped shaft.

Niklas made a desperate noise and surged forward to kiss him again. His mouth was hot, feverish, and he pulled at Theo's shirt with unsteady hands until Theo sat up enough to let him pull it up and off.

"You," Niklas husked as Theo lay back again. He was gazing down at him with something like wonder in his eyes. "I want—Theo... I want to make love to you. Please."

Theo slipped a hand under Niklas's waistband. He wasn't wearing underwear, and their eyes met, amusement in Niklas's matching the delight surging in Theo's chest as he dipped lower, until he could run a single finger down Niklas's stiff length.

"Are you asking to fuck me?" Theo asked, almost conversationally, but to his surprise, Niklas shook his head hard.

"*No.* I want—" Need was stark in his blue eyes, hunger and desire and vulnerability all mixed together but stark on his beautiful face. He took a deep breath and squared his shoulders. It was difficult to look dignified with your cock in someone else's hand, but he almost pulled it off as he gazed down at Theo, still waiting. "I need you inside me," Niklas whispered.

"You want me to bend you over the couch?" Theo teased, and they shared a smile at the memory, but Niklas shook his head.

"Just like this," he said softly.

It was Theo's turn to swallow hard at the mental image of Niklas riding him, sinking onto his cock as his head fell back and he fought to keep the noises in.

"Yeah," he managed after a minute, voice hoarse. "Yeah, okay."

Niklas pressed a kiss to his mouth, there and gone before Theo could respond. "Be right back," he whispered, and pushed himself to his feet.

Alone in the living room, Theo took the time to pull his pants off. After a minute of deliberation, he put them on the couch and sat on them, getting comfortable just as Niklas reappeared. He'd gotten naked too, miles and miles of glorious brown skin on unselfconscious display as he approached, eyes fixed on Theo, who suddenly felt too small, too pale, not... enough. He crossed his arms over the faint softness of the belly he couldn't get rid of no matter how much he worked out.

"Don't," Niklas said. He took Theo's wrist and drew his hand up to press a kiss to the palm. "Don't hide from me," he whispered. His eyes were hot as he stared at Theo. "You're so beautiful. You're—*fuck*, Theo, *you're* perfect."

Overcome, Theo pulled on Niklas's hand. "Come here."

Niklas obeyed, settling his weight on Theo's thighs and tossing a condom onto his chest. The lid of the lube clicked as he opened it and poured some over his fingers.

Theo felt for the condom and tore clumsily at it, unable to tear his eyes from Niklas's hands. He was reaching behind himself, brow furrowed in concentration and lip caught between his teeth.

"Let me help," Theo asked, and Niklas groaned but fumbled for the lube. Theo slicked up his left hand, holding his breath as he slid it between them. He grazed Niklas's balls, tight and full against his body, and over his perineum. Niklas wasn't moving, staring down at his face as Theo nudged up against the finger sunk to the first knuckle inside him.

Theo didn't immediately push inside. Instead, he traced the skin around Niklas's hole, urgency pounding in his blood but forcing himself to move slowly. He teased at the rim, making Niklas swear in a choked voice, then retreated, pressing a knuckle to his perineum and rubbing tortuously slow, until Niklas was shaking, one hand gripping the back of the couch next to Theo's head.

"Theo," he gasped, when Theo took hold of the hand he still had inside him and tugged gently. "Theo, *please—*"

"I've got you," Theo said soothingly. "Trust me, *älskling*." He guided Niklas's other hand to the back of the couch before he added more lube and went back to work.

Niklas was holding on so tight the wooden frame of the couch creaked under his desperate grip, but Theo wasn't worried. His furniture was built to withstand anything, even professional athletes fucking on it.

He circled Niklas's rim with a single finger, light and teasing, until Niklas was groaning with frustration, chasing his touch. Theo didn't give it to him until Niklas stopped trying and sagged above him with a helpless noise.

Then—

"Breathe," Theo advised, and pushed a slick finger inside to the second knuckle in one quick motion.

Niklas went rigid, eyes slamming shut.

Theo waited, throttling back the desperate ache to be sheathed inside him already and letting Niklas's body adjust to the intrusion. Only when Niklas drew an unsteady breath and nodded did Theo move. He kissed the wrist nearest his head, eyes on Niklas's face as he slid deeper, until the knuckles of his folded fingers were nudging the rim.

Niklas was impossibly hot and tight, muscles rippling around his finger, and Theo swallowed concern.

"Nik," he rasped.

A wrinkle formed between Niklas's eyebrows and he shook his head. "More."

Theo didn't move.

It took Niklas a minute to regain enough brain cells to open his eyes and glare down at him.

"Is this your first time doing this?" Theo asked.

"*Theo,*" Niklas said. He ground his hips, trying to draw Theo's hand deeper somehow.

"Answer me," Theo said, pulling his finger out instead.

"No, *no,*" Niklas almost sobbed, grabbing for his wrist. "Please, Theo, *please*—"

"Not until you tell me," Theo said.

Niklas hiccuped, fingers still bracketing Theo's wrist. "I'm n-not a virgin."

"I know, *sötnos*," Theo said gently. He rubbed Niklas's thigh reassuringly. "But have you ever been fucked?"

Niklas set his jaw, that familiar mulish stubbornness sliding into place. "If I say no, you won't do it," he said. "I *want* this, Theo, I want you to *be* my first. I know how it works. I've—I had a vibrator, back home." He gave him a defiant look. "I know what I'm asking for."

Theo closed his eyes against the tidal wave of emotions threatening to drown him. Awe mingled with fear—what if he couldn't do it? What if Niklas hated it and it was Theo's fault? Guilt snaked through his gut, too, slick and oily. It shouldn't *be* him here. Niklas should be having this moment with someone from the same century as him, who understood his jokes and could speak the same language. Not Swedish, but the incomprehensible back and forth references and jokes Theo didn't have the first clue how to decipher.

"You're thinking too much," Niklas said softly. He cupped Theo's face and Theo looked up at him. Niklas's eyes were warm, honesty shining from them. "I want this to be you. Isn't it better this way? To do it with someone I trust, who I *know* will take care of me?"

Theo sighed, and a smile flickered over Niklas's lips.

"Fine," Theo said, and the smile burst into a grin. "But we're doing this in bed."

Niklas pulled a face but swung his leg off Theo's lap and stood in one fluid motion. He held out a hand and Theo accepted it, allowing him to pull him to his feet.

Niklas wrapped his arms around Theo's shoulders and pulled him in close, tucking him under his chin, and they stood quietly for a minute. Theo could hear Niklas's heart thumping steadily against his ear, and he closed his eyes again. They fit so perfectly.

He pushed the thought away and slid his hand down Niklas's arm to tangle their fingers together. Then he led him down the hall to the bedroom.

Twenty-Six

NIKLAS WENT where Theo put him, heart banging crazily against his ribs as he settled himself on his back and Theo pushed a pillow under his hips. Theo's eyes were dark, a tiny furrow on his brow, but he smiled when Niklas caught his gaze, warm and tender.

"Try to relax."

Impossible. Not when the man he loved was settling between his knees and studying him like a puzzle to be solved, mapping out exactly how to touch him with that laser focus he brought to everything he did.

Still, he stared at the ceiling and did his best to obey, breathing deeply through his nose and exhaling through his mouth and running drills in his mind. *Long T-pushes. Keep your angles crisp. Rotate to face the puck. Come out to cut down the distance a shooter has.*

Theo smoothed a hand over Niklas's thigh, and Niklas wondered distantly if he'd ever get used to it, the familiarity of Theo's touch, the way it made his heart leap and twist. He hoped it wouldn't. Theo had popped the cap of the lube and was pouring some over his fingers.

Niklas was going to tell him how he felt. Soon, but not yet. Theo had enough to deal with—Niklas wasn't going to saddle him with this when he needed to focus on playing his best hockey. But soon.

A finger probed his hole and he caught his breath, hitching his leg higher on the mattress to give Theo better access.

"So good," Theo whispered, and pressed inside.

It wasn't much—his vibrator at home had been thicker—but the knowledge that it was *Theo* made Niklas bite back a noise. Theo took hold of his shaft with his free hand and added another finger on the down-stroke.

Niklas's eyes rolled back and he grabbed blindly at the blankets, skin hot and too tight for his body. Theo's grip was firm and steady—by now he knew exactly how Niklas liked it, and he was giving it to him, timing his strokes with the thrust of his fingers. The waves built, ebbing and flowing as they pushed him to the peak, and Niklas was helpless to do anything but take it.

Theo added a third finger and a hot tear trickled from Niklas's eye. Theo paused but Niklas shook his head fiercely, and Theo kissed his knee before resuming.

Niklas loved him so much he thought he'd burst from it. It wasn't the hero-worship from before they'd met, two-dimensional and flimsy, built on what Niklas had thought he'd known of him. No, this was real, a river deeper than he was tall, filled with everything he knew now.

He loved the way it took Theo a while to wake up in the morning, the way he forced himself to get up early on his days off because he knew it was good to keep to a routine, but deep down he secretly hated it and wanted to sleep all day.

He loved how Theo tried to hide his emotions, pressed his mouth into a thin line to fight the smile that burst free anyway, more and more lately. He loved the dimple that flashed in his cheek when he laughed. Theo should laugh more. Maybe then others would see him the way Niklas saw him, would *love* him the way Niklas did, the way Theo deserved.

Theo pulled his hand free and Niklas whimpered, reaching for him. Theo caught his wrist, grip firm and reassuring. He was just getting into position, Niklas realized, and he swallowed hard as foil crinkled and Theo rolled the condom on.

"You have to relax," he said, petting Niklas's thigh. "Otherwise it's gonna hurt."

"I can take it."

Theo smiled but there was a worried line between his eyebrows. "I don't *want* to hurt you. I want this to be good for you."

"It will be. It *is*." Niklas searched for words that refused to come as Theo studied his face. "Please, Theo, I need—" *You. All of you, everything that you are, the way you take care of me, the way you love me even though you think you don't.* He kept that locked behind his teeth and nudged Theo with a foot. "I need to come."

That won him the smile he'd been hoping for, dimple flashing, and even better, a kiss. Theo braced himself over Niklas's body and pressed their mouths together. There was no urgency to it, and Niklas tried to sink into the feeling, let it carry him away, but he hadn't actually been lying—he *did* need to come. Or at least he wanted to, desperately.

So he snaked a hand between them. Theo twitched when Niklas took hold of him, gasping against his mouth.

"I want you inside me," Niklas whispered.

Theo shuddered all over, pressed one more hot, desperate kiss to Niklas's lips, and sat up. "Relax," he repeated, and then there was a blunt pressure against Niklas's hole, growing steadily and feeling impossibly larger with every second. Niklas tensed, gulped air, and forced himself to go limp. Theo swore under his breath, pushed harder, and the head of his cock slipped past the tight ring of muscle. Theo immediately froze, bracing himself on one shaking arm.

It hurt. It hurt more than Niklas had expected, an overwhelming tsunami of sensations roaring through him as his body fought the unfamiliar intrusion. He hadn't lied about the vibrator, but it hadn't measured up to Theo's actual dick.

"It's too much," Theo said, but Niklas grabbed at him desperately, fingernails digging into his arms before he could pull out.

"If you—*kill* you if—" he rasped, and Theo's eyes widened.

He pressed his lips together but he couldn't hide the affection in his eyes as he slid another inch deeper. It might have been an inch. Might have been six inches. Niklas couldn't accurately gauge anything. He arched his back, squirming in a desperate attempt to find a more comfortable position. It was supposed to start feeling better, right? No one would ever do this if it hurt like this the whole time.

Theo had stopped again, waiting for Niklas's breathing to slow. Niklas loved him for it, distantly, and wanted to punch him. *Get on with it. Make it feel good. Help me.*

Then there was a hand on his cock, and Niklas jolted up into it with a helpless noise. The movement made Theo slide deeper, and Niklas opened his mouth to tell him to stop, he couldn't do it, he wasn't strong enough, but before he could, Theo shifted his angle and *thrust*.

Kaleidoscopes splintered behind Niklas's eyes and he bucked helplessly, unable to process anything but the pleasure suddenly pouring through his body.

"Fuck, *fuck*," he choked as Theo pulled out in one slow, steady movement. "What—Theo, what *was*—"

Instead of answering, Theo drove deep again. Niklas's eyes

rolled back as Theo found the spot he'd hit before, hooking Niklas's legs over his shoulders and pulling his hips off the bed until Niklas was bent nearly in half so Theo could pound into him, every thrust lighting him up from the inside until he thought he'd crack into pieces and flood the room with the brilliance building at his core.

Niklas flung an arm over his eyes so he didn't have to look at Theo's beautiful face, so intent and determined, the same focus he carried like an immovable force field when he was in net homed in on Niklas alone, like nothing else existed. It was heady and terrifying and Niklas was going to come untouched and it was going to be over and he couldn't bear it—

"Not yet," he begged, his voice thick and unrecognizable to his own ears. "*Please*, I can't—Theo, please—"

Somehow, Theo understood. He didn't stop the rolling rhythm of his hips, but he reached down and caught a fold of the thin skin over Niklas's hip, twisting hard.

The pain was sharp and shocking, scattering the building orgasm, and Niklas sobbed, grateful and overwhelmed and undone in every way.

"You're so good," Theo managed. His voice sounded unsteady, and Niklas didn't dare look at him, afraid of the truth he'd see there. Afraid of what Theo would see in *his* face. But Theo slowed, hips stilling for the first time. "Nik? Is it—are you okay?" There was genuine concern in his voice.

Somehow, Niklas managed to string enough brain cells together to nod, jerky and uncoordinated. He kept his eyes shut, but he groped for Theo's arm and followed the smooth line of it up to his shoulder, over his trap and the vein standing out in his neck to curve a hand over Theo's nape and pull.

Theo groaned at the undeniable message and ground deep briefly. "You'll be the death of me," he whispered.

Niklas resented the fact that Theo could still form sentences. He pulled again, insistent. Theo bent to kiss him, a clash and tangle of lips and tongue, and then sat up, shifting his position and folding Niklas forward again. His fingers were iron bars curving around his hips, and Niklas hoped dimly he never got free.

Theo's next thrust stole the breath from his lungs, and he would have sobbed with gratitude but he was too busy trying not to crack apart at the seams as Theo pounded into him, driving him up the cliff to the precipice one relentless, brutal pump of his hips at a time.

He wrapped a hand around Niklas's shaft and jerked him off, rough and brutal and unhesitating and exactly what he needed. Theo was everything Niklas could feel, smell, taste, invading his senses, and still he fucked him, his rhythm never faltering.

Niklas was flying so high, dizzying swoops and spirals, that he was only dimly aware as the pressure in his chest snapped. His back arched, muscles going taut as sweetness flooded his senses and wet heat splashed over his belly.

Theo talked him through it, still sheathed deep inside him, his voice rumbling through Niklas's core as he crooned sweet nonsense until Niklas collapsed, heaving desperately for air. His throat felt shredded, like he'd been screaming. Had he?

It took a few minutes for him to settle back into his body and regain awareness of his surroundings. When he finally opened his eyes, it was to Theo above him, holding very still.

"Did you—"

Theo shook his head, careful not to move the rest of his body.

Niklas's limbs were languid with the pleasure still curling like smoke through his nerves, but he reached between them, watching the way Theo's eyes slammed shut when he traced a curious finger over where they were joined. His arms trembled but he didn't move.

"Do you want to?" Niklas whispered.

Theo opened his eyes and gave him an incredulous look.

Niklas arched his back, making Theo's breath hitch. "Then do it."

"It's t-too much," Theo managed. "For you. I can just—" He held up a hand to illustrate and Niklas frowned.

"Do it," he repeated. "Fuck me, Theo, make me *feel* it."

The groan sounded ripped from Theo's chest but he obeyed, pulling almost all the way out and then slamming deep in one fast motion.

It *was* too much, just this side of it, every single nerve ending waking up to protest the onslaught, but Niklas was a professional athlete. He knew his body and he knew how much he could take. He hooked a heel over Theo's hips and encouraged him deeper, letting the shivery overstimulation roll over and through him until he realized, dimly shocked, that he was hard again.

Theo was folded forward, face buried in Niklas's throat. His breath was hot, teeth scraping against the tendon in Niklas's shoulder as his thrusts quickened and lost their rhythm, and then he wasn't breathing at all, utterly silent as he shuddered through his orgasm.

Niklas rolled his hips, grinding against the ridges of Theo's abs. Sweat and come slicked Theo's skin, and Niklas wrapped both legs around his hips to keep him in place as he searched desperately for the tipping point.

Theo moved, a twitch of his hips that nonetheless made Niklas jerk. Encouraged, Theo did it again, his face still pressed to Niklas's throat. He licked the sweat from his skin and somehow the wet drag of his tongue was what tumbled Niklas over the edge again.

If the first time had been a snapping of tension, this was an emptying of the vessel. Theo wrung his second orgasm from him with nothing but his mouth on Niklas's throat and the roll of his hips, and Niklas held on as he shook through it, tears leaking from his closed eyes and tracking hot and wet down his face, but Niklas couldn't wipe them away. He couldn't move.

"Look at me, *sötnos*."

Niklas shook his head blindly, eyes squeezed shut.

Theo huffed an unsteady laugh. "Nik. Sweetheart. Let me see you."

There was a hand on his face, warm and reassuring. Niklas burrowed into it briefly and then opened his eyes.

Theo smiled when their gazes met, something like worry melting from his expression. "Talk to me," he coaxed. "Tell me how you're feeling."

Niklas couldn't swallow around the sandpaper lining his throat. He tried to work moisture into his mouth as Theo raised himself just enough to slip free. Niklas couldn't stop the forlorn noise at the sudden emptiness, but Theo was still there, still blanketing him from head to toe, anchoring him, smiling down at him.

Niklas met his eyes. "I love you." The words slipped out before he could stop them and he flinched. He hadn't meant to say it, would give anything to take it back, but it was too late.

Theo blinked and the smile slid off his face. He tried to put it back in place, but it sat falsely below gray eyes filling with panic. He sat up and cold rushed over Niklas, making him shiver.

"No," Theo said. "You don't, Nik." His voice was gentle, patient, and humiliation rolled through Niklas.

He sat up, muscles protesting, as Theo shuffled back to give him room. "I didn't mean it like that," he said, working to keep his tone unaffected. Whatever happened, he had to make this believable. He couldn't risk fucking Theo up before the biggest challenge of his life. "I just meant—" He waved a hand. "You know. I *do* love you, but like... in a bro way."

"A bro way," Theo repeated.

Niklas lifted his chin. "That's all this is, remember? Orgasms for both of us, nothing more. So I love you for that. That's all I meant."

Theo slid off the bed and bent to remove the condom, expression unreadable. Niklas took the opportunity to roll off the other side of the mattress and find his bearings. He was lightheaded but he took a slow breath and let it out in degrees. When he was steadier, he turned to meet Theo's eyes, the king size bed a chasm between them.

"Thanks," he said, and found a smile somewhere. "Probably better if I sleep in my room tonight so you get enough rest. Tomorrow's a big day."

"Nik—"

"Goodnight, Theo," Niklas said, and slipped out the door.

Twenty-Seven

HE DIDN'T MEAN IT. If he kept repeating that, maybe eventually he'd believe it. But the memory of the hurt on Niklas's face when Theo had contradicted him stayed with Theo as he showered and dressed, moving on autopilot as his mind replayed those moments over and over.

He loves you.

"It's just infatuation," Theo said aloud to his empty bedroom, but his voice was hollow. What did the Americans call it? Puppy love. Niklas would grow out of it. He'd imprinted on him, like a duckling or lamb, and he'd forget all about Theo soon enough.

Theo swallowed the sick, greasy feeling that rose in his throat at the thought of Niklas with someone else, laughing with them, touching them, focusing all his formidable charisma on them, and instead pulled soft pants from the dresser. He couldn't think about it right now. They had a series to win and they weren't going to do it if Theo was distracted.

Twenty-Eight

LOGICALLY, Theo knew the entire population of Miami hadn't turned out for the first game of the Stanley Cup Final against the Spirit. Their building housed a little over 23,000, but not only was every seat sold out, the fans who couldn't get in had set up an unofficial tailgate party in the parking lot that was a seething mass of icy blue and navy, Spirit colors. Smoke drifted up from grills, the scent of sausage and hamburger and hot dogs coating the inside of Theo's nose and making his stomach twist.

"They've been here all day," Niklas said as Theo took the long way around to the players' parking lot. He sounded impressed.

"Everyone's a fan when we start winning," Theo said. He put the car in park and glanced at Niklas. "Ready?"

Niklas smoothed the lapels of the powder blue suit Anjali had given him and nodded. "Do I look okay?"

Theo rolled his eyes and stepped out. "Don't fish for compliments, you know you do." He did, too. The silky fabric followed the taper of his hips and hugged his legs, making them look even longer. Theo couldn't even look at him head on, too afraid Niklas would see the hunger in his eyes.

Noise buffeted them—fans chattering and laughing from the parking lot near them, music blasting, engines revving—as they headed for the building and nerves choked Theo again. He breathed deeply but that was a mistake—the smells of beer and frying meat and grease threatened to turn his stomach inside out.

"Hey," Niklas said sharply. He yanked the door open and pulled Theo through it. The noise cut off and Niklas backed him against the wall, crowding close until he was all Theo could feel. His broad shoulders blocked the light, his sweet-spicy cologne replacing the stench of grease and fat, and Theo shouldn't be letting it happen, anyone could walk by and get the wrong idea, but he wasn't strong enough to push Niklas away.

Instead, he closed his eyes and rested his forehead against Niklas's shoulder until the frantic battering of panic in his chest began to ease.

"Someone could see," he whispered after a few minutes.

"Let them," Niklas shot back. He didn't move. "No one's stupid enough to ask. We're goalies, remember? Think about something that makes you calm. Don't let anything else in."

Niklas's heart beat steadily against Theo's cheek as he formed an image in his mind. He was sanding a chair, putting the finishing touches on it. The tension, the stress, the fear of letting down his team again, when so much was on the line—all of them were blemishes he smoothed away one by one until the grain of the wood was satin-soft under his hands. Every joist, every post, every place where the pieces of the chair fitted together was done so carefully, so precisely, that it didn't even require nails. Nothing marred the clean, swooping lines. Satisfaction swelled inside him.

He opened his eyes.

"Better?" Niklas murmured.

Theo smiled up at him, wishing he could kiss him. They hadn't talked about the night before, but Niklas had been his cheerful, sunny self when Theo had found him in the kitchen that morning before their flight, no shadows lurking in his eyes. Maybe he *had* meant what he'd said the way he claimed, but Theo was just grateful they seemed to be back on solid ground. He'd sort the rest of it out later, when everything was over.

"Better," he said.

The away locker room was chaos, but people nodded to Theo as he picked his way around equipment bags and wadded up stick tape. No one spoke to him, but neither did they fall silent as he passed or whisper behind his back. Because of Niklas, Theo knew. Niklas had helped change the team's perspective somehow, made them accept him even though Theo still didn't fully understand how or why. It didn't matter. All that mattered was winning.

Despite everything, butterflies were still threatening to burst through Theo's ribcage as he pulled on his gear one piece at a time. So much was riding on this. His hands trembled as he tried to feed a strap through the buckle, and he swore under his breath as he missed. It was hard to breathe, like an anvil on his chest squeezing the air from his lungs.

Big hands covered his, Niklas kneeling in front of him. His movements were deft and sure as he pulled each strap to the perfect tightness Theo liked—of course he'd paid attention. Theo watched him, dark head bent to his task, and a different kind of butterfly surged, filling his throat until he thought they might fly out if he opened his mouth. He was head over heels for the young man currently checking his skate laces, and if he was being honest, he had been for awhile.

How he wished this could be real, that he could have Niklas forever, in his bed and by his side, always knowing what he needed and how to help. He wanted, more than anything, for Niklas to have meant it when he'd said he loved him, to know what he was saying and truly mean it down to his bones.

But Niklas was too young to understand what a sacrifice it would be, spending a life with Theo. He deserved more. He deserved someone with his life still ahead of him, someone his own age, who could keep up with him instead of forcing Niklas to slow down.

Theo would tell him that soon, when there wasn't so much on the line. He couldn't risk it yet, obviously, but when it was over, one way or the other, he would tell him. He was retiring, whether they won the Cup or not, and moving back to Sweden so Niklas wouldn't forever have his shadow looming over him.

His fingers itched to comb through Niklas's soft hair but he kept his hands in his lap. Niklas rocked back on his heels and smiled up at him.

"All done," he said.

Somewhere along the way, the butterflies had gone back to sleep. Theo's hands were steady again, the weight gone from his chest. *Thank you*, he mouthed, and Niklas's smile grew.

They lost. It wasn't even close, a humiliating blowout that left the Sentinels stunned and reeling as the Spirit celebrated their 5-1 win on the other end of the ice.

Everyone avoided Theo's eyes as he headed down the tunnel.

In the showers, he tilted his face into the spray and closed his eyes. The worst part was it was no one's fault but his. The Spirit had hammered their defense, chipped away with clever, deft plays until Theo's head was reeling and he was scrambling, unable to find his center. The pucks had found the back of his net over and over again, one trickling in under his elbow, another sliding between his pads, a third beating him clean over his shoulder. That one stung the most, he thought—he could forgive himself for the ugly goals and the bounces no one could predict, but he should have had that slapshot, and it was the goal that put the nail in their coffin.

His fault.

No one spoke to him in the locker room. Sunny and a few others were handling media, and Theo got dressed in silence. Niklas trailed behind him and they went straight to the hotel without speaking.

They were on the same floor, but Theo had his own room, while Niklas had to bunk with Joel. Instead of going to his room, though, Niklas followed Theo to his room.

Theo let them both in without questioning it, and Niklas went to the mini-fridge in the corner and the lasagna from the restaurant they'd visited the day before.

"Want some?" he asked.

Theo shook his head and took off his shoes.

"It's not as good as yours, of course," Niklas said as he lifted the slice out of the styrofoam and set it on a plate. His dimple flashed with the smile he sent Theo. "Remember the day we met?"

"Of course I remember," Theo snapped, but Niklas didn't flinch at his sharp tone. He just put the plate in the microwave and turned to throw the container away. Theo took another step into the room. "Why aren't you upset?"

Niklas was pouring water into two glasses. He slid one toward Theo before answering. "You're upset enough for both of us, I think."

Theo clenched his fists at his sides. "I have every right to be. This is the biggest fight of our lives and I fucking blew it. I *failed* us."

Niklas took a drink of water and didn't answer.

Fury welled in Theo's throat. "You're not going to argue? Tell me it wasn't my fault?"

Niklas regarded him calmly. "Would it help?"

"Of course it wouldn't," Theo spat. He turned away, then swung back. "You still think I can do this? After *that*?"

Niklas took another swallow from his glass. "My opinion of you hasn't changed."

"Your opinion of me is wrong and it always has been," Theo threw at him. "You're blinded by hero worship and you refuse to see me for who I truly am." He wanted to leave, storm away to make his point but this was *his* room.

Niklas moved quicker than thought, pushing him against the wall and looming over him. Theo's breath caught in his chest at the prospect of a fight, the chance to bleed off some of the rage boiling in his veins, and he tipped his chin defiantly.

"Hit a nerve?" he asked.

Niklas's eyes narrowed. "You're so determined to make everyone hate you," he growled. "Are you that afraid of letting anyone in, Theo? Letting someone *see* you? Why are you so afraid?"

"Fuck you," Theo hissed, and shoved him, hard. Niklas didn't even sway. "I'm *not* afraid. And if I was, I'd have good reason to be. But I'm fucking *not*, okay?"

"What reason?" Niklas asked. His tone was still level, and somehow that made Theo even angrier. He wanted a fight, not a calm debate. He balled his fists again, struggling for words.

Niklas waited. Theo had always admired that about him, his ability to sink into calm like a stone through clear water even as chaos raged around him. Right now, though, he hated it a bit. Hated *Niklas*, with his eyes that saw too much and his unwavering belief that Theo was a good person who deserved good things.

"It's easy for you," he finally said.

Niklas's brows winged up. "What is?"

"Your—" Theo gestured. "Everything is. You smile and the world falls at your feet. People meet you and instantly fall in love with you."

Niklas's eyebrows were nearly in his hairline by now but he said nothing, waiting for Theo to finish.

"You wanted to be a goalie, so you became a goalie. You wanted to play pro, so you did. You want to come out, and the only reason you haven't is because I asked you not to yet. You're not afraid of anything, because it's easy to *be* you." Theo's voice was rising as he found his stride. "And you have *no idea* what it's like to have to hide everything about yourself to play the sport you love, to see all your dreams stripped from you, your own team hating you, *laughing* at you because you're too stupid for your own good, you don't even have the decency to do what they all want and quit. You can't retire gracefully and hang up your skates *because you don't deserve to.*"

Theo snapped his mouth shut and silence crashed in, deafening and absolute. He wanted to crawl in a hole. Curl up and vanish entirely from existence. Anything to stop Niklas from looking at him like he currently was, with a devastating mix of understanding and sympathy.

"Let me go," Theo managed. Shame prickled his skin, crawled hot and stinging up his throat.

Niklas took a step back and Theo ducked out from under his arm and into the bathroom, shutting the door hard between them.

He slid to the floor, tile cold under his feet, and let his head fall back against the door.

"You're right," Niklas said, his voice low and muffled by the barrier.

Theo blinked. "I—what?"

"You're right," Niklas repeated. "It's been easy for me.

Not as easy as you seem to think, but I know I'm lucky. My parents supported my dreams, paid for them, pushed me when I wanted to give up. I don't know what it's like to have to fight every step of the way for what you want and never get there. Everything I've wanted, I've gotten eventually."

"Even me," Theo whispered.

"Parts of you," Niklas corrected. "The parts you were willing to let me have. And I cherish them. *You*. Because all you see are your failures, but I see everything else."

Theo shook his head. "There *is* nothing else."

"God, you couldn't be more wrong," Niklas said. "Look at where you are. Look at yourself! You're still playing professional hockey at the top of your game in your thirties, in a position that's known for how brutal it is physically. You won the World Cup, you took home a silver medal at the Olympics, you're one of Sweden's most well-known athletes. You're an artist, on and off the ice. You have more customers than you know what to do with for your furniture, and your vision between the pipes is legendary."

"Maybe it was once," Theo said. He pulled his knees to his chest and hugged them, abruptly exhausted. "It hasn't been for years."

"It still is," Niklas said, and his tone left no room for debate. "Tonight wasn't your fault. You know that, deep down."

Theo shook his head, not caring that Niklas couldn't see him.

"They were the better team tonight," Niklas continued. "But they're not the better team overall. We are. And you know *that*, too. Theo. Will you open the door? I need to say something."

Theo squeezed his eyes shut. He didn't *want* to. He wanted to wallow in his shame and misery, feel sorry for himself and forget about the rest of the world. But instead, he pushed himself upright and swung the door open.

Niklas smiled at him. "Thank you. Here it is. I guarantee Coach is ripping everyone in the locker room a new one right now. Because your defense *let you down*. The forwards did too. They all forgot to communicate, because the Spirit intimidated them and got in their heads. But I only saw you make one mistake tonight—that slapshot in the second. You should have had that and you didn't. The rest of the goals were *not your fault*. And everyone in that room knows it."

Theo blinked hard.

"We have an important day tomorrow," Niklas said, voice gentler. "You need to rest, because you're gonna need it when we beat the Spirit in front of their fans." His eyes were soft, and he reached out, cupping Theo's face in one big palm for a brief moment before dropping his hand. "Goodnight, Theo."

Niklas enjoyed being right a normal amount, in his opinion. He definitely didn't gloat when they came down for breakfast in the morning and the first player approached to apologize.

It was Cam, shooting an anxious look at Niklas and then staring at his hands as he mumbled something about working on his backchecking before he scurried away.

Theo shot a glance at Niklas, who pretended not to see it, suddenly busy with the food on his plate.

Kasha was next, shoulders drooping. "Sorry, Brick," he said. "Is not your fault, yes? You stand on head, but we not hold our end."

"I—it's.... Thanks?" Theo offered. He leaned over to Niklas as Kasha left. "What. The. Hell."

"Told you," Niklas said, and didn't bother fighting the smile this time. "Incoming."

Tanaka was heading toward them, dragging Cole behind

him. "You can punch me if you want," he offered when he arrived.

"Why would I punch you?" Theo demanded.

"I wasn't in position to block that shot in the first," Tanaka said. "I didn't read the play, and I should have."

Theo stared at him. "And what about you?" he asked Cole, still lurking behind Tanaka.

Cole flinched, eyes wide. "I missed my shot," he blurted. "Net was wide open and I fucked it up."

"A single goal one way or the other wouldn't have made much difference," Theo told him. "But thank you."

Tanaka bobbed his head and skittered away, casting a quick glance over his shoulder to make sure Cole was following him.

Theo settled back into his seat with a sigh. There was still tension in his shoulders, Niklas noted, and he frowned.

"What is it?" he murmured in Swedish.

Theo flicked him a look. "I—nothing."

Niklas jostled his elbow. "Tell me."

Theo sighed. "They're still afraid of me. Did you see Cole's face?"

"Have they ever apologized to you before?"

Theo frowned, then shook his head. "I don't... think so."

Niklas raised an eyebrow. "They're not afraid. They're ashamed of letting you down."

Sunny arrived before Theo could answer. "That wasn't my idea," he announced.

"What, the public groveling?" Theo asked dryly.

Sunny shrugged. "I told them they didn't have to, that you wouldn't expect it. But they didn't listen, because they're young and they know everything, obviously." He winked at Niklas and sauntered back to his table, hands in his pockets.

Theo stared at the tablecloth, eyes distant. "Huh," he said after a minute, and began to eat.

Niklas patted his knee and pulled out his knitting. His heart bumped briefly, but he concentrated on untangling the yarn from the needles and not checking the room to see who might be looking. If Theo could be brave, so could he. The gray fiber pooled in his lap and he smoothed a hand over the cables taking shape. It was coming along nicely.

"Dude, what's that?" Joel demanded, and Niklas jerked. Joel was leaning over from the next table, perilously close to tipping his chair. Niklas glared at him.

"What it's look like?" he snapped.

Theo's knee pressed briefly against his but he didn't look up from his food.

"It looks like crochet or something," Joel was saying, oblivious. "I didn't know you could crochet, dude! How come you never did in the rookie house?"

Niklas took a slow breath. There was no judgment, no mockery, in Joel's tone, only open curiosity. "Is not crochet, is knitting. And I was too busy then. Trying to get called up, trying not to die of—" He blanked on the English word. "*Stelkramp*," he said. "Because you are pigs."

Theo snorted a laugh, hastily stifled.

"What's stell—whatever?" Joel asked.

"Tetanus," Theo offered, voice rich with delight, and Niklas's treacherous heart jolted at the sound. "Let me guess—you only did dishes when there weren't any clean ones? Did you ever pile them in the shower?"

"That was *one time* and how did you even know about it?" Joel protested, wounded, and Theo laughed out loud.

"Cam would just buy new clothes," Niklas told him in English for Joel's benefit. "I think he not even know how washer works."

"*Hey*," Cam protested from two tables away.

"But yes," Niklas said to Joel. "Knitting. I knit. Okay?"

“It’s pretty,” Joel said. His eyes were fixed on the yarn and his fingers twitched.

The tension in Niklas’s chest eased and he held up the fabric. “Soft, too. See?”

Joel touched it with one careful fingertip. “What are you making?”

“Sweater,” Niklas said.

“Cool. Will you make me one?”

Niklas laughed out loud at that, but Joel just blinked.

“What did I say?”

“Sweater takes *long* time. I not—I *don’t* like you enough to make you sweater. Cost lots of money, time. You gonna pay me? Three hundred dollars, maybe I think about it.”

“Three *hundred*,” Joel muttered, and flopped back into his chair. Then he popped up again. “Hey, uh, Brick….”

Theo held up a hand, eyes on his plate as he forked another mouthful of fruit. “Forgiven. Play better tonight.”

“You got it.” Joel disappeared again and Niklas looked at his needles. Why had he been so worried? He should have known his team wouldn’t question him.

Theo bumped their knees together again. He was smiling to himself when Niklas glanced at him but he said nothing. Niklas bumped him back and began to knit.

Twenty-Nine

THAT NIGHT, playing in front of a packed arena that booed their every move, Theo posted a shutout with insulting ease, stopping every attempt as if he knew the plays before they unfolded. Niklas watched from the bench, heart in his throat every time the enemy attacked, but Theo faced each shot with the same unruffled air.

It helped that his team had remembered how to play. Kasha scored twice in the first period, and Joel put on a clinic in breaking up rushes and stopping shot attempts.

The Spirit were getting visibly frustrated, but the Sentinels kept their heads even when Sunny took a high stick to the mouth. He came up spitting blood and Orsher scored on the resulting power play. The crowd had been very satisfyingly silenced, Niklas thought, hiding a smile as fans left the arena in the middle of the third period.

The Spirit coach called a timeout with five minutes left and Theo skated to the bench. Niklas handed him a water bottle and Theo sprayed his face with it, then shook his head, sending droplets flying.

"Sorry," he said as Niklas tossed a towel at him. He didn't sound very sorry.

Niklas just grinned at him.

Theo returned it, his blond hair dark with water and sweat and plastered to his skull. There was nothing but happiness in his smile, pure and uncomplicated. This was the version of Theo Niklas loved the most—playing the game he loved so much, every move sure and unhesitating. Niklas could tell by the way he was carrying himself that his knee wasn't even bothering him.

"Watch Kelly," he said in Swedish, keeping his voice low just in case. "Number fifteen. He's looking for trouble."

Theo nodded and tossed the towel back to him. He scooped his helmet up and headed for his crease as he settled it in place.

The Spirit pulled their goalie as soon as play resumed, but even the extra attacker wasn't enough to break through the Sentinels' defense.

With ten seconds left on the clock, Kelly found the puck on a sloppy turnover and charged the net. Sunny was the only one there, skating backward as he paced him and looked for his opportunity.

Niklas gripped the wall, heart in his throat, as the huge forward bore down on Theo, who suddenly looked very small. Kelly wound up to shoot. Sunny threw himself to his stomach, still sliding backward, to block the shot. He stretched out with his stick, and Niklas couldn't see if it got under Kelly's skates or if he'd unbalanced him somehow, but either way, Kelly lost his footing. He went down in a wild sprawl, the puck spinning harmlessly off at an angle. Theo had less than a second to react. He jumped straight up from a standstill, tucking his knees, and both players crashed the net a heartbeat later, knocking it off its pegs. Net and players hit the boards with a bone-rattling thud. Sunny was on his feet a millisecond later and Theo spun and went to his knees by Kelly's limp form as the rest of the players caught up. Several players in ice-blue jerseys launched themselves at Sunny, who went down hard. More Sentinel players grabbed at blue jerseys, trying to pull them away. Punches flew, blue mingling with white as hostilities and frustrations boiled over.

Niklas leaped the boards. Theo was hidden behind a wall of large, angry men all doing their best to beat the shit out of each other, and Niklas could only catch glimpses of him between their legs. From what he could see, he was crouched over Kelly, keeping his head shielded with his own body. The referees were vainly trying to pull opponents apart, but no one was paying any attention to them. Fists flew, razor-sharp skates millimeters from Kelly and Theo on the ice.

"*Get away from him!*" Niklas shouted, knowing no one could hear him, and flung himself into the fray.

Men were shouting, shrill whistles splitting the air and fists flying, and Niklas took a punch that glanced off his jaw and made his ears ring, but he wasn't there to fight. He ducked under the swinging arms and shoved and pulled at the mass of bodies until he could force his way between them.

There was blood on Theo's sleeve when Niklas won through, nearly on top of him. Niklas's heart stopped briefly. But Theo still had his helmet on, and he lifted his head when Niklas hurled himself on top of him, shoving him and Kelly into the boards and bracing himself on his knees above them both.

Something hit his back hard—a player falling on him. An elbow dug painfully into his kidney. Something else connected with his head—a knee, maybe—and his ears rang but he hunched his shoulders and held on. Then Sunny was there too, hauling players away and hurling them bodily across the ice, a fixed snarl on his handsome face, and bit by bit, the chaos lessened.

As reason returned, several players stooped to check on Kelly and Theo. There was blood streaking Kelly's face, but his eyes were open and he nodded when Theo asked him a question.

Sunny gripped Niklas's shoulder. "We're clear, you can let go."

Beneath him, Theo turned his head and met Niklas's gaze.

Okay? Niklas asked with his eyes.

Theo nodded fractionally, and Niklas let go of the boards and pushed away so the arriving medics could attend to Kelly.

Theo joined him after a minute, helmet shoved up on his head.

"You're bleeding," Niklas said tightly.

Theo blinked and glanced at his arm. "Oh—it's not mine."

The wave of relief was almost dizzying, and Niklas bent to put his hands on his knees. Theo touched his back, a fleeting pressure against Niklas's chest protector.

"Thanks," he said quietly.

Niklas just nodded, still unable to find words.

They stretchered Kelly off the ice even as he protested it wasn't necessary, he could do it himself. The remaining fans cheered, and Kelly waved as he was carried away.

It took a few more minutes to sort out the infractions, and Niklas returned to the bench with the rest of the team to wait. Theo stayed by his net, now righted and in position, skating in slow, easy circles until all the penalties were handed out.

Not that any of it mattered, with ten seconds left on the clock. The puck drop was a formality, and Orsher won it cleanly, sending it sailing down the ice as the time ticked down until the buzzer blared.

. . .

Later, Niklas thought he'd done a pretty good job of getting through the rest of the evening without seeming too unhinged. He smiled in the appropriate spots when Sunny hailed him and Theo both as heroes, drank when prompted, and even answered when spoken to as they trooped onto the plane. They couldn't celebrate, not yet, not with another game so soon, but laughter flowed freely, arms flung around shoulders, backs slapped.

Niklas held it together for the flight. Luckily, Theo didn't seem to want to talk either, eyes closed and hands loose on his thighs. He was either asleep, meditating, or pretending to be one or the other so no one would talk to him, and that was fine with Niklas. What he had to say needed to be said in private.

He didn't speak in the car either. Theo glanced at him a few times, but didn't pry.

Safely in the house, away from the world, Niklas's self-control snapped. He pushed Theo up against the wall and kissed him, hard and desperate.

Theo made a soft noise and kissed him back, going up on tiptoe to wind his arms around Niklas's neck. "Mm—easy," he murmured between kisses. "I'm okay, *älskling*."

Niklas went to his knees in front of him, tears stinging his eyes. "I thought—"

"I know." Theo bent to kiss him again, fingers like silk in his hair, and Niklas took a shuddering breath and pulled him tight, pressing his face to Theo's belly.

"Are you *sure*—" he managed after a minute, looking up.

Theo pushed his hair off his forehead. "Not a scratch, thanks to you."

Niklas nodded and pressed his face to Theo's stomach again, taking a deep, grounding breath. Theo smelled like hotel shampoo—jasmine, Niklas thought vaguely—and clean cotton. He said nothing, seeming to understand Niklas just needed to hold him for a few minutes, needed the reassurance that he was okay.

"Are you good to play?" he finally asked.

Theo pulled him to his feet. "So far so good. I'll tell Coach if that changes."

"Promise," Niklas said, searching his face. "You won't play through an injury?"

A smile flickered over Theo's mouth. "I promise," he said gravely.

"Okay. You should rest." Niklas took a step back without looking away from Theo's slim form.

"I will," Theo said. "You should too."

"Yeah." There was so much Niklas wanted to say, the words clogging his throat until he thought he'd choke on them. *You mean everything to me. I'm so glad you're okay. Promise me you won't get hurt. Tell me you love me as much as I love you.*

Theo blew his hair out of his eyes and offered Niklas a soft smile. "Sleep well, *älskling*."

Stop calling me that, Niklas wanted to say. *Stop making me think there's a chance.* He kept his mouth shut and nodded instead.

Niklas slid under the covers in his bed, burrowing into the pillows. He could still taste Theo on his lips, smell his shampoo on his fingers.

How did he make Theo realize this wasn't a crush, wasn't some stupid puppy-love or infatuation? The man was somehow more stubborn than Niklas, so damn determined to be the white knight and sacrifice his own chance at happiness for some misguided attempt to set Niklas 'free', as if that was something he wanted.

Niklas punched the pillow. Now wasn't the time. He had

to be steady for Theo, not distract him from the most important fight of his life. He could do that. There would be time, later, to figure out how to get through to him. For now, there was hockey to be played.

He fell asleep with a pillow hugged to his chest, his back cold.

Thirty

GAME THREE, home ice. Theo stretched with Niklas but instead of peeling off to meditate, he followed him down the hall to the group playing two-touch.

Niklas gave him a quick look, surprise arching his brow, and Theo shrugged.

"Sometimes it's good to shake things up a bit, you know?"

The players made room for them without comment and Theo bounced on his toes a few times, waiting for the ball to come his way. His knee didn't hurt, but he was more aware of it than usual, of the way it bent and flexed. It wasn't stiff or even tight, though, so he pushed it away and jumped forward as the ball sailed at him. He bounced it off his head toward Sunny, who deflected it in turn to Cole.

Sunny sent him a quick grin but didn't say anything. Theo smiled back and then it was his turn again. Everyone cheered when he twisted to ricochet the ball off his shoulder toward Cam.

. . .

This game wasn't going to be easy. The Spirit were eager to bury the shame of losing at home, but the Sentinels were just as determined to give their fans a win. It was chippy and vicious, more than a few ugly hits and covert trips tried when the referees weren't looking.

Theo didn't let any of it touch him. None of it was his problem. All he had to do was stop the pucks that were fired at him and ignore the ones that slipped through.

The Spirit drew first blood in the opening period, and the Sentinels equalized it late in the second. It stayed locked at one apiece for the next nineteen minutes, both teams jockeying desperately for an opening, until Joel somehow caught a flying puck and batted it toward the net with a wild swing of his stick. The Spirit goalie lunged but his skate slipped and the puck sailed over his shoulder. The goal light went off and the crowd erupted.

Two wins down. Two more needed.

The flight back to Miami was subdued. Everyone knew better than to celebrate too soon. Niklas barely looked up from his knitting for the entire flight. Theo watched his hands, the rhythmic back and forth of the yarn, the clicking of the needles, and let everything else fall away.

The part already knitted—Theo didn't know if there was a term for it—had grown significantly. He wasn't sure if Niklas was especially fast or if that was normal, but he didn't ask. Instead he followed the stitches that twined their way up the fabric, looking without touching. They looked almost like brambles, the way they twisted and flowed into each other. Every few rows, there was a break in the pattern, some of the vee stitches branching off and then clustered together in a little orb.

"Cloudberries," Niklas said, startling him.

"What?"

Niklas pointed to one of the clusters. "It probably doesn't look much like them, but the pattern was inspired by cloudberry bushes. These are leaves—" He touched the rounded points of the leaf. "And this is a berry."

Theo shook his head. "I still can't believe you just... designed this yourself."

"I can't believe you take plain wood and make art from it," Niklas teased.

"Are you making it for yourself?"

Niklas shook his head.

"Who's it for?"

"A friend," Niklas said. He was already knitting again, and Theo leaned his seat back just enough that he could rest and still watch him. "I did this before games in Sweden," Niklas continued.

"Did it help?"

"Yeah. It's like meditating. Helps me put everything away. Couple of the guys laughed at me but our captain put a stop to it." He slanted a smile at Theo. "Too bad you can't do your woodworking in the locker room, huh?"

Theo snorted a laugh. "Maybe I should. I'd pay good money to see Benson's face when I bring my deck sander in there."

"This one's not going to be easy," Benson said, surveying the room. His feet were spread, hands behind his back and shoulders straight.

"Because the others were a cakewalk?" Xander muttered, and Kasha hurled a roll of sock tape at his head. Xander ducked with a squawk of outrage and Kasha glared at him.

"Shut up! So stupid!"

"Thank you, Kasha," Benson said calmly. "But let's not

injure our own team, eh? The Spirit's more than happy to do that for us."

Theo tuned them out again, stretching his legs straight in front of him and setting his heels on the carpet. He folded forward at the waist and gripped his toes, letting his face rest against his knees. His hamstrings and calf muscles protested briefly but slowly released and he concentrated on his breathing, slow and steady. His knee felt good today. No stiffness at all, not even that bothersome awareness that sometimes popped up. He was ready.

Game four. They were 2-1, looking for their third win in a row. Miami had turned out in force again, the booing taking an ugly undertone when the Sentinels took the ice for warmups. Someone hurled popcorn on the ice and a few kernels bounced off Theo's helmet as he did his stretches at center ice.

Niklas stiffened in outrage, looking for the culprit, but Theo shook his head at him.

"Don't give them a reaction. They'll be dealt with."

Sure enough, when he glanced over his shoulder a minute later, security guards had reached the offending fan and were escorting him up the stairs as he protested his innocence loudly.

Theo smiled at Niklas. "Can't let it touch you."

Kelly skated by and tapped Theo on the pad in greeting. Theo waved back.

"Glad to see him in the lineup," he said to Niklas.

"Gonna remind you of that when he scores on you," Niklas muttered.

Theo snickered and popped to his feet. "See you on the other side."

. . .

They were going to win this game. Theo had premonitions sometimes, superstitious hunches he tried to ignore, not wanting to fall into the trap of being defined by them, but he'd never felt one this strong before. It went all the way to his bones, an unshakable conviction. A Spirit player—not Kelly—slipped a puck past him but Theo barely noticed. It didn't matter. They were going to win.

Kasha scored once, then twice in the second period, and then a third time in the last period, his first hat trick in the NHL, and Theo flung his arms in the air to cheer for him as the Sentinels tackled him. Their whoops rang in the silent arena as a few hats fluttered onto the ice from the handful of Sentinel fans in attendance.

Niklas was hanging half over the bench as Kasha skated by for the traditional fist-bumps, a massive grin splitting his face. He snaked his arms around Kasha and yanked him off his feet for a rough hug, hauling him over the boards and yelling something in his ear.

Theo watched, smiling so hard his face hurt. For the first time, he let himself think about it, for just a second. The dream of lifting the Cup, the culmination of everything he'd fought for his entire life. It was within reach.

When the final buzzer went off, the score was 4-1. They were one game away from winning the Stanley Cup. Theo didn't feel the aches and pains accumulated over the grueling postseason as the crowd of celebrating players engulfed him, slapping his helmet and yelling joyfully in his face until his ears were ringing. He yelled back, tears stinging his eyes, hugging everyone within reach.

Thirty-One

HE SLEPT most of the way back to Saskatoon. He was good at it by now, and the celebrations faded pretty quickly after takeoff, in any case. The whole team was tired, and most of them were well aware of the importance of grabbing as much rest as possible.

He was woken by the plane's descent and sat up, yawning. Niklas was still asleep, head at an uncomfortable angle but his face peaceful. Theo touched his arm.

"Almost home," he murmured when Niklas blinked blearily up at him.

Benson came down the aisle from the cockpit and held his hands up to get their attention. "Be careful on the drive home, gentlemen—apparently there was a cold snap and freezing rain while we were gone. The roads are clear now, but I don't need anyone ending up in a ditch." *Especially not with so much on the line* hung unspoken but clear in the air.

Theo stifled another yawn and pulled their carry-ons out of the locker. The players shuffled down the aisle and off the plane in twos and threes.

"Get home safe, Brick," Joel called in the parking lot.

"Yeah," Tanaka chimed in. "We need you rested."

They were smiling, no trace of teasing in their eyes, and Theo snuck a quick glance at Niklas, who was upright but seemed to still be mostly asleep.

"Uh—yeah," Theo said to the rookies. "Will do. Um—you too."

Niklas was asleep again before they were out of the airport, seat reclined and one hand under his cheek. Theo resisted the impulse to smooth the hair out of his eyes and concentrated on the road. He'd been on the receiving end of Benson's ire before and had no real wish to have the experience repeated.

The house was dark when he pulled into the driveway. The headlights illuminated a few scrawny icicles hanging from the eaves—from past experience, Theo knew they'd likely be gone once the sun was fully risen.

He parked in the garage and turned the car off. Niklas stretched, his back a long, graceful arch, and yawned. Theo glanced away and stepped out.

The house was warm and dark, utterly silent but the velvety black somehow welcoming as he carried his bag through the hall. Niklas stopped at his door and Theo wanted to beg him to come to bed with him, wrap his arms around him and let Theo finally get some decent sleep, but he kept the words locked behind his teeth and managed a smile.

"Get some rest."

"You too," Niklas murmured.

Theo's bedroom felt emptier than usual when he stepped inside. He dropped his carry-on by the bathroom and tossed his phone on the bed to change into comfortable clothes. It occurred to him, as he was brushing his teeth, that it was mid-morning in Sweden, and he hadn't talked to his parents since before the last game.

He set his toothbrush back on its stand and turned to grab his phone. But instead, his left foot caught in the strap of the bag on the floor. Halfway through the step, off-balance, he jerked desperately to get free.

It worked, sort of. His foot came free, but he was already tipping forward. He landed hard, right knee taking the brunt of impact, and caught himself on his hands.

Fuck. That was all he needed. *Stupid, stupid idiot—*

He rolled to sit on the floor and carefully stretched his legs out in front of him. His right twinged in protest, sending shockwaves of pain rippling from under the kneecap. Theo gritted his teeth and gingerly tugged his pant leg up. The knee was an angry red, but maybe if he iced it, he could get it going again before the game.

Halfway to his feet, Niklas knocked on the door and Theo froze.

"Theo?" Niklas called softly. "I heard a noise—"

"I'm okay," Theo said, forcing his voice to sound normal. "Just tripped over something, nothing's wrong."

"You sure?"

"Positive. Go back to bed. Thanks for checking on me."

He waited until he heard footsteps retreating down the hall before he tried to take a step.

His right knee buckled and he caught himself on the bed. *Goddammit.* Back on his feet, weight on his left leg, he centered himself and slowly tried again.

He made it three awkward, halting steps before it buckled this time. Easing himself onto the mattress, he sat for a minute and looked down at his legs. The knee felt hot when he put his palm against it and he thought there was already some swelling, but maybe he was being paranoid.

One thing was sure, he needed ice, but he couldn't make it to the kitchen like this, not without Niklas catching him. *So tell him*, a tiny voice whispered.

Theo shook his head hard at the thought. If Niklas found out—if *anyone* found out—that he was injured, there would be panic. They'd doubt him, and they'd have reason to. After everything they'd fought for, knowing their goalie wasn't at his best behind them would do nothing but destabilize them.

Eventually, he shuffled haltingly back into the bathroom and filled the tub with cold water. At least it had been cold outside recently—the tap water was just a hair above freezing. It would have to do.

He lowered himself into the frigid water with gritted teeth, hissing at the shock. Fully seated, he stretched his legs back out and leaned back against the porcelain.

There was no question of him sleeping, not in a nearly-freezing tub of water. So he crossed his arms in a vain attempt to conserve upper body warmth, closed his eyes, and let his mind drift.

He had to play. He *had* to. He couldn't give up now, not when the team needed him so badly. Niklas didn't have playoff experience; it wasn't fair to shove him in net and force him to bear the weight of this run. If they lost, it would be on Theo's shoulders, not Niklas's.

The cold water seemed to be helping. The pain had lessened, the throbbing muted. Theo rested his head against the wall. It would be okay. His knee would be fine by morning, he'd be able to walk, move, skate again without issue.

If he told himself that enough, maybe he'd believe it.

Maybe it's a good thing, that same tiny voice whispered.

Theo examined the idea, turning it from side to side in his mind. *How* would it be good?

Niklas is stronger than you. More resilient. If he does have to step in, he'll be up to it. He's proven he can handle whatever's thrown at him.

Water sloshed as Theo shifted his weight, catching his breath as cold licked up his sides.

He didn't want Niklas to *have* to. He wanted to do this himself. How many people got a second chance to fix their worst mistakes? To come so close and fall short *again*—it didn't bear thinking about.

The water was warming up but he was already close to the fifteen minutes maximum his body could handle. He levered himself out and dried off. The swelling had gone down, and the knee bore his weight when he took a cautious step.

Hope unfurled a tiny shoot. Maybe he *could* do this.

Theo made his very careful way out of the bathroom and crawled into bed, not bothering with clothes. He'd take another ice bath before they left for the rink. It would be enough.

Thirty-Two

SOMETHING WAS WRONG. Niklas didn't know *what* yet, but there was something off about Theo. He still smiled at Niklas, answered easily when addressed. But a furrow appeared between his brows when he thought no one was looking, a worried set to his mouth that made Niklas want to grab him and demand to know what was going on.

Not that Theo would tell him. Niklas knew better by now than to try and force him to open up. Theo would talk to him in his own time, or he wouldn't.

At least they had two days off before the next game. They went to the rink for video review the morning after they got home, then had the rest of the day off.

Theo drove them home, content as always to not fill the silence between them with empty words. Niklas watched him, wondering what was going on beneath the surface, but didn't speak either.

His phone buzzed as Theo was pulling into the driveway and he fished it out.

"Cam wants to come over," he said, and glanced up to get Theo's reaction.

"Okay," Theo said easily. He put the car in park. "Just don't be too loud, I'm going to rest."

"Theo—"

Theo paused, door half-open. "Yes?" His eyes were clear, nothing but curiosity in them.

Niklas couldn't think of how to ask. "Is it okay if Joel comes too?" he finally said.

"Sure," Theo said. "No ragers in the living room, right?"

Niklas rolled his eyes and stepped out of the car. "Not even one?"

"Not even a little one," Theo said, smile widening.

Niklas smiled back and followed him inside.

Theo was in the kitchen when Cam arrived, and Niklas set his knitting aside and bounded to the door to let him in.

Kasha grinned at him over Joel's shoulder. "Wren has work," he said.

"You know he can't be left on his own," Cam said. "We're performing a public service."

"Extroverts," Niklas sighed, and stepped aside so they could come in. "Don't be loud or Theo will kill me."

Joel snorted as he shoved a case of beer into Niklas's arms. "As if Theo doesn't worship the ground you walk on."

Niklas trailed after them down the hall, trying to come up with a convincing counter argument for the laughable idea that Theo cared that much. Fuck English for being such a confusing language, anyway—how was he supposed to have a good comeback when half the time he couldn't even conjugate a word properly?

"Hey Cam, remember that time Nik told us he had a crush on Theo? That's what his face looks like right now," Joel said. He fell onto the couch in a sprawl of long limbs as Niklas froze.

"Hey Joel, remember how we don't go outing people without their permission?" Cam sniped, and hurled himself on top of Joel, who yelped.

Fists flew as Kasha turned to Niklas, eyes bright. "You have crush on Theo?"

Cam landed a particularly hard punch and Joel made a strangled noise.

"Hit him again," Niklas said.

"I have crush on Saint," Kasha said with the air of someone imparting a grave secret.

Niklas laughed in spite of himself. "We know, Kash."

Joel briefly freed himself from Cam's headlock, out of breath. "Aren't you dating Wren?"

Kasha flopped onto the other couch, careful to avoid Niklas's knitting. "She has crush on Saint too. Most people do."

Cam rolled Joel off the cushions and they hit the floor with a heavy thud. Niklas edged away from the flying limbs and glanced at Kasha, who met his eyes with a raised eyebrow.

"Can I have beer?" Kasha prompted. Clearly, there was nothing more to discuss.

Niklas tore open the box and tossed a can to Kasha. He set three more on the coasters Theo must have put out earlier and hefted the box. "Gonna—fridge."

Theo was at the stove, stirring something. He greeted him with a smile. "Food is almost ready, I made enough for everyone."

"Shit—Kasha's here too," Niklas said. He set the beer in the refrigerator and turned. "Sorry, I didn't know."

"I made enough for at least six," Theo said serenely. "Honestly, I'm surprised Cole isn't here too, they tend to travel as a pack." As if on cue, the doorbell rang, and Theo threw his head back to laugh.

Niklas stared at him, a rush of love swamping until he

couldn't breathe. This man who hated surprises and didn't like crowds had *expected* more visitors, had known Niklas's friends would show up en masse, and had planned for it.

"You should get the door," Theo prompted.

"Right." Niklas shook himself. Halfway to the hall, he stopped and spun.

Theo made a startled noise when Niklas pulled him around but kissed him back, free arm snaking around Niklas's neck to pull him closer.

Niklas poured everything he couldn't say into the kiss, hot and desperate. *I love you. I miss you. I'm so proud of you.*

He tore away before anyone came looking for him, backing up several steps. Theo stared at him, hair mussed and cheeks pink.

"Sorry," Niklas said, breathless. "Won't happen again." He turned on his heel and jogged for the door.

Sure enough, Cole gave him a winning smile and held up another case of beer. "Joel texted me."

Niklas sighed and let him in.

Joel and Cam had settled their differences by the time Niklas got back with Cole on his heels, and were comfortably bickering about who got to play Fortnite first. They settled in and Niklas picked up his knitting.

"Who it's for?" Kasha asked, indicating the project with his chin.

"Theo," Cam and Joel said in unison.

Niklas stared at them, needles frozen in midair. "How—"

Cam crowed in triumph and pointed at Cole. "Pay up, loser."

Cole dug a bill out of his wallet, muttering something under his breath, and crumpled the money into a ball so he could throw it at Cam's head.

"The only reason I took the bet in the first place is because Theo said he had a girlfriend," he said to Niklas. "But I figured out pretty quickly he was talking about you."

"Oh come on," Cam said, noticing the look on Niklas's face. "Who else?"

Footsteps in the hall—Theo.

"Don't tell," Niklas implored, and then Theo appeared, a big tray in his hands.

"Hungry?" he said by way of greeting. "I made a few things for you to snack on."

The others flocked around him as he set the tray on the coffee table. Niklas watched from the couch, still reeling. Was he just that bad at keeping secrets? Did the entire team know he was in love with Theo and just... didn't care?

"Thanks, Brick!" Joel said with his mouth full, and Cam punched his arm.

A smile flickered over Theo's lips. He met Niklas's eyes and dropped a quick wink. "Try to keep it down, okay? I'm old and need my rest."

"Nik, get over here before Joel eats it all," Cam ordered.

"Not hungry," Niklas said. He looked at his friends as they made themselves comfortable again, plates piled high with food. Cam was complaining about Joel's manners. Joel was grinning at Cam, mouth open to give him a good view of his half-eaten food. Kasha was texting his girlfriend, and Cole had his eyes closed, making little whimpering noises as he chewed with cheeks so full they bulged.

"I love you guys," Niklas blurted.

Joel choked and Cam pounded his back, staring at Niklas in alarm.

"Are you dying?" Cole demanded.

"You'd tell us if you were, right?" Joel managed, voice strangled.

"Can I have your Xbox if you're dying?" Cole added.

Kasha put his phone down. "You okay, Nik?"

Cam sighed through his nose. "He's having a moment, guys. We love you too, Nik, are you sure you don't want some of this food?"

"I'm sure," Niklas said. His eyes stung and he smiled, clutching Theo's half-finished sweater to his chest. "I have next game against Cam."

"Why not me?" Joel objected.

"Because you're terrible at Fortnite and everyone knows it," Cam said, and picked up his controller.

"Oh shit, is this popcorn spicy?" Cole demanded. "I swear, Nik, if you don't wife Theo up, I will." He shoved another handful into his mouth, chortling as he chewed, and Niklas laughed helplessly.

Theo disappeared into his bedroom and Niklas spent the rest of the afternoon relaxing with his friends, letting the stress of the past few weeks drain away. After several hours, Theo reemerged and put his head into the room to make sure no one needed anything. His hair was rumpled and there was a crease mark on his cheek from his pillow, but his smile was genuine.

"More of that spicy popcorn?" Cole asked. "What was on it, anyway?"

"Sriracha," Theo said, smile widening. "I'll bring you some more."

He disappeared and Joel, lying flat on the carpet, stretched with a satisfied noise. "I dunno why we were ever afraid of him."

Cam nudged him with a toe. "Cuz you're stupid."

"Sounds right," Joel said. "Yo Nik, does he want to join us? It's not weird, us hanging out in his house without him?"

Niklas shook his head. "It's too much of stress for him. Is… tired?"

"Tiring," Cam suggested.

Fucking conjugations. Niklas nodded. "Theo don't like lots people in his space. But he knows I do. He's not need… lots friends, but I'm happy?" He shrugged. "He's happy."

There was silence as the others worked their way through his mangled syntax.

"So what you're saying," Cam finally ventured, "is that Theo doesn't like or want a lot of people around because it's exhausting for him, but if *you* have guests, he likes it because it makes you happy. Even though it's something *he* would normally hate."

"What I said," Niklas pointed out.

"Forget about wifing him up," Cole said. "You guys *are* married."

Niklas threw a coaster at him as Theo came back, carrying a big bowl. Was he moving more stiffly than usual? But Theo shot him a smile and crossed the room with his usual grace to put the bowl into Cole's greedily outstretched hands. *Imagining things*, Niklas told himself, and smiled back.

"Are we watching the movie or what?" Cam asked.

"Brick, you wanna join us?" Joel asked.

Theo shook his head. "I have some work to do before dinner. You boys have fun."

Thirty-Three

GAME DAY dawned crisp and clear, frost clinging to the grass and crunching underfoot. Theo was up early for another ice bath and didn't emerge until he heard Niklas stirring. His knee had been stiff when he woke up, but the cold had kept it from swelling. He wrapped it with a soft cotton bandage once he was dry, and did some slow, careful stretches to test it after he was dressed. So far so good, he decided, and padded out to the kitchen in his slippers to make breakfast.

It wasn't long before Niklas joined him, and they ate porridge with apple mash in peaceful silence, feet bumping together occasionally under the table.

They drove to the arena and Niklas stretched in the hall beside him, eyes distant as he focused on how his body was responding. Theo watched him, wondering if the urge to kiss him breathless would ever go away. Probably not, he thought.

He turned his attention inward. His knee was still a little stiff, but the ice baths had done their job and the more he stretched, the easier it was to move.

The arena was sold out again, fans driving several hours to watch what might be the deciding game. Theo knew it was game five, he knew if they won, they had the Cup, but he pushed the thought away every time it tried to surface. He had to play in the moment or he'd collapse under the weight of the expectations on his shoulders. The rest would follow. It had to.

The first puck slipped past him on a freak bounce off a Spirit's skate, three minutes into the first. The officials held a quick huddle to determine if it had been kicked in. It hadn't. Theo could have told them that. He took a gulp of water and settled himself between the pipes again.

The second puck came on a breakaway, the forward closing on him like a freight train as the Sentinels gave desperate pursuit.

Theo took a long drink, sprayed his face with water, and shook himself. They'd come back from worse. His knee wasn't hurting more than usual, still responding to his demands. This wasn't because of him.

Was it?

He pushed the thought away as the players got in position for the puck drop.

Things just got worse from there. Kasha managed to tip in a goal just before the buzzer, but when the first period ended, the score was 4-1 and they'd been outmatched in every possible way. Outskated, outshot, outplayed.

"Where the fuck are you?" West roared at the miserable players huddled on their benches in the locker room. "You're hanging your goalie out to dry, you've all fucking collectively forgotten how to hit, how to *score*?" He focused on Xander, who'd fumbled a pass and left Theo all alone with no protection for the third goal. "You." West was not an intimidating man, most of the time. This was not one of those times. Theo drank more water as West advanced on Xander. "Is it Aruba? Or maybe Jamaica? Somewhere hot and sunny with lots of girls in bikinis?"

Xander blinked at him. "Coach—"

"Because you're sure as fuck not here in Saskatoon," West interrupted. "So tell me where you are so I can hop on a plane and drag your sorry ass home."

"It's not my fault," Xander whined. "Maybe if I had more ice time—"

"You could, what? Let in even *more* goals? That's a great idea! Let's do that next time we want to throw a game!" West flung his hands in the air and turned on his heel.

"It's not all on him," Theo said mildly.

West spun. "You wanna talk about your performance, Wallin? You really want to go there?"

Theo drained his water bottle. Niklas was holding another one out before he could even set down the empty one. "Go ahead," Theo told West, thanking Niklas with a quick glance. "I can take it."

"Why don't you tell *me* what you're doing wrong?" West shot back.

Theo drank half the bottle before answering, savoring the sweet water sliding down his throat. "Other than letting pucks in?" he finally said.

West glared at him. "You think you want to maybe stop doing that?"

"Do my best," Theo said, and drank more water.

Niklas scooted closer as West turned to find another target. "Are you okay?" he asked under his breath in Swedish.

Theo evaluated. Oddly, he was, he realized. A sense of fatality had settled over him somewhere around the third goal. Some games were like this—dirty bounces and ugly plays and no matter how hard you tried, nothing went your way. It sucked that it had to happen for them on game five of a championship run, but there was nothing to do but shake it off and reset.

"Yeah," he murmured. "What's up with the boys?"

"They're rattled," Niklas said. "There's so much riding on this—"

Theo looked around the room. Other than him, Sunny, and Orsher, most of the players there didn't have much playoff experience. Sunny was talking to a knot of rookies clustered around him and Orsher appeared to be meditating.

West rolled the whiteboard in and clapped his hands for their attention. "Here's what we're doing," he announced.

Theo leaned back, tuning him out. "West's a pro. The boys just need to trust him and remember their game."

"How come you're not freaking out?" Niklas asked quietly.

Theo glanced at him. Niklas's eyes were worried, hands clasped in his lap and tension thrumming through his body. Theo's hand was halfway up to tuck a curl behind Niklas's ear before he remembered himself. He smiled ruefully.

"I've been here before. If it happens, great. But if it doesn't —" He lifted a shoulder. "It's like I said when we met, do you remember? I've had such a good career, done so many things with people I love. I'm so blessed." He smiled again, holding Niklas's eyes. "And this time I mean it."

Niklas searched his face for a long moment before finally nodding. "I'm glad, Theo. But—" He smiled, eyes creasing. "I do want you to have this."

Theo patted his knee. "I know you do. I want it too. So let's go get it."

By the middle of the third period, though, Theo knew it wasn't going to happen. His knee was stiffening again, making him slower to react, and the Spirit's offense had figured out his weakness. They drove hard to the net on his right over and over, forcing him to lunge and pivot and thrust his right leg out in save after desperation save.

The Sentinels had scored once more in the second period, but they were locked at 4-2 and none of their efforts were enough to break through.

A defenseman had the puck and he cut close, seemingly committed to a five-hole play. Theo fell for it, throwing himself to the ice to stop the shot that somehow didn't happen. He realized with dawning horror that the d-man had fooled him but it was too late, he was already belly-down in his crease as the player ripped the puck up over his shoulder.

There was only one chance to stop the shot. Theo didn't think about it. He just wrenched his right leg up and sideways. *Classic scorpion*, he thought dimly as something in his knee ripped. He didn't have time to think about it. He'd deflected the shot but the puck was still in play. He scrambled to all fours and then to his feet. His right leg wouldn't hold him and he landed hard on his left knee.

Where's the whistle? Theo couldn't see anything through the legs and sticks directly in front of him. He turned, searching for the puck as men shouted and shoved above him. *There*. The puck was a flash of black, there and gone again, and Theo hurled himself forward. Someone fell on top of him, driving the air from his lungs, but he didn't care. He had the puck in his glove, and as soon as the referees realized it, they'd blow the whistle.

Skate blades flashed near his face, gouging divots in the ice. Theo huddled in on himself and waited.

It felt like centuries but was probably under five seconds when the whistle blew, shredding through the noise in Theo's head like a scythe through cotton. He didn't move even when the players around him had shuffled back enough to give him some room.

"Theo?" That was Sunny, bending to put a hand on his back. "You okay?"

Theo let go of the puck and tried to get up, but fell forward again as agony knifed through his knee. "Julie," he gasped.

"She's coming," Sunny said.

The athletic trainer was there within seconds, going to her knees beside him. "Hey Theo, how we doing? Wanna talk to me?"

"My knee's fucked," Theo managed. He tried to push himself up again but Julie put a hand on his shoulder and stopped him.

"You're gonna stay right there until I'm sure you're okay," she said firmly. "What happened? Was it the scorpion?"

Theo nodded mutely. The pain in his knee made it hard for him to feel anything else, so it took a minute for him to realize the arena had fallen silent as they watched. He tried again to sit up and this time Julie let him.

"Nice and easy," she said, hand still on his shoulder.

Theo put his hands flat on the ice and got his left foot underneath him. *Nice and easy* was just going to make it hurt worse. He straightened in one swift move, swaying on his left foot as sweat broke out on his forehead from the renewed pain. His right leg dangled uselessly from the knee down.

"Can you put weight on it?" Julie asked.

Theo shook his head.

"Do you need a stretcher?"

"Absolutely not," Theo said through his teeth.

"Okay. Sunny, on his right. Arm over your shoulder. Theo, let him take your weight. Easy now."

Somehow, Theo made it off the ice. Scattered applause broke out and grew stronger as he made his way down the tunnel, past Niklas warming up, eyes huge with worry and terror. Theo wanted to touch him, calm him with a kiss or a few words, but Sunny didn't slow down, half-carrying him down the hall to the trainer's room.

"I got it," Julie said once Sunny had Theo on her table. "Go back and finish the game."

Sunny lingered, looking at Theo, who nodded.

"Go."

Sunny firmed his mouth and ducked back out of the room.

"Let's see what we've got here," Julie said cheerfully. "Do you want to help me get your pads off or should I do it?"

"I can help," Theo said, and struggled to a sitting position.

Between them, they managed to strip him to his UnderArmour, his gear set to the side in a neat pile because Julie knew how particular he was.

Her hands were quick and deft as she poked and prodded his knee, muttering under her breath. Theo did his best to obey her directions to stretch the leg, wiggle his toes, turn his foot this way and that, clenching his teeth so hard his jaw ached.

"You need imaging," Julie finally said. "But from what I can feel here, I think you've probably torn a ligament. ACL, if I had to guess."

Theo nodded dully. He'd known it was coming.

"I'll call the ambulance," Julie said.

"*No,*" Theo said, one hand out. "Please, just... can you wrap it up for now and let me watch the rest of the game? There are only a few minutes left."

Julie frowned, glancing at the television in the corner and back to him.

"Please, Julie," Theo said quietly. "I'll stay right here, I won't move. Don't make me leave yet."

Julie sighed and grabbed her stool, parking it beside his

bed and dropping onto it. She took his hand and Theo gripped it, unsure how to say thank you through the lump in his throat.

Niklas looked shaky when the camera panned to him, movements hesitant like he was constantly second-guessing himself.

"He'll be okay," Julie said.

Theo didn't answer. The score was 4-3—someone had scored while Julie was examining him. But it wasn't going to be enough. The seconds ticked down, slow and inexorable, as the Sentinels brought their full weight to bear on the Spirit's goalie, who somehow stopped every single shot they hurled at him.

"God, he's good," Theo whispered, his lips numb. West had pulled Niklas to put a sixth attacker on the ice, but even that wasn't enough to break through.

The final buzzer made Theo's teeth vibrate. The Spirit players flung themselves on their goalie, celebrating like they'd already won the Cup, as the Sentinels filed off the ice, shoulders sagging.

Julie squeezed his hand. "You still have two more chances."

"They do," Theo said quietly. "We both know I'm done."

Thirty-Four

"I CAN'T DO THIS," Niklas said before he even had the phone to his ear. "Theo, I can't, I *can't* do this—"

"Stop it," Theo said sharply. "*Breathe.*"

Niklas drew a shuddering breath. Theo could hear ambient noise around him but couldn't pick out specifics.

"Where are you?"

"Hallway," Niklas managed. "Outside... locker room."

"Find somewhere quiet," Theo ordered. "Even the bathroom, if you need. Somewhere you won't be interrupted. Go there right now and tell me when you're there."

The doctors had refused to wait until their Cup run was over for surgery, telling him over and over how time was of the essence and every minute they delayed was a chance for something else to go wrong. If they didn't operate immediately, they wouldn't be responsible for the inevitably disastrous results.

It wasn't like he could back Niklas up anyway, and traveling to Florida was out of the question with a severed tendon and a leg that wouldn't bear his weight. They didn't need him there to win, anyway. But still—

"I found a room," Niklas said. His voice was still shaky. "No windows. Just a desk and chair."

"Is there room to stretch?"

"I—yes. Mostly."

"Put me on speaker." Theo listened as Niklas obeyed, the rustle of fabric loud over the tinny microphone mixed with his still too-rapid breaths, sharp and short in his lungs. "Do the splits," Theo ordered. "And then hold it until you've got your breathing under control."

He knew Niklas was sliding to the floor, knew he'd have his palms flat against the short carpet to ease his descent as he stretched those endless legs of his out. He'd fold forward once he was all the way down, until his face was nearly touching the floor. Theo loved Niklas's flexibility, envied it as it got progressively more difficult for him to match it. Had he ever been that supple? He didn't think so.

Niklas's breathing was steadying, the familiarity of the pose helping ground him, just as Theo had hoped.

Theo started counting out loud. Breathe in for five seconds, out for seven, hold for three. Repeat. Niklas knew this part too. He could have done it on his own, but Theo was selfishly glad he hadn't, cradled the thought that Niklas had reached for him close to his chest even as he knew he'd have to break him of the habit sooner rather than later.

Not yet. Please, not yet.

He shifted his weight on the couch and his knee twinged.

"How are you feeling?" Niklas asked, as if he'd seen Theo's wince.

"This is about you, not me," Theo said. "Now, I want you to listen to me, because the chances of me saying this again are slim to none."

"Okay," Niklas said, wariness ringing in the word.

"You have the potential to be the best goalie in the league," Theo said baldly.

Niklas sucked in a shocked breath.

"You've worked for it," Theo continued. "You've handled every challenge thrown at you. You've got the speed, the agility, the puck sense—you read body language better than Felix."

"*Theo*," Niklas managed.

"You're ready for this," Theo said. "I know you think you're not. I know you're scared. I know I've been hard on you and pushed you to do more, be better. It's because I know it's in you. *You can do this.*"

Silence.

"Better than Felix?" Niklas whispered.

"You heard me. But if you tell him I said so, I'll deny it to my grave."

"Of course." A tiny thread of amusement wound through the words. He was fighting a smile, Theo knew, that dimple flashing as he pressed his lips together.

"It kills me to not be there with you," he said.

"I didn't want this," Niklas blurted. "It feels like I took it from you."

In spite of everything, Theo couldn't help the laugh. "Of course you did. You're human and a professional athlete—you're going to want this. I'd be worried if you didn't. But you didn't take it from me, *älskling*." He took a deep breath. "And if I had to give it to anyone else, I'm glad it could be you."

Niklas made a noise, a hiccupping breath like a strangled sob. "Theo—"

"Go out there and play hockey," Theo said. "And then come home."

He hung up before Niklas could say anything else, pressing the heels of his hands to his eyesockets and grinding them hard.

"Still not admitting it, huh?"

Theo dropped his hands and glared at Anjali, leaning

against the doorjamb. She was holding two mugs, wisps of steam curling from them.

"Not only was flying out here when I could have managed on my own completely unnecessary," Theo snapped, "but I *really* don't know what you're talking about."

"New York is closer than Sweden," Anjali said serenely. "And if I hadn't done it, your mother would have." She settled beside him, her weight barely denting the cushion, and handed him a mug. "And you know exactly what I'm talking about."

Theo wrapped his hands around the mug and took a deep breath of the fragrant steam.

"Are we really playing this game?" Anjali pressed.

"Anj," Theo said, and closed his eyes. "It's not—there's nothing to admit. There's... nothing. Okay? Can you just... let it go, for once in your life?"

"Well, I would," Anjali said thoughtfully. "Except that young man is so head over heels in love with you he can't even look in your direction without it oozing out every pore."

"Gross," Theo muttered.

"I notice you're not actually denying it."

"Would it help?"

Anjali squirmed into a comfortable position and picked up the remote. She turned the tv on, found the game, and muted the talking heads currently having a heated discussion onscreen. "I don't understand why you won't let yourself have this," she said softly.

Tears pricked Theo's eyes suddenly and he set the mug on the table beside him. "Because it's not fair to him," he managed.

"God, I know," Anjali sighed.

Theo looked up sharply. "I'm serious."

"And you're right! Poor Niklas, falling in love with someone with one foot already in the grave." She pitched her voice high and mocking. "'Oh Niklas, you just don't understand, I'm so old I need a minder, I couldn't possibly fall in love with you, I've already got my headstone picked out—'"

"*Stop it*," Theo hissed. "How dare you? You think this is *funny*?" Fury and hurt blinded him and he blinked hard. When his vision cleared, Anjali was glaring at him, just as angry.

"I think this is the stupidest thing you've ever done, and you are a *stupid* motherfucker," she snarled.

"My career's over!" Theo flung at her. "His is just beginning! How do I shackle him to me with a clear conscience when his whole life is ahead of him?"

"Your *first* career is over," Anjali shouted back. "Eleven years, Theo! That's all there is between you, but you act like you're a doddering, drooling corpse that hasn't got the memo to stop breathing yet! You're *in your early thirties*! You have *so much* to offer a partner, your *own* life is still ahead of you, so why are you so terrified to reach for it?"

"Because!" Theo yelled. "Because *I don't deserve it*!" He covered his face. Tears scalded his cheeks and seeped through shaking fingers. He didn't fight them.

Anjali set her mug on the other table with a soft clink and then her cool hands were wrapping around his wrists and she was pulling, gently so she didn't hurt his knee, until he sank into her lap. She bent over him, arms around his shoulders, and Theo let the tears flow, body shaking with his sobs.

When the storm finally burned itself out, he'd lost track of time. The first thing he registered was Anjali's hair in his face, the silky strands sticking damply to his flushed cheek. She smelled like cinnamon and lavender, her arms steady and unwavering.

Theo drew a slow breath and rubbed his face against her sleeve. "Sorry," he mumbled thickly.

"Cool, we're not done being stupid," Anjali said. She let

go with one hand and leaned away, then she was back and dropping a box of tissues on his chest. "Clean yourself up."

Theo maneuvered himself upright and did his best to obey. On the tv, the announcers were still earnestly talking as players whirled through warmups in the arena below them. He couldn't see who was in net from the camera angle, eyes still blurry and unfocused.

"You've worked so hard to protect yourself for so long, it's really not surprising you can't drop the walls," Anjali said. "You blame yourself for what happened in Sweden, even though you were just a kid and couldn't have stopped it—probably would have gotten hurt too. And you withdrew from everyone after that, because they can't hurt you if they don't know you, right? But when no one tried hard enough anyway, it still hurt you, and that made you hard and bitter. And angry."

Theo opened his mouth to argue and then closed it again. Anjali arched an eyebrow at him.

"I've been in therapy for a while." Her voice was impossibly dry. "You were bound to come up eventually. I recommend it, by the way."

Theo just shook his head, too tired to find a rebuttal.

"It's easier to be an asshole than it is to be vulnerable," Anjali said quietly. "It doesn't hurt as much when they leave that way." She took his hand, folding her fingers around his. "Except you're *not* an asshole, Theo. You never were. And you deserve happiness as much as anyone."

Theo squeezed her hand. "What if he changes his mind?" he whispered. "What if… what if he gets older and realizes he has better options than a half-crippled retired ex-goalie who can't express emotions?"

"What if he does?" Anjali countered.

Theo looked up at her and she met his eyes steadily.

"I'm serious," she continued. "What if you're together for

five or seven years and then he *does* decide he wants something else? What happens then? You're alone again. Well, you're alone now, aren't you? You know you can survive being single, and you'd have five years of good memories with a man you loved, even if he did become someone who couldn't stay with you in the end. Isn't that worth something?"

Theo sat very still, her words ringing in his head.

"For the record," Anjali said, sliding closer and curling up against him, "I don't think he will. I think he'll be in love with you for the rest of his life even if you never say another word to each other." She poked him in the ribs and he twitched. "Which isn't going to happen because I will personally staple you together to talk this shit out if I have to."

Theo hugged her hard, making her wheeze. "I love you."

"And you love him." It wasn't a question.

The announcers had stopped talking and the camera was panning the players as someone sang the national anthem.

"Game's about to start," Theo said.

"Say it."

Theo sighed. "I love him."

"Damn right you do," Anjali said contentedly, and turned up the volume.

They watched the game in silence. Theo tensed every time a Spirit player came near Niklas's net, but there was no evidence of the nerves he'd heard in his voice earlier. He batted every puck away or smothered it, showing no hesitation.

Unfortunately, the Spirit goalie was still on his game. The Sentinels attacked over and over, driving hard and forcing the Spirits to give ground under the onslaught, but he stopped every scoring chance and made it look easy.

"You can let one in," Anjali reassured the tiny image of

him on the screen. "It's okay, we won't be mad." She glanced at Theo. "You think he's gonna get a shutout?"

Theo laughed and didn't answer.

The minutes ticked down. Five minutes in the third. Four, then three, both sides still scoreless.

"Come on," Anjali was muttering under her breath, leaning toward the tv like she could somehow influence their team to score. "Just one, you guys. Come *on*!"

Thirty seconds left. Overtime loomed. Theo was holding his breath, something he only realized when he got lightheaded.

The Sentinels had managed to stay disciplined for most of the game, but desperation was bleeding into their movements. Theo watched, heart in his throat, as Kasha lost the face-off and the Spirit stormed Niklas's net.

He fended off one, then another, but he couldn't freeze the puck. It bounced wildly off a player's helmet on a desperation shot. Hung suspended for a heart-stopping moment. Niklas lunged, glove out. But a Spirit was there first, stick reaching.

"*No*!" Anjali screamed.

The puck glanced off the top of Niklas's glove and careened into the net.

The goal light went off. The arena erupted.

Theo fell back into the cushions, ashes in his mouth.

"No!" Anjali repeated. "Was that legal?" She twisted to look at him. "That looked like a high stick."

Theo shook his head numbly. "Below the shoulder. Lucky bounce. It was a good goal."

The Spirit was mobbing their goalie as the Sentinels filed off the ice. Theo muted it and dropped the remote.

"I thought the shutout curse was supposed to work," Anjali muttered, slumping beside him.

"Only when it's against us," Theo said. He reached for his

phone and pulled up Niklas's texts, but hesitated, unsure what to say.

"I know I'm not a professional," Anjali said, "but I thought he looked good out there. Did he?"

Theo stroked a finger down his phone case. "Yeah. He looked good." He typed, *Proud of you. See you soon*, and hit send.

"One more game," Anjali said. "One more chance. At least it's at home."

"I need to work," Theo said abruptly. "Can you hand me my crutches?"

"*Now*?" Anjali stared at him like he'd grown a second head.

"Crutches," Theo repeated.

He was panting with effort, sweat rolling down his face, by the time he levered himself into his workshop. The air was rich with the smell of cedar and maplewood, sawdust dancing in the golden light of the lamp he switched on.

His latest project was sitting on the workbench, a simple rosewood bowl measuring six inches around the base and tapering to four inches at the top in a graceful curve. A dala horse in traditional tack stood proudly on the side, etched in painstaking detail right down to the buckles on the bridle. Flowers marched around the rest of the bowl, the largest standing under the horse's nose. A gap split the lip of the bowl, curling in a meandering spiral down to the center of the flower.

Theo picked the bowl up and inspected it. He liked the way he'd made the crack blend into the petal of the flower, but the wood was still rough. It needed to be sanded and sealed so he could polish it and make sure there were no snags or crevices.

He perched himself on the stool and got to work. It was exacting work, demanding precision and care, and he forgot the rest of the world as his focus narrowed to the bowl in his hands, teasing blemishes out of the wood one at a time. Distantly, his knee ached, but he ignored it and worked on. It had to be perfect.

Anjali picked Niklas up from the airport at three A.M. and Theo woke from his drugged doze on the couch to the door opening. Anjali had bullied him into taking something when she found him falling asleep at the workbench, ignoring his protests as she chivvied him back into the house.

Cobwebs clung to his brain as he rubbed his eyes and fought to wake up.

Niklas appeared in the doorway, bag over his shoulder. There were shadows under his eyes, a bitter twist to his mouth.

Anjali cleared her throat from behind him. “Going to bed,” she announced. “If anyone cares.”

Theo and Niklas regarded each other. There was guilt in Niklas’s eyes, Theo realized with a jolt, and he held out his arms, a silent request.

Niklas dropped the bag and went to him, dropping to his knees in front of the couch and burrowing into Theo’s midsection. His hair was damp, frost crystals on the ends stinging Theo’s cheek as he pressed it to Niklas’s head.

“I’m sorry,” Niklas whispered, voice muffled. “I couldn’t win it for you. I—”

“Hush,” Theo murmured. “Come to bed.”

“Anjali—”

“She knows.”

Niklas jerked his head up, eyes huge. “She—is she—”

“It’s... complicated.” Words refused to cooperate and

Theo shrugged, frustrated. "I'll explain later. Will you sleep with me tonight?"

Niklas nodded and climbed to his feet, holding out a hand to Theo. "Do you want me to carry you?"

Theo shot him a look. "You just played a sixty minute game and flew across the country. My crutches will do just fine."

A ghost of a smile played around Niklas's lips but he said nothing, scooping his bag up from where he'd dropped it and following Theo down the hall.

He waited until Theo was settled in the bed, his knee supported, before sliding close and wrapping an arm around his waist. His breath was warm on the back of Theo's neck.

Neither of them spoke. Theo fell asleep to Niklas's breathing, heart beating steadily against Theo's ribs.

Niklas woke the morning of game seven to an empty bed. He found Theo in the kitchen, leaning on his crutches as he stirred something on the stove. Anjali was nowhere to be seen, so Niklas came up behind him and kissed the nape of his neck, breathing in the sweet fragrance of his shampoo. Theo had lost weight during the playoffs and his vertebrae were still too prominent. It made tenderness ache in Niklas's chest. He kissed one of the bumps, pulling the collar of Theo's shirt aside just enough to find another and kiss it next.

Theo shivered. "Don't start," he warned, a satisfying roughness to his voice.

Niklas smiled against his skin but regretfully eased away. "Why are you making breakfast?"

"Because Anjali needs a mandate from the government to be awake before noon and you need a filling meal."

"I can make it myself. You shouldn't be on your feet."

Predictably, Theo ignored him and kept stirring. "It's just

oatmeal, but my mother sent me apple mash and I have pecans."

Niklas wanted to wake up to Theo making him breakfast every morning. He wanted to carry him back to bed and make love to him for hours, slow and syrupy-sweet until they were both sated. He wanted to tell him how much he loved him again, make Theo *believe* him somehow.

Instead, he kissed Theo's neck again and stepped away to make himself coffee. He couldn't think about that right now. All he could afford to focus on was the game that evening, his last chance to win Theo a Cup. He'd failed twice. The thought of the look on Theo's face if he failed again made his stomach twist.

They ate in the breakfast nook, morning sun creeping across the cushions, gilding Theo's profile and setting his fair hair ablaze. Niklas tucked his feet under himself and shamelessly appreciated the view until a faint flush crept up Theo's throat and dusted his cheekbones.

"Stop looking at me like that," he said, but it was half-hearted.

Niklas stretched out a leg to prod gently at Theo's left thigh. "I missed you."

"God, I can't believe you're actually horny," Theo muttered, biting down hard on a smile. "We have game tape to watch."

"Multitask," Niklas suggested.

"Since I guess it has to be said, we are *not* having sex today," Theo told him sternly. "We're watching tape and talking strategy, and you're resting until tonight."

Niklas took a bite of oatmeal and thought about it. "What are my chances of sex if we win?"

"Baby, if you win, you can fuck me in every room of this house," Theo said, and Niklas choked on oatmeal.

It took a minute of spluttering and coughing, Theo

muffling laughter as he pounded him on the back, before he recovered.

"Consider it won," Niklas rasped, wiping streaming eyes. "No take backs."

"No take backs," Theo agreed. His eyes glinted with amusement, and Niklas tilted his head to consider him. "What?" Theo asked after a minute.

"I don't know." Niklas kept looking at him. "Something's... different about you."

Theo rolled his eyes. "Nothing's different. I'm still just me. Game tape, let's go."

When it was time for Niklas's pre-game nap, Theo declined to join him.

"First of all, you'll try to talk me into sex, and my defenses are only so strong. Second—" He held up a hand before Niklas could pounce on that. "I'm working on something. So you go sleep—" He gave Niklas a light shove toward the door. "And I will see you when it's time to go to the rink."

Niklas paused in the doorway, looking at him over his shoulder. "Are you sure you're up to it?"

Theo gave him a smile blinding with its sweetness. "You think anything could keep me away? Now *go*."

Niklas went, grinning to himself.

The strangely buoyant good mood lasted until they got to the rink. Theo was slow, struggling with his crutches and swearing under his breath as his bag bumped against him, but he refused to let Niklas help with it.

Niklas held the door for him instead. The smell of popcorn and rubber and ice hit his nose and he took a deep breath. No one but staff was in the building yet, but there was a charged feeling to the air as they entered the locker room, an energy that almost crackled. *Last chance. Do or die.* What if he couldn't do it? What if he just wasn't good enough?

A wadded up ball of sock tape sailed toward him and he snatched it out of the air before it could bounce off his head.

Kasha grinned at him. "Reflexes good!"

Niklas hurled the tape back. Kasha ducked and Cole took the opportunity to wrap an arm around his neck and give him an old-fashioned noogie. Kasha squawked and flailed but Cole hung on, impervious.

"That's what you get for attacking our starting goalie," he shouted over Kasha's protests. "Want me to beat him up, Nik?"

"We need him," Niklas said regretfully. "But if he not score tonight—maybe then."

Kasha straightened, indignant. "I'm score tonight! I'm score *so much*!"

"Prove it," Theo told him as he set his bag carefully by the locker and settled on the bench.

Niklas stripped to change into his UnderArmour, focusing on the familiar ritual of getting each item into place, getting it settled just right, but even as he pulled on his pads and bent to tie his skates, the nerves simmered in the back of his throat, threatening to boil over at any second.

The Spirit was such a good team. They wanted this badly, every bit as badly as the Sentinels. If they were hungrier, if they fought harder, if the bounces favored them—

Theo's hand closed hard over the nape of Niklas's neck and he pulled him around and down until their foreheads were pressed together. The noise of the room faded around them as Niklas stared into Theo's beautiful brown eyes, so dark he couldn't see the pupils. He focused on the feeling of Theo's hands on either side of his face, the hard press of his skull, the steadiness of his breathing.

Slowly, so slowly, Niklas's breaths evened out into a ragged approximation of Theo's. Theo searched his eyes, so close he was slightly out of focus.

"You can do this," he said in Swedish, so low only Niklas could hear him. "You're better than he is. Remember that."

Niklas opened his mouth to protest and Theo let him go abruptly. He wasn't leaving, though—just bending to pull something from the bag he'd guarded so jealously earlier.

He came up holding something wrapped in tissue paper.

"This is for you," he said, and shoved it at him. "To remind you there's nothing you can't do."

Niklas took it, looking at Theo's face for a hint, but there was nothing to read there. He looked at the gift in his hands. It felt heavy, solid.

"Open it!" Cole yelled.

Theo twitched, clearly having forgotten their audience.

Niklas almost laughed and unwrapped the tissue. It fell apart in folds to reveal a gleaming wooden bowl. Light and dark pieces formed the squat belly of the bowl, joined so neatly it looked like the wood had grown that way. Niklas didn't know wood, not the way Theo did, but he was pretty sure trees didn't grow in swirls like this. A dala horse had been burned into the outside, standing in a field of sunflowers that marched all the way around the base.

"Is it broken?" Cole asked, startling Niklas out of his reverie. He pointed at the gap in the wood spiraling up from the largest sunflower in front of the horse's nose. "Why is there a hole in it?"

Niklas touched a petal with a wondering finger. Theo was watching him silently, waiting for his reaction, but words refused to form.

He loves me. The thought was so crystal clear, so loud in his head, that Niklas looked around to see if he'd said it out loud.

Faces gazed back at him in various states of confusion and interest. Sunny was smiling, looking at Theo, who was carefully not looking at anyone but Niklas.

"All I'm saying," Cole said loudly, "is that it's gonna be hard to eat cereal out of it!"

Niklas clutched the bowl protectively to his chest and glared at Cole. "Is not for food!" He looked back down at it and then at Theo, still waiting for his reaction. "Is yarn bowl." He wanted to kiss Theo so badly it was a physical ache in his chest, but somehow he held himself still. Theo had made him a yarn bowl, had spent who-knew how many hours creating it. Niklas could picture him, bent over his workbench with his tongue caught between his teeth as he poured all the love in that bottomless heart of his into this declaration.

He loves me as much as I love him. If there had been any doubt, it was swept away when Theo met his eyes. The truth shone there, stark and absolute. The corner of Theo's mouth twitched briefly and he nodded, but stayed silent.

Niklas could do this. He was one of the best goalies in the league, and he was in love with *the* best goalie in the league, who loved him too.

"What the *fuck*," Cole demanded loudly, "is a *yarn bowl*?"

Thirty-Five

ANJALI WENT with Theo to the Sentinels' suite where the scratches and players' partners watched games. They were welcomed with open arms and Anjali was pulled into a knot of statuesque women, all of whom had questions about her latest designs.

Oscar and Lilly hurled themselves at Theo's knees and were caught just before impact by Inga, who grabbed them both by the collar.

"We talked about this!" she scolded them as they hung in her hands, looking abashed. "Uncle Theo has a sore knee and we are what?"

"Careful," the twins chorused, hanging their heads.

"Sorry, Uncle Theo," Lilly added. Tears were welling in her big eyes and she scrubbed them away angrily with a small fist.

Theo bent and held out his arms. Lilly stepped into them first, followed by Oscar, both of them being careful not to jostle him.

When he straightened, Inga was smiling. She tousled Oscar's hair and laughed at his ferocious scowl. "Go get something to eat," she told them both, and turned to give Theo a hug of her own once they'd scampered off. "Sorry about that."

"No damage done," Theo said. "You look lovely." In fact —he stopped and gave her another once-over. Her hair was shinier than ever, skin glowing, and her face seemed fuller, like she'd gained a few pounds. Theo narrowed his eyes. "Are you —"

Inga made a shushing motion. "Don't say it!"

"You *are*?" Theo demanded, and a pretty blush touched Inga's cheeks as she nodded. Theo pulled her into another hug. "Congratulations," he said against her hair.

Inga's laugh was a little watery when she stepped back. "Sunny doesn't know yet. You won't tell him?"

"Of course not."

Anjali popped up by Theo's elbow, a plate in each hand. "Hi Inga. Theo, you should be sitting down. I got you food." She bullied him to one of the seats overlooking the arena and Theo eased himself into it. The rink was empty but the stands were already filling.

"Sold out again," Inga said as she sat beside him and Anjali took the chair on his other side. "It's going to be a good night."

There was a knock on the door of the suite and Anjali hopped up to answer it.

"Theo, it's for you," she said, and Theo swiveled in his chair in time to see Felix step through the door, a tall, bearded man close on his heels.

Shock and relief crashed over Theo. He grabbed for his crutches to meet him but Felix crossed the room in a few quick steps before he was halfway upright. Theo found himself hauled into a crushing hug and he closed stinging eyes, clutching at Felix's jacket.

It was a long time before he could let go, but when he

finally did, wiping his face surreptitiously, Felix's eyes were suspiciously bright too.

"Hi," Theo managed. "I didn't—you came. You didn't have to—"

Felix rolled his eyes. "Yes I did, stupid." He put a hand out to the man who'd followed him inside and drew him closer. "Theo, this is Fisher. Fisher, meet Theo."

Fisher was even taller than Felix but with the breadth to match, a huge refrigerator of a man with the kindest eyes Theo had ever seen. His hand dwarfed Theo's when they shook, a white flash of teeth splitting his short beard.

"I've heard a *lot* about you," he rumbled. "It's great to finally meet the legend in person."

Theo shoved Felix. "'Legend'," he muttered, and Felix laughed. "It's good to meet you too, Fisher. Felix never shuts up about you."

Fisher's grin widened and he slung an arm around Felix's waist. "Does he ever shut up about anything?"

Theo laughed out loud at the mock outrage on Felix's face. "I'm so glad you're here."

They sat again, Anjali and Inga withdrawing to give them privacy. Below them, the lights dimmed and players spilled out onto the ice for warmups in chaotic swirls of color.

Joonas Ratia had been called up from the Bandits as Niklas's backup, but Theo barely even saw him, all his attention on Niklas's lanky form as he made a lap around the half-ice and then settled between the pipes.

Felix nudged him with an elbow. "He looks good."

Theo nodded but didn't answer. Felix was right. Niklas seemed relaxed, not as tense and strung up as he had before the previous game. He stopped shot after shot, even kicking a saved puck after Kasha when he tried a fancy move on him.

"Feels good too, looks like," Felix said with a quiet laugh. He leaned closer. "Are you two still—"

Theo gave him a quick glare. "None of your business."

"As your best and oldest friend, I think it is very *much* my business, *ami*," Felix countered.

Theo ignored him, leaning past to address Fisher. "When did you get into town?"

"Today," Fisher said.

"Have you been to Saskatoon before?"

"First time," Fisher said. "It seems... nice."

Felix snorted a laugh. "So diplomatic, you are." He patted Fisher's thigh. "We got a hotel, we thought we'd stay a few days. One way or the other, you can probably use the company."

"Cancel the hotel," Theo said impulsively.

Felix's eyes widened. "Theo—"

"I mean it," Theo said. "I have the room, I want you to. Please?"

Felix studied him for a minute. "He's good for you," he said in French, voice low.

Theo dredged up his high school French to translate and then ducked his head, feeling a flush crawl up his throat.

Felix squeezed his hand and took pity, turning back to watch warmups and talk to Fisher.

Theo rested his elbows on the bar and leaned forward to do the same. He was smiling but he didn't try to stop. It felt good, surrounded by his friends, watching the man he loved getting ready to play the most important game of his life.

The Spirit wasn't going to make it easy. They'd come to win, and they were prepared to do whatever was necessary, which apparently included egregious tripping and slashing penalties whenever the referees weren't looking.

Theo's throat was raw from yelling by the time the first

period was over, both teams still scoreless. He unclenched his hands and shook them out.

"What's *wrong* with these refs?" Felix demanded. "That player swung his stick at Kasha's head, why wasn't he ejected?"

"Trying to seem unbiased," Theo said. Rage simmered in his throat, acidic on his tongue. If one more Spirit player ran over Niklas, he was going to cause some damage of his own.

"Are you going down to see him?" Felix asked.

Theo had thought about it but he shook his head. "I don't want to distract him."

Period two was more of the same tense action, an undercurrent of vicious fury fueling both sides. Niklas stayed steady, blocking shot after shot, but Theo could tell he was feeling the pressure from the way he reset before each play.

The Spirit were outshooting them, forcing Niklas to stand on his head more than once as they peppered him, but they couldn't find a chink in his armor.

Unfortunately, the Sentinels couldn't break through the Spirit's defense either. They circled each other, play after play, exhausted desperation clear in the lines of both teams. It had been a long, bloody road to this game, and there wasn't a single fresh player in the arena.

The players left the ice for second intermission still scoreless and Theo slumped in his seat, dragging in a deep breath.

"This is a lot," Fisher said. "And you do this on purpose?"

Felix leaned against his shoulder briefly. "It's worth it when we win."

Theo didn't say anything. Every fiber of his being longed to be in the dressing room with Niklas, not stuck up here in the box so far away he might as well be watching at home on the television. He could *see* him in his mind's eye, elbows on his knees and head hanging as Coach talked, conserving his energy and staying dialed in.

"You should go see him," Felix murmured.

Theo shook his head. "He needs to stay focused."

"You are anything but a distraction, *ami*," Felix said gently, but Theo set his jaw.

"It's too important."

Felix sighed but didn't argue.

Third period. Every time the puck was in their zone, Theo held his breath. Niklas didn't waver, though. He was as graceful as ever, reading plays before they developed, anticipating where the puck would be, and shutting down rush after rush.

Anjali was holding Theo's right hand and Felix his left, both of them gripping so hard Theo could barely feel his fingers. He didn't care. He leaned forward as Sunny stole the puck and sent it to Kasha, who danced past two players and drove for the net, but the Spirit goalie snatched the shot out of midair and Theo sagged back again.

Felix was swearing under his breath in French. Fisher rubbed his thigh as if trying to soothe him but didn't speak. Tension hung in the air, so thick Theo thought he would choke on it.

The minutes ticked down. Ten-minute mark, then eight. Three minutes left. One. Overtime loomed, and Theo swallowed hard against the dread. The team was already so tired, and now they were going to have to play longer?

"Seriously," Fisher rumbled as the buzzer blew, "*how* do you guys do this?"

Felix said something but Theo didn't hear him. He was watching Niklas skate to the bench and wait for the team to file down the tunnel. Just before he stepped off the ice, though, he looked up, locking eyes with Theo. They gazed at each other for a minute and then Niklas turned and made his way down the tunnel.

"Fuck it," Theo said abruptly, shoving himself upright. "I need to get down there *right now*."

Felix's grin was blinding. "I thought you'd never ask. Fisher?"

Fisher was halfway across the room already, opening the small closet by the door and pulling out a folded wheelchair.

Theo stared at them both.

Felix shrugged. "Anjali and I wanted to be prepared."

"Let's go," Fisher said impatiently. "We don't have long."

Gratitude would have to wait. Theo folded himself into the wheelchair and handed the crutches to Anjali, who took them with a wink. Then Fisher was whisking him out the door and they were jogging for the elevator, Felix close on his heels.

They rode it to the basement floor in silence, Theo sitting perched on the edge of the seat as if he could make the elevator car move faster. The break between regular periods and overtime was much shorter and they didn't have time to dawdle. When the doors begrudgingly slid open, Fisher pushed the chair through and into a dead run down the hall, Theo directing him.

They got to the locker room just as the door opened and the players began filing back out. Sunny's eyes lit up when he saw Theo but he didn't stop to talk, pushing several rookies along with him when they wanted to see what was happening.

Theo struggled to his feet, heart in his throat, just as Niklas stepped into the corridor.

"Nik," he managed, and Niklas's eyes went wide.

"Are you okay?" He closed the gap between them, hands outstretched for Theo's, but seemed to remember himself and dropped them before they touched.

Theo reached for him, slipping both hands into Niklas's

and pulling him nearer. "I'm fine. I just—wanted to see you." He was vaguely aware of Felix and Fisher moving away to give them some privacy, of the team clustered by the entrance to the tunnel pretending not to watch, but he didn't care. None of it mattered. The *only* thing that mattered was that the man in front of him knew exactly how he felt. "Nik—" His throat closed up.

Niklas squeezed his hands. His hair was sopping wet, curling damp over the collar of his jersey and sweat beading at the tip of his nose.

Theo looked at him for a minute. He was so beautiful, and somehow he was *his*. "No matter what," he said, and stopped again.

Niklas waited, one eyebrow arched.

I love you," Theo said in a rush, loud enough for everyone in the tunnel to hear. "It's crazy and you'll figure out soon enough that I'm actually a nightmare to live with and change your mind but I want to be with you. Forever. Or... at least as long as you'll have me." There. He fought the impulse to hide and instead squared his shoulders and waited for Niklas's reaction.

Niklas was... laughing? Theo stared at him, bewildered, as Niklas gripped his hands tighter and laughed until tears rolled down his cheeks. He refused to let go when Theo tried to pull away though, sobering like a switch had been thrown.

"Oh Theo," he managed. His eyes were brilliantly blue in the dimly lit hall. "I know."

"You—"

"No one gives a present like that before such an important game, in front of our entire team, unless he's trying to make a statement. I know you love me, Theo. I know you love me as much as I love you." And then Theo was being pulled close, dragged in against sweaty goalie gear as Niklas claimed his mouth and overwhelmed his senses.

Someone cheered behind them and applause echoed down the hall. Niklas's arms tightened and Theo melted against him, pouring all his feelings into the kiss until his head spun.

Sunny coughed reluctantly behind them and Niklas growled, deepening the kiss briefly before breaking free and lifting his head to glare at Sunny as Theo clung to him, thoroughly disoriented.

"Still have a game to win," Sunny said, sounding faintly apologetic.

Niklas sighed and tipped Theo's chin up. "I'll be right back." Soft lips brushed over Theo's and then he was gone, striding up the tunnel to the ice.

"So that went well," Felix remarked.

Theo tried to glare at him but he could feel the dopey grin that wanted to break free instead. "I'm staying down here," he said. "Until it's over, I mean."

"Thought you might." Felix set the brake on the wheelchair and winked at him. "We'll see you after, yes?"

Theo nodded, heart so full he couldn't speak. "Fee—"

Felix's eyes softened. "I know. We'll find you when it's over."

Fisher gave him a quick wave as he followed Felix back to the elevator, and Theo limped slowly up the ramp to the curtain at the entrance.

The security guard was one of Theo's favorites, a tall man in his fifties named Ron. He grinned when he saw Theo and gestured to the chair beside him.

Theo gave him a grateful nod and eased himself into it. He had a good view of the arena here. The faceoff was at center ice, with Kasha, Orsher, and Sunny starting on the top line.

Three-on-three hockey was a beautiful thing, in Theo's opinion. It was cleaner, faster, more elegant somehow. Mistakes were more obvious, harder to recover from—it demanded the best from everyone on the ice, no room for fumbles or lapses in judgment.

Theo had never hated anything more. He watched with his heart in his throat, leaning forward so much he was in danger of toppling, swaying with the movements of the players, tensing every time a shot was fired at Niklas and slumping with relief when it was batted away or smothered.

Niklas was unhesitating, though, every movement perfectly calculated and smooth as silk. Theo watched him, awestruck all over again by his beauty, the grace in the long lines of his body, the coiled power in his muscles and the way he unerringly read each play. He was going to be the best goalie in the league, Theo knew it deep in his gut, and pride welled until he thought he'd suffocate with it.

Playoff overtime wasn't the same as in the regular season. There would be no shootouts. Instead, the three-on-three play would continue, twenty minutes at a time, until someone scored, no matter how long it took. Theo had seen and heard of games going five or even six extra periods before a goal found its way in. Distantly, he spared a prayer that it wouldn't come to that.

Kasha, Orsher, and Sunny were back on the ice. A Spirit forward had the puck, but Kasha picked his pocket neatly and spun away with it. The Spirit gave chase. Kasha was already one of the fastest skaters Theo had ever seen, but somehow he seemed to find another gear, outstripping all three players like they were standing still. He was completely alone as he crossed the blue line.

The Spirit goalie floated forward to cut down Kasha's reaction time, low to the ice, glove ready.

Kasha slowed briefly, cutting to the left. He faked a shot, back foot popping up, but the goalie didn't fall for it. The enemy players would be there within seconds. Kasha had milliseconds to make his play.

He swerved right, directly in front of the goalie. Dropped the puck between his feet, behind him. Followed it with his stick. And scooped it up and over the goalie's desperately reaching glove. Time slowed. The puck smacked into the back of the net. The Spirit goalie collapsed forward in despair. The goal horn went off, the red light flashing as the arena erupted with screams.

They'd done it. They'd won the Stanley Cup.

Theo nearly fell off the chair, Ron catching his arm at the last minute, and stumbled for the bench. In front of him, the Sentinels were already flooding the ice to converge on Kasha, but all Theo could think about was Niklas. The net was empty —he'd already joined the celebration. Theo couldn't see him. He slipped on the ice and caught himself, and then Sunny was there, hauling him into a crushing hug.

"We did it!" Sunny screamed in his hair, and Theo pounded on his back, screaming with him.

"I need Nik!" he yelled over the din, and Sunny let him go but kept an arm around his waist.

Theo let Sunny guide him to the knot of players and push and shove until they opened enough for Theo to slip through. He was buffeted and battered as players shouted in his face, grabbed him for hugs, then pushed him forward again into the thick of the group. Theo hugged them back, his throat raw from screaming, smiling so hard his face hurt. He could barely see for the tears.

He fell forward into the center of the crowd and Niklas grabbed him before he went down. The players thronged around them, shielding them from view, and Theo and Niklas were caught in a suspended moment of calm, staring at each other.

Theo launched himself forward and pulled Niklas into a desperate kiss. He let everything go in that moment, aware of nothing but Niklas's hot mouth against his, the arms around his waist pulling him tight, promising to never let him fall. Theo went on tiptoe and wrapped his own arms around Niklas's neck. *I love you so much,* he told him silently, more tears sliding down his cheeks.

Niklas kissed him back just as hard as players pounded them on the backs, shook their shoulders, screamed in their faces. Neither of them noticed.

Theo was done being a coward. He was tired of hiding from the world. The only thing that mattered was the man in his arms, kissing him as if his life depended on it. Niklas loved him, and that was better than any trophy in the world.

Printed in the USA
CPSIA information can be obtained
at www.ICGtesting.com
CBHW060730280524
9077CB00004B/7

9 781949 936803